Tom Evans

Tom Evans
All Is Not Well

Published by BooxAi

ISBN: 978-965-577-997-4

ALL IS NOT WELL

TOM EVANS

DEDICATION

For Dodie

The specific indignities of girlhood – the dehumanising demands of men, the casual violence with which those demands are enforced, the constant 'campaign for her own existence' that every girl will eventually be defeated in.

EMMA CLINE, "THE GIRLS"

CONTENTS

Prologue 11

PART ONE

Chapter 1 19
Chapter 2 25
Chapter 3 31
Chapter 4 39
Chapter 5 43
Chapter 6 55
Chapter 7 63
Chapter 8 73
Chapter 9 79
Chapter 10 89
Chapter 11 97
Chapter 12 101
Chapter 13 113
Chapter 14 119
Chapter 15 127
Chapter 16 133
Chapter 17 145
Chapter 18 153
Chapter 19 163
Chapter 20 175
Chapter 21 185
Gracie tells her story 197

PART TWO

Chapter 22 243

Epilogue 295

PROLOGUE

Most of Wilsonville is sleeping, but all is not well, not only because there wasn't a black person within miles (most would think that was a good thing), as black people were *persona non grata* there and still are to this day. It wasn't even because many of its denizens grew wealthy through ill-gotten gain because, let's face it, the same can be said for many places around the country. The main reason was because Wilsonville thought it was much better, not much worse than it actually was. Not that anybody living there should be out in the streets (that would come soon enough), but enough people knew what was going on down south and in the ghettos (including in their own city) to do something about it, but chose to look the other way. Everyone was complacent and complicit, and all things were exactly as they should be. God was in His heaven, blessing them abundantly on the backs of the poor.

Consider this, then, the antithesis of a Wilsonville Chamber of Commerce campaign, an attempt to set the record straight. No judgement, merely a forthright account of what might have been observed during an innocent bystander's own peculiar experience growing up there in the late fifties through the sixties, when it was abandoned for more enlightened climes, i.e., the city.

Wilsonville is a paradigm of Cheever's suburbia, with its swimming pools, manicured lawns, country clubs, cul-de-sacs before they were a thing, and chilled martinis. Many, many martinis. The village, nestled in the midst of a larger town, grew from humble beginnings as most places did. You have to start somewhere, after all. It evolved ever so gradually over a period of years from the time of the French and Indian War to the present, with the concomitant accretion of land, property, and material goods, until, with little left to spend their money on, it merely became a matter of keeping up with the Joneses.

It was the early beneficiary of its location on one of the principal land routes (ironically named The Great Iroquois Trail, whose namesakes were literally trodden over in the march of progress) between the East and West, serving the much less prosaic function as a rest stop for various wayfarers, be they pilgrims or preachers, confidence men or speculators, stagecoach drivers or just ordinary settlers who did most of the living and dying along the way.

Although it's difficult to imagine when looking through the jaundiced eye of planned obsolescence, before Wilsonville was even a gleam in the eye of future town fathers, there were Native Americans (mainly Algonquin) in the area, who, after being displaced, left behind artifacts of pottery, flint arrowheads, tomahawks, and sundry other weapons and implements, as well as the skeletons of their ancestors, in a large burial ground right in the middle of what would become the village proper, a profoundly mute record of their existence.

Like most towns, which came to be because of the nationwide land grab otherwise known as "manifest destiny," the origins of the deeded territory were murky, with many nebulous land transactions eventually resulting in the majority of real estate being parceled out among a few families, who controlled it for a century or more.

One of these families was the Wilson family, whose patriarch

Josiah grew relatively wealthy from establishing the first tavern in the area, as well as the first brewery adjacent to it, an oasis for the thirsty sojourner. This gradually morphed into a full-fledged inn, again the first one in these parts, offering rooms for travelers wishing to stay the night, as well as, for an additional nominal fee, partaking in the evening's particular bill of fare, usually cornmeal mush and beefsteak in the winter, and tomatoes and beefsteak in the summer, as well as mugs of hearty ale or cider, mulled in the winter if so desired.

As it will, competition came as a slew of small taverns sprung up seemingly overnight, but they could never overcome the foresight (or cash) of Josiah Wilson and gradually vanished as though mirages from the landscape.

New settlements were often given the name of the first postmaster or a prominent storeowner, or another type of merchant. Thus, the dubbing of "Wilsonville," after its most prominent citizen, who wouldn't have it any other way.

Gradually the population grew, aided in part by people fleeing there from the nearby city of Buffalo after the British burned most of it down. In addition, other settlements were being formed around Wilsonville in all directions, with their own dwellings and civic institutions (modest though they were), and eventually (unavoidably), political organizations, who held town meetings, wrote and passed laws pertaining to their peculiar constituents, mostly mutually exclusive to their neighbors.

Interestingly enough, one of the first orders of business and the first examples of cooperation between villages and towns was for the supervisor and overseer of the poor of each town or village to get together to divide them up and "assign" them to towns and villages along with the tax revenues apportioned to each, and that each town would "forever thereafter" support their own poor with said tax revenue, affirming the Biblical prophecy that their poor would always be with them.

What was once primarily an agricultural area was rapidly

becoming urbanized, and consequently, even if its older citizens caviled, they were being overruled by the town fathers, and more and more small farms gave way to more and more small businesses and industries.

As a result, just after the Civil War ended and through the turn of the century, Wilsonville was acquiring all the trappings of a thriving, if small, village.

Among these were the Wilsonville Hose Company, the whole gamut of Christian church denominations: Catholic, Lutheran, Episcopalian, Methodist, Presbyterian, and Baptist-much later even a synagogue; several elementary schools, and a junior and a senior high school were budgeted for and built. The XL-o Sponge Factory, the latest iteration of the building owned by the Wilson brothers (no relation to the founder, though they often tried to take credit for it), a quaint little industry, the only manufacturing concern in the area for many years, giving steady employment to a dozen men, rapidly polluting the streams it had been built on, and ultimately abandoned. Development of new subdivisions with attendant street-building and road-paving plans and sewer and water installations were announced practically on a monthly schedule.

Yet, no matter how hard the little village tried to modernize, no matter how many high rollers moved in, it was still and always would be in the main a small village with a turn of the century flavor and mores, with remnants of hitching posts, a blacksmith shop (now an auto repair garage), ice house, the Mennonite church, a water mill (there had once been several), and the houses.

And what houses they were! Large stone houses with wide verandas and fireplaces made of the same stone as the exterior, with expansive yards and copious shade trees, houses for the town fathers, and other assorted movers and shakers. The rest of the townsfolk (many proud first-time homeowners) made due with turn of the century housing, postwar tract houses, with many new prefab houses interspersed everywhere, and to the north, where acre upon acre of wooded land was being cleared for endless subdivisions. What all had in common was their unshakeable belief in God, country, and upward mobility.

All of this by way of explaining how Wilsonville, as we now know it, came to be, for better or for worse.

PART ONE

CHAPTER 1

I*'ve seen it all, boys, I've been all over, been everywhere in the whole wide world...*

It was true of him, all right, he'd seen it all, seen it all, Jim Weatherly had done it all, from riding the blinds, dishwashing, following the seasons as a migrant worker, gold-mining in Alaska, semi-pro baseball player at a mill town down south, roughnecking in West Texas, hoboing to shoveling shit- you get the drift- jack of all trades, master of none, weathered to the max. Lasted him through his thirties, but it's a rough road to hoe, and he realized he had to settle down after a fashion eventually. Still, every now and then, when he got the urge for going, he picked up and hitchhiked wherever he pleased. He's got a good gig at Muck's Car Repair garage and hires himself out in village households to repair whatever needs repairing- stoves, furnaces, water heaters, toilets, lawnmowers- you name it- anything at all that needed fixing. In his spare time he walks up and back Main Street through the village all the way to the town line, so much so that he's called "the Wilsonville Walker" (which he doesn't mind), stopping in at stores along the way or talking to people he knows (and he knows most everybody). He even lives above the shop. Simplify, simplify. Other than that, he just sits out in front of the garage in a chair up against the wall, whittling, watching and listening. His handiwork is considered a "collectible," so he's told, but he gives it away, mostly to kids or passersby that take an interest. He grew up here in the town orphanage, never knew his parents, had been on his own since he was eighteen. You can learn a lot about a place, especially a small town, by observing and listening. He'd come to find every person has a story, whether they tell it, someone else tells it, or it remains untold. He had no doubt if people knew they were going to be in a book, they'd either be better or worse than they already were, but they wouldn't be their true selves, that is, life as they've lived it, because you can't both live life and portray it at the same time. But nevertheless, he's chosen a few characters in the small village in Western New York whose story you may or may not be interested in. Nevertheless, here they be.

Chief Grimes, for instance, walking what he called his "beat," a misnomer in that the whole damn village was his beat. It was a daily ritual after having lunch, usually in his office, then it was downstairs and out the door and he was practically in the park. Oakgrove Park was its name, after the many oak trees that lined its perimeter. It was usually deserted at this time after the mothers with their children had left off their swinging to go home and have lunch.

In addition to the swings, there was a gazebo with a recently erected bandstand inside, raised in preparation for Old Home Days, an annual week-long event the village sponsored, lending a carnival-like atmosphere to the town. A carnival indeed, the very path he walked on would be surrounded by the brightly lit midway filled with all sorts of games, arts and crafts, clowns, food, even a Ferris wheel, all culminated by the Friday night beer tent. The beer tent, a conglomeration of the townspeople and their families, also an informal annual class reunion of sorts, classmates catching up on their success and failures, whatever the case might be, asking about others who hadn't made it that particular year, which spilled over across the street into the Eagle House after the beer tent closed at eleven sharp, for the more serious drinkers. He could see it in his mind's eye, even though it was hard to believe, given the usual quiet, pristine, almost stately nature of the place he was used to. But at the beer tent all hell might break loose at any time, and then there would be plenty for his men to do: keeping the riffraff (bikers and such) out, arresting a few drunk and disorderly persons nursing an old grudge here and there against someone they hadn't seen in a while, one year even making a drug bust in the men's lavatory.

He didn't mind; it was just one week out of the year, his only objection being having to sit up on the dais with the Village Board while the politicians made their introductory remarks before the parade began, marking the official opening of Old Home Days, part of the price for being a duly elected public official. At least he wasn't expected to say anything, just smile and wave at the proper time and otherwise look official.

As he returned to his office, he saw Joseph Wilson standing in the parking lot conferring with several of the Board members, never a good sign as far as he was concerned, as it was no doubt some money-making scheme concocted by his lawyer to sell some property for more commercial development.

He didn't look forward to that resulting debacle because, while not involved, it made his superiors on the Board surly, half of them all for progress, the other half wanting no part of it. He had a feeling whoever got paid off last was often the deciding vote.

He ducked in the back way before anyone saw him.

"Muckety-muck warning," he winked and said to his office assistant Betty as he closed his door, "do not disturb unless absolutely necessary."

Before he was Chief John Grimes, he was Deputy John Grimes, and before that, Johnny Grimes, who'd grown up in Wilsonville and witnessed many of the changes that had been wrought there since he was a boy, and that continued to change, not always to his liking. He hardly recognized the place anymore. It was getting to be almost crowded and busier than he ever remembered it. It just didn't seem like the place he'd grown up in any longer, a place where a kid could just get up and roam around in the wide-open spaces, with less land and more houses and people now, at least that's how he saw it.

He was a mild-mannered man, even-tempered, not easily riled, but all these changes happening and forthcoming in his town were bringing him to a slow boil, and you wouldn't like him when he was angry. He cared about his village, and it seemed to him these out-of-town city boys (he privately referred to them as carpetbaggers) were taking it over. Enough is enough, was his thought.

Widening Main Street, for instance, to twice its original size, and for no good reason that he could see, except for the added tax revenue. It took away a lot of greenery, and for what? So a lot more cars could clog up the road and things could get noisier and more polluted? He had to bite his tongue at those mandatory Town Board meetings (though most of it went in one ear and out the other, as far as he was concerned, and he would never really say anything, knowing which side his bread was buttered on), hearing how they planned on building more subdivisions across Sherman Drive and were already talking about how the influx of families might cause them to have to build another high school when the one they have (Wilsonville High) is already twice as big as when he went there.

They're getting ahead of themselves with all this, he thought, but, as all the other proposals floated out there, he would have to wait and see. Some of those Village Hall blowhards were just blowing smoke, liking to hear themselves talk, with their schemes not amounting to a hill of beans. Not old man Wilson, though, when he wanted something (or was told he did (Wilson never had an original thought in his head), it was his mouthpiece Bill Burnham, the Village Lawyer, who did the dirty work and got it rammed through with a strategy, the result of his business acumen, inculcated to bring about a favorable resolution, at least for Wilson.

It was all greed if you asked him, though nobody would. Build up the tax base. That's what it's all about; that's the master plan. Still, despite all this, even he (who always tried to look on the bright side) had to admit there might be a silver lining to all this: the bigger the town, the more manpower he'd need to police it. He'd take that in a heartbeat.

A constant stream of strangers was moving in and settling down, although the village proper was still pretty much the same, as there was very little turnover of property there if it could at all be helped, and it could. A cadre of sixth-generation WASPS (including the Wilsons) had definitely kept it in the family. Mostly comprised of the wealthiest class, they'd had things to their liking for as long as they could remember, a case in point being able to choose from several Protestant denomination churches throughout the village, whereas the Catholics, mostly working-class types, were relegated to the one church/school (albeit by far the largest of them all) right at the halfway point on the village's Main Street.

"Dirty Catholics, keep 'em all herded together, I say," he'd heard one board member remark, "easier to see what they're up to that way."

Some of his best friends were Catholic, and though they'd often given him a hard time growing up because he wasn't, he took that remark as a shot across the bow. 'That guy's due for a ticket of some kind,' he figured and vowed to keep an eye on him.

CHAPTER 2

If there was ever an example of someone being born with a silver spoon in his mouth, Joe Wilson was one. As is usually the case, he did nothing to deserve or perpetuate it except being born, while his brother Jim, the brains of a family whose line would soon run out, infinitely the better man, expanded and diversified the business during his lifetime, which was cut short by his suicide after his wife left him for another man a few towns over. Unfortunately, there seemed to be a streak of insanity and misfortune running through the family, usually with dire consequences, as with Jim. That left the family fortune to Joe, who was fortunate to have a smart man to oversee things, who literally thought and spoke for him. Due to his (Bill Burnham Esq.'s) machinations, everything seemed to turn to gold for Joe Wilson, but a more dull, obtuse person you would be hard-pressed to find. Everyone in the village knew the way he was but had to give him his due as the wealthiest man in town, earned or not. There would always be enough sycophants tapping into his influence to give him his due, which he never acknowledged if he was even aware of it. He was not a bad man. He was just unaware of the things he should have been, i.e., like what was going on in his own family. If and how much longer this luck will last, we will soon find out.

Mr. Joseph Wilson (not to be confused with the original Wilson family, whose line by then had died out, although the current clan claimed this distinction for themselves when convenient, and who was still around to refute them?) was no dummy. Well, actually, he was, but, as they say in the sewers, he was one of those people who could fall into a pile of shit and come up with a $100 bill. And boatloads of money could cover up any past mistakes or indiscretions he had blundered into, one of which was a failed attempt to rebuild old man Altman's amusement park and nightclub after it was burned down, which, ironically, against his vehement wishes, was ultimately turned into a recreational park after.

His father may have been an old fuddy-duddy, but Mr. Wilson could read the handwriting on the wall, and it said Progress! Progress! Progress! Onward and upward! Secretly he wished his old man had lived long enough to see the rapid expansion happening in Wilsonville after WWII. That alone would have killed him, his father being a man who in his early years proudly drove through the village on a horse and buggy when he could have easily afforded an automobile and a luxury one at that if he so chose. 'The old skinflint,' his son thought unceremoniously. Not being a sentimental man, soon after his father's death, he felt it was incumbent on him to bring the village into the twentieth century, which meant constant development, investment, reinvestment, and expansion everywhere possible, never mind that it was its pristine quaintness that had drawn many from the city to live there in the first place. Live in a beautiful setting, get away from the rat race, jump on the new expressway and be to your downtown office in ten minutes. The best of both worlds- that was the ticket!

Mr. Wilson cared nothing about this. It was up to him to overcome his father's anachronism (certainly not his word) and enable his village to catch up with the relative modernity of the surrounding villages whether it wanted to or not. In other words, there was a lot of money to be made in developing and expanding the village, and he made sure other businessmen of his ilk would see it that way also.

Befitting the patriarch of a minor fiefdom, the Wilsons lived in a colonial brick and wood mansion on Main Street, in a prominent spot in the village, the house being the site of the original tumbledown dwelling erected by his great-great grandfather, who'd come to these shores from Scotland in 1840 or thereabouts. The Wilson clan had done it all - sheep ranching (including purportedly being the original sheep-dippers in the area), farming, running a distillery and eventually acquiring a lot of land in the area, whether by hook or by crook or merely being at the right place at the right time. At the time most of the land was prairie land for a long stretch, culminating in hills blanketed with large stands of trees further south and densely forested land to the north. That the land could be had for a reasonable price was self-evident, as the Wilsons never overpaid for anything.

Mr. Wilson had inherited a quarter of the land (by then a vast amount) in Wilsonville from his forebears. His older brother James had inherited slightly more, so between them, they owned over half of Wilsonville, a good position to be in, on the ground floor of what promised to be booming times. James ran a factory that produced many different products over the years, prophylactics and gelatin, to name a few. The rest (mostly several buildings lining Main Street and the factory) they held jointly, believing, as wealthy families are wont to do, that every thin dime should be kept in the family. Having a degree in chemical education (he got the brains in the family), he was constantly experimenting and, shortly before World War II, began working with polyurethane, landing a highly lucrative contract with the DOD producing high-gloss finishes for a massive airplane factory nearby. After the war he came up with the idea of manufacturing sponges made of it. After his tragic death he left his brother with not only all the family's land holdings, but the business, too, which, despite his general incompetence, still managed to thrive, as, consequently, did Joseph Wilson.

And since, thanks to James Wilson, the XL-o Sponge (*the sponge that wipes it all away*) Company was run so smoothly and was self-sustaining, after his brother's demise, Mr. Wilson became a so-called man of leisure, having his accountant and financial adviser ensure the business continued to thrive and helped him acquire even more land. This enabled him (as advised) to become a member of every club in the village: country, trap & field, curling, and sit on the boards of several important institutions, including the school, village, Rotary, Kiwanis, as well as being a Freemason. In short, a veritable mid-century Babbitt!

That these were merely figurehead appointments was a given, as he had not one iota to

contribute, becoming more addled the older he got. But it would be a scandal of major proportions if the richest man in village didn't maintain a high visibility in body if not in mind.

Mr. Wilson was tall, tan, and angular, with a salt-and-pepper brush cut growing in, and a constantly bemused smile on his face, as if not quite believing how he got where he was or how much he was worth. Being taciturn and dull himself, he was a hard person to warm up to and seemed to live in his own little world. He was prone to walking around stores in the village, not buying anything, mind you, just picking up items and checking the price, then putting them back. He was also a notoriously cheap tipper, oftentimes leaving only loose change no matter how large the bill.

As previously mentioned, he couldn't have accomplished what he had if he'd not had a more than competent adviser (brilliant actually), Bill Burnham, bank president as well as lawyer, who also doubled as his accountant and informal real estate agent. A very astute man, assiduous in all his duties, Mr. Burnham, was a devout Catholic, with a requisite passel of kids as testimony.

They were also golf partners (though you would never call them friends) and could be seen most summer days (except Sunday, Mr. Burnham at least) on the links at one of the village's two country clubs. All in all, it seemed a strange pairing, Mr. Wilson towering over the short squat florid Mr. Burnham, which was tolerated by all parties concerned (Mr. Burnham usually being the only Catholic in the group, back when those things mattered)) because it was seen as a purely business arrangement mutually beneficial to everyone. And that's what most of these golf outings were, informal business meetings either with just themselves or a foursome with a couple of clients who could be ad men, investors, village cronies, high-powered salesmen, professionals, and executives from all sectors of the business community. They seldom played with other members of the club and, despite the frequency of their play, were both hackers.

No, you couldn't by any stretch of the imagination call them friends. They never socialized together (though neither socialized all that much anyway), the families hardly knew each other, and the rumor was that neither had ever darkened one another's doorway. While that was never challenged, the nature of their relationship would later prove to be scandalously otherwise.

CHAPTER 3

As a chronicler of Wilsonville's oral history, Jim Weatherly noted the rapid influx and efflux that was taking place in the Village proper as well as the burgeoning neighborhoods cropping up north of Sherman Drive, which had previously been mostly woodland. After the War was when this all began, although in the Village proper, it was more like musical chairs, where people were becoming "upwardly mobile," leaving their old neighborhoods behind but still staying in the village. Whereas in the new neighborhoods, there was a lot of turnover, many of its residents being corporate executives and upper management types, which often required moving around the country at their company's beck and call, not unlike the military. Sometimes you needed a scorecard to keep track and Jim Weatherly was that scorecard. While there was no real animosity between the villagers and newcomers, and vice versa, not one single newcomer ever moved into the village, and vice versa.

Chief Grimes was a Wilsonviller through and through. A hefty, likable man with a bum knee, the result of an old football injury, he had worshipped at its churches (not so much anymore), attended its schools, played sandlot baseball on its playgrounds, fished, trapped and hunted in its woods, streams and fields, and played on the greatest high school football team in Wilsonville history, if not the state.

But that was a long time ago, so long only the old-timers remembered it, and he wished they wouldn't bring it up practically every doggone time they saw him. It only made him feel that much older and often made his bad knee flare-up, though Mrs. Grimes said it was psychosomatic or some such thing. He'd torn the anterior cruciate ligament (the surgeon having told him it had been gradually wearing away for a while) in his knee playing tackle on both the offensive and defensive lines right through to the state championship game, even though in excruciating pain the entire time. They had to help him off him the field then after the chop block that finally severed it completely in the waning moments of the game, not because he was a conquering hero (nobody paid any attention to linemen), but because he couldn't walk off under his own power. He'd had it operated on shortly after but was never the same again, as was the case back in those days. At the time it had seemed worth it, he supposed: state champs and local legends with shiny trophies and their names permanently in the record books, but now he wondered. It seemed that ever since then, the guys on the team had been cursed with more than their fair share of problems, especially the best players, a quartet who all played in the backfield, save one.

Swede Patrick, the quarterback who could throw a football from end zone to end zone and seemingly run under and catch it at the same time, he was so fast. They didn't have hardly any passing attack, but he was a good runner on the option play and could bootleg his way out of trouble if need be, throwing a bomb every now and then to one of the lonesome ends on the team to keep a defense honest. He was the penultimate of five tough brothers in a family willing to throw down at the drop of a hat, often at the dinner table. After high school he had become an alky working odd jobs around the village and hustling pool at the Pool Hall, hooked on vodka stingers. Not that he was one of those "I coulda been a contender" guys, crying in his beer (or stinger in this case) about how great he once was. He merely took his frustration and inadequacies out on some pour soul in the bar who looked at him cross-wise, intent on beating him to a pulp unless the other patrons tore him away.

Joseph Pierre, their scatback, part Indian, was a squat, quick, tough runner who exploded through a hole or flashed around end on a sweep and an excellent pass-blocker out of the backfield. He was barely ever seen at school, just enough to keep him eligible. Rumor had it he was working full-time at his old man's gas station out in the boondocks. He was immensely strong, though you couldn't tell it to look at him unless you saw him up close when he somehow seemed twice as big as he was. Right out of high school he became a Golden Gloves boxer briefly until he accidentally killed a guy in the ring. He never got over that and became even more of an erratic recluse. His feats of strength were legendary. One night, driving home in a blizzard, he noticed a car in the ditch near his house. He got out of his car and went over to it and, seeing someone was in there, picked up the back end of the car and pulled it out of the ditch with his bare hands. Incredible as that was, no one had any trouble believing it when they heard about it. He once walked two miles in another blizzard (Buffalo being the Blizzard City, as you're probably aware) just to punch a guy in the mouth who insulted his girlfriend, immediately turning around after cold-cocking the unfortunate soul and heading back from whence he came. He was reputed to be slightly off, a fair assessment in light of the things that transpired when he was in the vicinity. He was rarely seen after his dad's gas station closed shortly after his death, relegated to collecting disability and food stamps, which he most likely spent on booze, if the ramshackle condition of the house he inherited from his dad was any indication.

Still, as unfortunate as these are stories are, Gary Graham's was the worst, being that Johnny Grimes had known him since he was a kid, even considered him a friend, albeit at times, a very difficult one. Who wouldn't be after the childhood he'd endured? Oh, not that he'd ever once mentioned it in all the years Johnny had known him, no sir. But word gets around quickly in Wilsonville, and Johnny gradually learned he'd lived in a bunch of foster homes after he was born and finally was adopted when he was five, but the mother was an alcoholic and the father, a ne'er-do-well traveling salesman, was on the road most of the time, with very little to show for it. They lived just down the street from the Grimes family, and while Johnny knew his mother was strict, which might imply she cared for him, like most alcoholics, she somehow had no idea what his life with them was like, or how she could make it better for him, leaving him pretty much to his own devices, which mostly meant playing by himself out in the yard, or up alone in his room.

It was always sports sports sports with them when they were kids, especially baseball, but Gary never participated in the neighborhood games, though Johnny'd ask him to time and time again until he finally gave up. He never really learned how and where Gary spent his time when he wasn't in school. He was just never around. Johnny always spoke up for him when people talked about him behind his back, which was the only thing they could do. They'd never say it to his face, him being so massive and all. Massive is the only word for him. He'd had a lot of baby fat on him when he was younger, but even then, he was strong, as he proved time and time again in any gym or recess activities he was forced to unwillingly participate in, and, not only that, he was fast, beating all challengers in any speed races they made him run during gym class. It was hard to believe anyone that big could move so fast. In short, he was a natural athlete. Because he was the biggest kid in the class (if not the whole school), gym teachers picked on him, making him wrestle, rope climb, or throw a ball against their favorites, assuming he'd be humiliated. Instead, it backfired. It was no contest, he won easily against all challengers. And as he grew older, he shed the fat so sudden-like it was as if he'd been wearing a fat suit up to that point. He was now muscle on muscle, never having or having to lift a weight. One of the gym teachers, who was also the varsity football coach, was salivating just thinking about what he could do with him on the team. But Gary showed no interest, no matter how many times the coach and Johnny begged him to come out for the team.

Around that time, the police were at Gary's house so often, Johnny's parents didn't want him associating with Gary any longer, worried that the blowback from him doing so might somehow affect the course of his future, which they were constantly worrying about. Johnny didn't think this was fair, as, like most kids his age, Johnny never gave his future much thought at the time, and, to be honest, the few times he did, he didn't think it looked too bright anyway.

Then suddenly, Gary's mother was institutionalized with a diagnosis of schizophrenia, just as he was starting high school, and his father, unable or unwilling to take care of him, never returned from his weekly business trip. It was thought he'd moved away to parts unknown, as no one ever heard from or saw him again. As a result, with no guardian, Gary was also about to be institutionalized. Johnny didn't dare ask his parents to let him live with them, and none of the town's churches, including his, would help. He couldn't believe no one would take him in. If no one did, being too old to likely be adopted, he would become a ward of the state and spend the remainder of his adolescence at "The Home", a county facility for wayward boys. That was, in fact, where he stayed the first few nights until a more permanent situation could be found.

At this critical juncture, help, though not entirely altruistic, arrived in the person of Coach Jenkins. Gary could live with him, no strings attached until he finished high school. Married with no children and always wanting a son, it seemed a win-win situation. Some of the barber shop wags may have been skeptical of the coach's motives but were as happy as anyone when Gary showed up for JV football practice that fall. Played sparingly that season while he got the hang of things, the few times he got in (mostly in crucial situations), he made the most of it, bulling into the endzone from five yards out to win one game and stuffing an opposing runner on a goal-line stand in another.

He was a man among boys physically, if not mentally. He quickly became a good teammate and a great football player, the greatest in that area's history, not to mention Wilsonville High School football. And State Champs said it all! As a middle guard, he knocked over hefty linemen like bowling pins, often getting to the runner right as the quarterback handed it off to him. But it was at fullback he became a holy terror, with his chiseled 232 lbs. and immense strength (with his shoulders, humped like a bull's, he was literally capable of bending iron bars), and was as fast as anyone on any defenses in the league. Defenders hung off him like sheets on a clothesline flapping in the breeze, if not already having been run through and stomped over. He carried the ball the old-fashioned way, cradling it in both arms in front of him, and you couldn't pry it loose with a crowbar. And Johnny Grimes (no lightweight himself at 225 lbs.) had been honored to pave the way for him to get a full head of steam from his tackle spot, not that he often needed it, usually getting a face full of turf for his efforts, having been trampled over by Gary on his way to pay dirt. He looked as if he didn't even need to wear a helmet, if he could even find one big enough to fit him properly.

But while he became well-known, he still kept pretty much to himself, and people, even Swede, a perpetual burr in anyone's saddle, learned to leave him alone early on after snapping a towel at Gary's posterior in the locker room after practice one day and getting himself jerked off the ground above his head with one hand for his efforts. 'Let him take that pent-up anger out on his opponents,' was Coach Jenkins' thought when he heard about it. He admonished everyone on the team to leave him alone. Not only didn't he have to ask twice, he needn't have asked any of them once.

Lest it be forgotten, there was a fourth star on the team, the sole non-backfield member, who was perhaps the strangest of them all. His name was Paul Brennan, a 167- pound pulling guard and middle linebacker. He was a workout demon, running up and down the bleachers at Billie stadium year-round in work boots, with not an ounce of fat on him and the look of the zealot in his eye. Purportedly mild-mannered off the field, he was a silent assassin on it, flying around to make bone-jarring tackles (breaking several helmets in the process) and crushing blocks well down the field, picking off impediments one by one as Pierre or Gary tailed closely behind him, their escort to the end zone. He was the quiet leader of the group, the most respected and dreaded, and the unquestioned captain of the team, though because of his size, it seemed difficult to fathom why at first glance. Of course, it didn't hurt that he had Gary Graham playing in front of him, anchoring the middle of the defensive line and controlling the line of scrimmage almost single-handedly. When Coach Jenkins gave an order, Paul could be counted on to enforce it. Johnny Grimes saw it up close and personal, so to speak. Well, actually, he didn't really *see* it because his job was to engage the defensive end by any means necessary so Paul could go around him and pull for Joseph on a sweep, and it happened so fast that often by the time he had looked over to see if he'd done his job correctly, Paul was already gone.

The original Fearsome Foursome (except for Gary) were as close-knit on the field as off it, and even Gary joined the frat they formed with a couple of other motorcycle crazies named Marty Modifari and Greg Zimmer, their ostensible purpose being to raise hell both in school (the rare times they were all there) and out, where they threw weekend beer blasts, and rumbled with frats from neighboring towns, often hanging out at Greg Zimmer's father's auto parts place near the high school.

None of the backfield trio were at their high school graduation, Joseph and Swede because they never graduated, Gary because he had no family to see him graduate, even though Coach Jenkins was hurt by that because he was going anyway. Paul graduated in the middle of his class though it was common knowledge he was the smartest guy around.

Joseph and Swede both stayed in town after school doing much of nothing, while Gary, with Coach Jenkins pulling some strings and calling in several favors just to get him noticed, had gotten a full ride at the University of Nebraska, a national powerhouse at the time. No one questioned his motives for taking Gary in after that. It had worked out just fine for both of them. He was rumored to have done pretty well, making All-American at fullback as a freshman, in fact, though it wasn't mentioned in the *Wilsonville Bee*, most likely because he'd only lasted one season before he half-killed someone in a bar fight shortly after being honored, and was banished permanently from the team, All-American or not. He came home with his tail between his legs and more pissed off than ever.

Paul Brennan was indeed an especially talented and intelligent individual. No one heard much from him after he graduated high school, though several crazy rumors surfaced from time to time: that he was studying to be a doctor, that he'd entered a monastery in Kentucky, that he'd become a demolitions expert and was working in Alaska, finally, even joined a commune, all plausible scenarios.

Whatever their situations, it seemed the Fearsome Foursome was no more.

CHAPTER 4

For most average people life is earnest, from the cradle to the grave, a long struggle to keep your head above water and keep it there if you are successful. Not so for the Wilsons, who were playing at life, neither engaging with the community and letting their children run roughshod over them. Both Mr. and Mrs. Wilson were the end of their line, which was a good thing because while they were physical specimens, their minds were weak. In short, they hid behind their money. Jim Weatherly hadn't known many people of their ilk, not personally, but he'd studied them from afar, and in all his years, he'd never seen anything like the Wilsons. He felt bad for the children but knew with every fiber of his being, things weren't going to end well for the family. Whether intentionally or not, they were playing with fire and things were bound to come to a head; they always do.

As in most cases with the wealthy (literally wanting to keep everything in the family), Joseph Wilson had married well to the only daughter of the Village's lone doctor, Dr. Lapham, a shy, reclusive beauty named

Marilyn. The whole village marveled at what a handsome couple they made (mostly due to Marilyn Lapham), and she played the role to the best of her ability, but with each baby's arrival her public appearances diminished until with the fourth and final one, they ceased altogether. She was also reputed (which in this village meant she did) to have an unfortunate drinking problem, which only added to her reclusiveness.

Mr. Wilson's firstborn, a son, also named Joseph (dubbed Joey and eventually just Junior), was the apple of his eye, given anything he wanted, and thus spoiled beyond belief. No one knew what kind of hold he had on the old man (besides being the firstborn) to allow this to happen, but the other children (two girls and a boy) seemed merely an afterthought. Everything revolved around Joey. It was he who reaped the benefits of his father's many club memberships, becoming adept at shooting, golf, and even curling. Just bright enough to become a savvy conniver, he would become a thorn in the side of just about anyone he came into contact with, especially adults and peers. He was an Eddie Haskell who didn't even attempt to butter up any parents and was always scheming and playing pranks and getting others (even his few friends) into trouble. Being popular because he had good looks and money, he always had a coterie of people who hung around him (the older he got, the younger they got), but there was never any question who was the ringleader. They just could never pin anything on him. Any idea Mr. Wilson may have had of them being buddies was peremptorily jettisoned at an early age. Neither of them would prove to be capable or seemingly even in need of such intimacy. They never became enemies because Mr. Wilson was an enabler, and things would be fine as long as he remained that way.

Determined to dispel any remaining whiff of the stuffy paternalism of his past, Mr. Wilson, whether through confidence gained by a recent judicious and extremely remunerative land sale, or on the advice of the shrewd Mr. Burnham—more probably the latter— made a bold move. Whatever the reason, he moved his young family from the family mansion on Main Street to a house on Elliott Creek he had built in a new residential area (on land he formerly owned) that was springing up not far away. It was now the most desirous location in the village, one of the choicest pieces of real estate in the area. You'd expect nothing less from a burgeoning land baron. All the best people were relocating there, and, as a bonus, he'd one-upped Bill Burnham, who lived just around the block in an older split-level (one of the first of those in the area) on a street so contiguous to their back yards they practically overlapped one another.

The new house was a sleek brick split-level with white siding and a picture-window in the front, looking out on a putting-green lawn in the front, and a rock garden in the back, surrounded by a wide expanse of lush green carpet that led gradually down a gentle slope to the creek. In the freshly tarred, hosed-down driveway stood his silver Cadillac Coupe de Ville, equipped with all the latest amenities that came standard in the top luxury car of its day. It was just like in a commercial of the time, the one where you had the perfect home (split-level, of course) and family, car (usually a wood-paneled station wagon, which the adverts were for, and was indeed Mrs. Wilson's car, though rarely driven), and a dog, of course, a setter named Mickey, after every boy's favorite baseball player, Mickey Mantle. In short, the American Dream in all its untrammeled beauty.

Meanwhile, unbeknownst or wished away (as most family matters were) to Mr. Wilson, vestiges of behavioral problems concerning Joey were beginning to manifest themselves.

"Lookit' these power windows, locks, and seats," Joey'd brag to his little friends as they stood around his father's car, "I bet your father's car doesn't have those. It's even air-conditioned!"

Most of the kids were both impressed and a little intimidated, except for one quiet boy hanging on the periphery of the group. He wasn't even from the neighborhood, didn't go to the same school as the other boys. He merely knew Joey from little league football and baseball. He wasn't impressed because his father drove an Oldsmobile Ninety-eight with the same power features and air-conditioning as Mr. Wilson's Cadillac, and, even better, it was a convertible. And his father didn't use his car to tool around the village in, either, he used it for his job as a traveling rep for a large insurance company, his territory stretching from Virginia to Vermont. The fact that his father's car was a company car never crossed his mind, nor would it have mattered anyway, except possibly to Joey. He drove it fifty-thousand miles a year, ten months out of the year spent on the road, home weekends, with summers off, getting a new car every two years. The boy never mentioned any of this to Joey, not wanting to contradict him or incur his wrath at some future date, even though he seldom (if ever) saw him when those sports weren't in season.

Joey laid on the horn until his father came outside to tell him to stop horsing around, but by that time they'd all run down to the creek. It was usually at that time Toby (the quiet boy) parted company with them and went on his unobtrusive way, usually to the Wilsonville Library or a friend's house. He couldn't imagine anyone treating their father like that. He knew he wouldn't even do it if he could (he couldn't). He wouldn't dare, not that he even wanted to (he didn't).

CHAPTER 5

Though Jim Weatherly, ever the optimist, swore up and down that just being alive was good enough, no matter when, as long as you were true to yourself, it was the early sixties, still a great time to be alive, with a few years yet before the proverbial shit hit the fan, leaving the country torn and raging. The war was over (except for the cold war, of course), the next war had yet to start, the GI Bill afforded vets the opportunity to buy new, affordable, and readily available housing ("will build to suit," a big catchphrase of the time, merely meant, "we'll get the cookie-cutter out and erect a house indistinguishable from any other on the street"), wages were good, things, in general, seemed a bit more relaxed, simpler back then. It was a prosperous, even booming time for all concerned if you were white and in the right place at the right time. It was no different in Wilsonville.

This new housing was almost exclusively being built away from the city, engulfing formerly small villages and municipalities—of which Wilsonville was one—creating what became known as the suburb (from the word suburban), just beginning to become a widespread phenomenon across the country. This mass migration from the cities was dubbed 'white flight' by the sociologists, and for the most part, cities, now mostly comprised of segregated colored people and poor but proud second-generation German and Polish immigrants, were left to fend for themselves. It was no coincidence the cities deteriorated inversely to the rate suburbs were prospering. This was called urban planning.

Still, the city, with its movie theaters, the biggest and best stores, fine restaurants, gin mills and dance halls, jazz clubs, the baseball stadium and basketball and hockey arena, even a theater (formerly an infamous strip club) for Broadway plays and musicals, if you were so inclined, continued to thrive (if you were just visiting), as they were still the only places for a special night out. The fact that one needed to be mindful of where they were at all times, especially at night, was common knowledge. And last but not least, this is where the jobs were, the city bustling during the weekday, then like a ghost town weeknights until Friday and Saturday rolled around, to be deserted again on Sunday.

For sure, things had changed a lot since he was a kid growing up in Wilsonville, it was obvious to anyone who had lived there any length of time, but Deputy Grimes wasn't complaining, mind you, quite to the contrary. He'd gotten farther ahead than he'd ever thought he would in life, especially at a fairly young age. He had a cake job, you couldn't beat the pension, and (so far) he hadn't been asked to do anything he couldn't tell his wife about in order to keep his job. No, he enjoyed almost everything about the job and had taken his pledge to do his duty with integrity and honor to the best of his ability, and he was a man of his word.

Deputy John Grimes (most of his friends called him Jack, which he preferred, with a few exceptions, one being his wife, who favored the more formal name, befitting his informal status of Assistant Chief), was in his early thirties, with a shock of almost black hair, which he mostly wore as a flat top, but let grow out some for extra warmth in the winter. He still retained the broad shoulders, thick legs, tree trunk thighs, and biceps of a former high school lineman, but in the midst of losing the age-old battle against becoming more and more sedentary with age, was getting a bit thick about the middle. Husky, beefy, burly, brawny, whatever you desired (his wife preferred brawny), he was, and his bum knee pained him plenty, but he was still a positive, fair and gentleman, with a good sense of humor.

He'd gotten back to his hometown at just the right time after the Korean conflict (in which, thankfully, he was a non-combatant). Things were affordable (a house, believe it or not, more so than a car) because of, again, the GI Bill, courtesy of Uncle Sam, and he immediately took advantage of it, purchasing a cozy little bungalow on Howard Street, right off Glen Avenue, the same street he'd lived on as a kid, which was right behind the same Catholic church whose playground he and generations of kids had played on. Lest you think it strange, he now lived on the same street he'd grown upon. It wasn't intentional, it just happened that one of the few houses in the village he could afford was on that street, so he jumped at the chance.

He took a job at the DPW but had bigger aspirations, though at the time, he didn't realize it. He was perfectly content to own (after a few renovations and painting inside and out), a home, no matter how small, and have steady employment. He didn't really need a car at that point because he could walk to work. How great was that? Some of his old high school classmates, Gary Graham and Billy Martz, to name a couple, worked there too, though Gary wasn't in a good way, drinking too much, known to be packing a knife and a gun at all times, ramping up his activities in a motorcycle club.

He minded his own business and counted his blessings. He knew that he was very fortunate to be where he was, having half-assed it through the service and come back home with nowhere else to go and no prospects whatsoever, no family left. Not that he had ever had much of one anyway, everyone having either moved away or died, and no one in Wilsonville he was close to anymore. Gary would have been the closest, but he was a changed man, and not for the better, and the future Chief stayed clear of him.

He was young, the world was his oyster, with not really a care in the world and no big plans for the foreseeable future. He only needed to keep body and soul together for now, and, although he'd never imagined himself working there, his job at the Wilsonville DPW suited him just fine. Good honest labor, decent wages, and regular hours. On top of that, a house, something else he'd never imagined himself having, which would be a good investment down the line should he need a nest egg, or if he should eventually settle down, get married, raise a family. Not that he was unsettled by any means, but having a family would be the icing on the cake.

If it was true, he caroused a bit too much with the boys on a Friday payday over at the Crow's Nest or the VFW, or a Saturday night "on the town," what of it? He never got in any trouble to speak of, wasn't hurting anyone but himself, with only a severe hangover and depleted wallet to show for it.

He usually went to church the Sunday after a toot to atone for it, it being merely a short walk up Main Street to the Lutheran Church by the NYS Thruway, a walk he was used to and enjoyed, having done it since he was a kid. He'd been raised a Lutheran and went to Sunday service with his parents without fail, brushing up his suit and polishing his shoes the night before. He didn't mind it so much, except for the formalness his strict parents insisted on, and actually began to enjoy it once he got a little older. It was a way to get out of the house on Wednesday nights for Youth Group and during Lent. He even sang in the choir, not only because he had a good voice, but because he was expected to be there on Saturdays for choir practice and arrive before his parents on Sunday to warm up before the service, giving him a few more hours of freedom. He found he especially loved the liturgy and the hymns; they comforted and gave him peace while he was there. As you've probably already figured out, comfort and familiarity were the two beacons guiding his life at that point in time.

Of course, Pastor Brand's sermons could be a little long-winded, but he was an all right guy, as he'd found out during his time as an acolyte, altar boy, and candidate for confirmation.

He lost what little faith he had left when he set out on his own after his Dad died his senior year in high school (it was after the high school football season, so at least he got to see them bring home the state championship) and his Mom went to live with relatives in Michigan shortly after he graduated. He chose not to go with her because he didn't want to uproot his life, start over again, as it were. Though there had never been anything unpleasant, he often found them looking at him in puzzlement, as if they didn't recognize him or wondered why he was there. It gave him a very unsettling feeling like he didn't belong. While there was no animosity as far as he was concerned, there just was no emotional attachment of any kind with her or her relatives, or even his father, for that matter, which bewildered him ever after because he couldn't understand why or how that could be. Nevertheless, the feeling seemed to be mutual. He never saw her again, wasn't even notified when she died a decade later.

Instead he went into the service mainly because he had nowhere to go and nothing else to do. It was there he found out he'd been adopted by them as a baby and, though initially devastated, was somewhat relieved, as it partly explained the many things which had perplexed him so as he was growing up.

It was at this church he met his better half, Roberta. One Sunday, sitting in a pew near the choir loft, nursing a frightening hangover, he noticed a brown-haired, healthy-skinned young beauty with enough meat on her bones to satisfy him (he didn't go in for the pale, wispy WASPY type then in vogue with the in-crowd). After the service at the coffee hour, seeing her unattended for a moment, and figuring they at least had common ground with him having been a former and her a current member of the choir, went up to her and introduced himself, hoping she wouldn't smell the booze on his breath. Normally something he would never do, he figured it must mean there was a strong attraction, at least on his part.

Not so much, it seemed, on hers, if their initial conversation was any indication.

"Hello," he began, "my name is John Grimes. I used to be in this very same choir myself when I was a boy."

"Hello," she said politely, "I'm Roberta Kane. If you're interested in rejoining, the Choir Director is right over there," she said, pointing to a reed-thin gentleman sipping a cup of tea. "Goodness knows we can always use some new blood. Now, if you'll excuse me, I have to be going."

"I'll think about it," he said as she nodded and walked away, and "Nice to meet you," he said to her retreating form.

There was no way he wanted to be in the choir at this or any other time, he knew. Those days were long gone and brought back only painful memories of growing up, even if partly retroactive from when he found out he'd been adopted.

Still, it was an in, he thought, and at least now she knew who he was. He'd figure something out in the meantime. He had to see her again.

Gradually getting to know her better by attending church more frequently (which for him meant less drinking, which to him meant some kind of commitment) and asking around, if not actually talking to her, not wanting to be too forward, it became evident she was everything he could have hoped for. She was an elementary school teacher right there in Wilsonville, having just moved there from a few villages over after taking the job at the beginning of the school year.

He knew that she was kind of shy from the few times they'd chatted awkwardly at the coffee hour, but so was he. She gave no indication what she thought of him one way or the other or if she even thought of him at all, for that matter. He figured his only chance was to keep talking to her, no matter how awkwardly, until he could screw up enough courage to ultimately ask her out on a date.

"Maybe you'd like to go out to dinner sometime?" he finally asked her tentatively after doing so.

"I don't see why not," she responded immediately (or so it seemed to him), "look me up, I'm in the book. It'll have to be on a weekend, though, work and all."

He was pretty excited when she said yes, though even then, it took him another couple of weeks to actually make that phone call, during which time he avoided church, not wanting to run into her and have her think he was wavering or even worse, chicken.

Thus, she seemed surprised when he finally got up the nerve to call her, wondering why he hadn't been at church lately.

"Oh that," he mumbled, "no reason, I guess. But here I am now," he said awkwardly.

She accepted right away, which did his heart glad. He figured they might as well make a night of it and told her he'd like to go into the city to a favorite Italian restaurant of his. It was a dark, quiet, candlelit place, as he described it, perfect for getting to know each other, he thought, and the food was simple but terrific.

Although loathe to even think it lest he jinx things, and given no indication either way by her, he thought they had hit it off right away. She hadn't been into the city since she was a kid, it turned out when it was always a big adventure to make their annual visit to the big city, usually around Christmas, to see all the lights, decorations, holiday storefronts, even visit Santa at Sears when they were very little. She was an only child, too, her father a factory worker, her mother a housewife, and, as a dutiful daughter, she still went to visit them as often as she could, though it had been good to get away from what she described as a gloomy place way out in the sticks.

She didn't drink, so he made sure he kept it to one beer and a glass of chianti with his spaghetti Napoli under the broiler that evening if only to take the edge off his nervousness. After dinner was over, not wanting the evening to end, he even surprised himself (being lousy at it and knowing it would wreak havoc on his knees) by asking her if she'd like to extend it by doing a bit of dancing.

To his relief, she said, "I'll have to take a raincheck on that, but I'd love to some time. A real gentleman that can dance," she said, smiling, as she got out of the car, "and not half-bad looking, who would have thought it?"

He even walked her up to the door of her rooming house on Grove Street and said goodnight, telling her what a good time he'd had, and maybe they could do it again soon.

"Call me," she said, "you know my number, and don't wait so long this time."

Smiling once more, she thanked him for the lovely evening.

While he wouldn't call it head over heels, he thought it had gone well. Regardless, he knew he liked her just fine. He felt comfortable with her and she seemed to be with him as well, and, before long, it became a regular thing between them. He popped the question to her at that same Italian restaurant they went to on their first date a year to the day later.

Blushing, then smiling (she smiled a lot), she said "yes" with no hesitation.

They had a small wedding at the church and a reception at a local restaurant called The Rose Garden. Neither of them being big travelers, they went to Niagara Falls, it being "the Honeymoon Capital of the World" at the time, after all, with the caveat that they'd go someplace further away when they were more established.

This, among other things, made him realize he could and would do much better for her. They bought a car (a first for both), a Ford Fairlane, and Bobbie (he called her that now) redecorated and repainted the whole house indoors while he repainted the outside. "It's the perfect place for raising a family," she often said, both realizing they'd need a bigger income if she took maternity leave, however brief, at her job.

To that end, on a day off, when he was at Village Hall for something or other, he saw a job posted for a police officer right there in Wilsonville. He'd never thought of that for a career, but now that it was there in black and white, it seemed perfect for him. He followed the instructions on the posting and immediately went over to the Wilsonville Police Station, which was conveniently located right next store. He talked to the secretary and told her he'd seen the job ad and would like to apply for it. She handed him a bunch of papers to fill out and told him to come back when he'd completed them. Not wanting to waste any time, he immediately went to the library for the first time since he was a kid to fill them out, hoping to have them completed by the close of day.

He barely managed to do so, and it was a big pain, in triplicate to boot and a few weeks later got a letter telling him to come to the Police Dept. on a certain day and time. Even though it said nothing more, he thought he'd gotten the job, wondering how it could have been that easy. Bobbie, ever the cautious one, said not to get ahead of himself, and she was right. After reiterating his desire to become a police officer, he was given a complete physical and mental evaluation on the spot, and some more lengthy forms to fill out, which, while again a pain, would be more than worth it if he got the job.

Even then, that was just the beginning. First, he had to be accepted and attend classes at the Police Training Academy. When he got in, both Bobbie and he were pretty excited, although he was nervous about making the grade (literally), specifically school of any kind, not being his forte, as well as about his mediocre military record. Bobbie said she knew he could do it and do it well, and he knew she was right if he could just make it through that final hurdle.

Still, it was rough having to dabble in criminal law, community policing, firearms training (he would never feel comfortable carrying a gun), and investigation and defensive tactics, along with a whole lot of physical exercise. Six months later, though, he was very proud to be walking across the stage svelte and more confident upon graduation. But not as proud as Bobbie.

The process still wasn't over, however, as he had to undergo still more physical and psychological testing, pass a polygraph, and interview first with the Wilsonville Police staff and, finally, the Village Board.

He began to wonder if he'd made the right decision and if he'd ever be finished, but he finally made it through and, almost a year later, became a full-fledged member of the Wilsonville Police Department.

Again, right place, right time. If he thought he'd had it bad, it would be much tougher for the new guys trying to make the grade. Big changes in the process had occurred since, requiring even more rigorous mental and physical standards and what amounted to basically a college education at the brand spanking new and improved Police Training Academy, just a few blocks down from the high school. He wasn't sure he could even qualify today, but it hadn't held him back. He mostly subscribed to the Andy Griffith method of policing, figuring it was always better to get along with people, treat them fairly, give them the benefit of the doubt, and mostly it's proven to be true. And he hasn't regretted it for a single moment.

Bobbie came to his swearing in, of course (she wouldn't have missed it), and, while he disliked all the pomp and circumstance of such affairs (he only went to his high school graduation at his mother's vehement insistence) and military rituals in general, he was glad she did and could tell she was proud of him because she said it about every five minutes. And while he kept his uniform clean and pressed, his shoes shined, and his hat blocked, that was just part of his overall neatness, a result of his military training, not that he was all that gung-ho about it or thought he was superior to any civilian. Not like fellow inductee Deputy Rains, who was all spit and polish, giving crisp salutes to all the top brass he saw, lording it over the citizens of Wilsonville. Not in a mean way, but just enough to tell he did. Chief Grimes could just imagine him going back to his boarding house room and standing in front of the mirror for hours, quick-drawing, preening, and saluting.

He and Bobbie went out afterward for a real nice feed put on by the Police Auxiliary people at the most popular restaurant in town, Maitland's, where they all gathered in their big banquet room and really chowed down. That was on a Friday, and the next Monday it was off to work.

Early on, his favorite thing about the job was going out on patrol. He started off on the night patrol, which in Wilsonville consisted mostly of trying to stay awake. Back in those days, you didn't have 24-hour convenient stores or fast-food drive-ins, it was only the 2-quart thermos of coffee and a couple of sandwiches Bobbie made him, every now and then slipping in a couple of homemade oatmeal raisin cookies (his favorite) that kept him from Mr. Sandman. He had certain nightly rounds to make each hour- the banks, churches, Main Street stores, houses where people were away for vacation in the summer, the local lover's lane by the new airport, and lastly, the cemetery. It was mostly uneventful and usually needed to be stretched out to last the whole hour. Every now and then, his routine might be interrupted by the odd bar fight, false fire/building alarms, and domestic disputes, which, although not as prevalent back then, were the worst because he usually knew the people, although they rarely resulted in bodily harm, that being reserved for the household items damaged in the process. Every now and then, there was a call-in on a driver speeding or driving drunk, or a stray dog or cat, even a wild critter (skunk, deer, or raccoon mostly, although Mr. Bradley reported seeing a pink elephant every time he went on a bender) now and then, mostly just your garden variety disturbances, requiring little or no action, arrest-wise, or subsequent follow-up.

Come to think of it, if you want to know the truth, over the years he'd come to find it was the villagers who perpetrated (and perpetuated) most of the offenses just named, for the most part, the result of too much boozing.

And then there were the Wilsons, the oldest and wealthiest family in Wilsonville, who were in a class of their own, the old man gradually relegated to a doddering fool by his eldest son, a kid from hell. There were all types of rumors concerning them, in fact, you'd think they were the only thing to talk about, and when you thought about it, they just might be. Rumors of illicit sex, affairs on many sides, major theft-nothing proven, of course, and no charges made, but it had been his experience that where there was smoke, there was fire. That's in addition to the alcoholism and mental instability that was prevalent in the family history. Hopefully, it was the end of the family line because it sure as hell had run its course.

Regardless, he was in the dual honeymoon phase of his job and marriage, and he wasn't going to let that rain on his parade. That could wait 'til later if it was to be.

Still, he couldn't shake the feeling that in regard to that, and with the influx of people, things in Wilsonville were going to get worse before they got better, and that naturally, he'd have to be right in the middle of it. Unavoidable, as that was what he was getting paid for, but he had no idea at the time how bad things could really get.

CHAPTER 6

It was a thriving time, the sky was the limit, and it seemingly would last forever, but the old values still applied if seldom followed any longer. Teach your children well, instilling in them good values, compassion for others, always striving to be the best you can be, working hard every day, no matter what you are doing, and living life to its fullest. And TELEVISION! TELEVISION! TELEVISION!

Yes, Joey Wilson and Toby Klein both had fathers with luxury cars, but the resemblance ended there. In fact, they couldn't be any different. Whereas Joey was bragging loudly and constantly about how rich his father was, Toby went on his quiet way, content to merely observe, and was thankful for what he had.

In fact, that experience in Joey's driveway served to begin to change his perspective on life somewhat, see things in a different way, a path he would follow from that moment on. While his house wasn't in the wealthy part of town, he loved it just where it was, down the street from the Catholic Church schoolyard, where he could shoot hoops practically any time he wanted (except when church or school were in session), and get the guys together on a moment's notice to play a pickup basketball or baseball game. For baseball they'd mostly use a tennis or rubber ball, and a ball hit over the Bentley's backyard fence in left was a home run, as well as one hit above the cement line girding the brick school building was a home run in right. Any ball hit to center was an automatic out because there was nothing to prevent the ball from rolling downhill out of the parking lot right out of the school yard into the street. All this, of course, unless you hit one of the many windows above the cement line, after which the custodian, old man Gangnagle, would come charging out, and they'd all run home to live another day.

The baskets in the schoolyard were sturdy affairs, with metal backboards painted white and chain nets, which jangled loudly when you hit nothing but. If you did this enough times, they'd eventually break and you'd have to play with no net at all, which was a pain, but they were usually replaced sooner rather than later. Mr. Gangnagle was nothing if not a stickler who took pride in keeping everything inside and outside the school shipshape.

Another great advantage of where he lived was that all his friends were no more than a few blocks away and easily summoned for games on short notice in the aforementioned sports but also football games in the street or in his ample backyard. His street was a dead-end and, therefore, an ideal place to play as traffic was pretty much reduced to the residents. The curb was the out-of-bounds sideline and the field was three telephone poles long. You could only play three-on-three there and you couldn't dive for a ball or tackle in the street, obviously, but when there were more players, they'd take it to his backyard where they could dive and tackle to their heart's content. The only thing to be aware of was the dog's cable running the length of the yard, easily and sometimes painfully tripped over if you didn't watch yourself. His dog's leash was fastened to it so he could run the length of the yard, which he enjoyed immensely if his smiling face was any indication. They might have to take a rare timeout now and then when it was the dog's time to come out and do his duty, but that was no big deal, all the kids loved Rocky, his Irish setter.

The yard was the length of half a football field, which made it ideal for long bombs and broken field runs, as well as kickoff and punt returns, and the lush grass made for a soft landing. The only time they couldn't play was if the ground was too wet, with Toby's father deciding that. There was even a low-hanging branch on a very tall lilac bush over which they could kick field goals if they eschewed punting. No one else's yard was as well-suited for this and it made Toby a very popular boy in the neighborhood.

There were a couple of drawbacks to him being an only child and his father being away all the time, but those were out of his control, so he didn't dwell on them. His Mom was diminutive, with dark brown hair, and just like a TV mom, not only because she was a great cook, always smelled and looked nice, and kept the house sparkling clean, but because he could talk to her about anything, and she was super smart, always giving him good advice, and encouraging (not very successfully at first) him to read, even giving him books she thought suitable for his age from her Book-of-the-Month Club.

His father, on the other hand, tall and lean, with sandy hair growing sparser each year, was taciturn and mostly unapproachable, speaking only when he was giving a command (not that he needed to very often, as everything in their home was as regimented as clockwork, his father almost making a career out of the military) or when something wasn't done the way he wanted.

While he would never say anything, Toby could see his mother was unhappy, so he did anything, no matter how slight, and whenever he could, to cheer her up, including drying the dishes with her every evening, and as he grew older even reading the most recent BOTM offering she had given him, and discussing it with her when he was finished. He was also (thanks to his dad) adept at fixing things and would do so immediately should she ask him or when he saw something that needed fixing himself, so she didn't have to ask his father when he returned from his week on the road. "He's so exhausted when he comes home from those trips," she'd say, feeling she needed to excuse his behavior.

But not too tired to ensure that Toby's chores were done on time and done properly, which they always were, though it elicited no praise or thanks from him. He would help his son when it was absolutely necessary, when something was too heavy for one person to lift, for example, or when he saw Toby didn't know how to do something he was doing for the first time. Oddly, it was in that situation he was at his best, patiently teaching Toby how to do it, step-by-step, with no hint of the usual recrimination in his voice. And Toby could be assured he was being taught right, and remembered what he was taught from then on. That, of course, was when Toby liked his father best, but he knew he'd never change, and, while overall he loved him the way a son is supposed to love his father, it was more from a sense of duty, not with affection.

He knew all about how rough his father had it as a child, orphaned at an early age, growing up at the County Home, where it was survival of the fittest, then straight out of there into the military, the Air Force specifically, to fight in WWII and become a flight instructor afterward. He never talked about it, but Toby's mother told him he'd seen some horrible things, including his best friend from the Home being torn from his plane and hurtled through the sky, his remains never to be found. "Your father always felt like he should have been the one to die, and that he definitely would have taken his place if he could have. And I believe he would have, and not only that, wished he had," she said.

They'd met at a USO dance in New York City shortly after the war ended. His mother saw how broken he was and felt that maybe she could help him heal. She'd been very much in love with him, he was so handsome and strong (and a very good dancer, I might add, she'd say), and she'd had such high hopes for their life together. But she saw early on it was not to be. He was a loner who had the worst job possible for someone "in his condition," as she put it, and at the beginning of a marriage. She saw very little of him all those years he was on the road. He would have "spells" where he was also off somewhere in his head, and he would just sit and stare. Oftentimes he was just plain uncommunicative, especially after a night of little rest, having been woken from a nightmare in a cold sweat or crying out in his sleep.

"But I have you, my little man, and that's made all the difference," she'd say to Toby when she got what she called "a little blue." Toby hated to see her like that and later came to realize that feeling "a little blue" meant she was going to drink an extra martini or two that evening. He was worried (with good reason) that she'd develop a drinking problem. That was one more thing she and her husband didn't have in common. He was a teetotaler and often berated her for drinking too much, so much so that she rarely drank when he was home for the weekend, only if they went out to dinner. When Toby got older, he found bottles and unfinished martinis stashed all over the house- in corners, under chairs, in closets and drawers, even behind the curtains. He never saw her drunk, only tipsy a few times after a night out at a restaurant.

One night when she was in her cups, she even told Toby his father never wanted to have children and only acquiesced so she wouldn't be so lonely all those weeks on the road (and even when he was home, if you want to know the truth). She felt awful the next morning for having told him and apologized profusely until Toby reassured her that everything was fine.

But his mom was always there for him and he for her, a case in point when they found a tumor on Rocky's leg. They took him to the vet and the doctor said it should be all right if they just let it heal and washed and bandaged it each evening. Soon the bleeding stopped and the leg seemed back to normal as if there had been no tumor at all. It was OK for about a month and then it came back with a vengeance. Toby helped his mother take him to the vet, where they left him overnight. When Toby came home the next day, he saw his mother had been crying. He knew it wasn't a good sign but asked anyway.

"How's Rocky doing?" Toby asked.

His mom just shook her head and said, "He's in doggy heaven."

They both had a good cry and it hurt for a long time after and they didn't know if they'd ever get another dog again, but gradually came to think they might, but not just yet.

Somewhat of a burden for a young boy to bear, yet overall, Toby was a happy, well-adjusted kid with a good head on his shoulders. He preferred his regular friends to boys like Joey, neighborhood kids, other kids he had met playing little league football and baseball, and kids from school. Kids who weren't afraid to get dirty didn't need to be chauffeured everywhere, didn't eat cold soup (which he'd been forced to choke down at one of the team's mandatory pool parties so as not to be impolite) on purpose, content to be just one of the guys, ready to play an impromptu neighborhood game of baseball, football (and later on basketball) at the drop of a hat, swap baseball cards as soon as each new pack came out each week in the summer, or head down to the local swimming hole to cool off.

He loved the normal rhythm he and his mom slipped into when his father was away, where he could depend on three squares a day, lived in a nice house in the village proper, had his own room, and, even if he had parents who didn't quite seem the same as the other kids, at least knew what to expect.

He went to the local elementary school where all his friends were and liked it just fine. Although bright, he was a middling student, much to the consternation of his parents, who knew he could do better. But Toby was a modest boy who didn't want to stand out or show up his friends and was content with the Cs he got along with the rest of them.

It was recess he lived for, just like at home he couldn't get enough of the kickball, dodge ball, running races, baseball, and basketball games at all times of the year, with rough and tumble in the winter months, anything he could display his athletic prowess in. There he wasn't afraid to shine, and, if not the biggest and strongest, he was fast enough and tough, with endless stamina, all of which allowed him to excel.

The only thing Toby might begrudge Joey was his freedom, as his mom was pretty strict about his comings and goings (keep it in the neighborhood was her prevailing ground rule), but he wouldn't ever have wanted to disappoint her even one little bit, nothing could ever be worth that.

CHAPTER 7

Time moved along, as it tends to do, and also as it will, disappointments came, and, though not to minimize it, they came to everyone. As we shall see, how you react to it determines the course of your life, and just as many disappointments there were, so too there were the many ways of dealing with that disappointment, perpetuating the misery, accepting it, or turning it into a positive direction in your life. We shall see how everyone reacted or, instead, were swept along by the tides of time with little say in the matter.

Things went pretty smoothly over the course of the next several years for the Grimes's, and before long, Deputy Grimes was "promoted" to working days, and, with that, he and his wife began to plan and save in order to start a family.

But it wasn't to be. For one reason or another, they weren't able to conceive, and though, trouper that she was, Bobbie tried to hide it, she was heartbroken.

They finally began to think about the possibility of adopting a child, but at first, didn't have the heart to go through the process or give up entirely on trying to have kids of their own. Though neither would admit it, they were hoping for a miracle, and if that miracle was aided by fertility drugs, so be it. They put off the adoption option for a few years, knowing they could always do it as a last resort, having already been approved, though they'd have to make a decision soon, as they weren't getting any younger. In the end, after the Thalidomide scare, they decided not to go that route, and nothing else they tried worked, so, unless they adopted, they would remain childless.

Though it seemed ludicrous at the time, Gary Graham was rumored to have fathered a child (a daughter specifically) out of wedlock with an unnamed partner. Deputy Grimes first heard it at the station and casually mentioned it to his wife at dinner one evening. Perhaps it was only his imagination, but he noticed his wife, who had been down in the dumps recently, perk up when she heard that. She didn't say anything that night but brought it up "in passing" several days later. Not much at first, just a general inquiry wondering if he'd heard anything more at the station, such as had the rumor been substantiated? When he said he hadn't, she became a bit more insistent, asking if he'd inquire if there were any new/further developments or any corroboration whatsoever. He agreed he would, though he doubted there was anything to it, but even if there was, why was she so interested?

"I want to know that's all, deputy. Do I have to have a reason?" she responded sharply.

He knew something was up when she called him that and with such deprecation. Her response was demeaning and rude, which was a very uncharacteristic way for her to behave. He cut her some slack, at least this once, not fully comprehending the situation.

When he continued to come home with nothing, however, she prodded and poked further, finally accusing him of not doing his job, which was even more strange. Usually when he talked about police business, it was in one ear and out the other with her, which made it unlikely she even knew what he did most of the time. When he merely shrugged his shoulders as if to say, "can't help you, dear," she responded with a peremptory, "OK then, I'll have to find out for myself, I guess." And when he asked how she planned on going about doing that, she would only say, "I have my sources."

At the time Deputy Grimes hesitated to speculate on the reason for this line of inquiry, but as time went on, he grudgingly realized it was more serious than he thought and even began to entertain the crazy notion it was because she wanted to look into the possibility of adopting Gary Graham's daughter. That worried him, as it was so unlike her to live in a fantasy world. She was usually so level-headed, sober, and pragmatic. This was so far-fetched he didn't know what to think. She didn't even know if the rumor was true, and, even on the slight chance that it was, how in her right mind did she think she would be able to adopt someone else's child? Of course, she was a woman, he told himself, and regarding babies, they were apt to think or say anything. Then again, maybe he was being a little paranoid himself. She'd never given any indication that's what she wanted to do.

He said nothing, figuring he'd let it play out on its own, which he anticipated would lead to a dead end. If he didn't know beforehand, though, he certainly would find out how resourceful Bobbie could be when she set her mind to something.

She waited a month, checking the "Vital Statistics" listings that appeared in the paper each month, and saw that, indeed, a daughter had been born to Mr. Gary Graham early the previous month, no mother listed.

She didn't even mention this discovery to her husband. Instead, she took matters into her own hands, and when eventually her husband got wind of what she was up to, he was fit to be tied.

To begin with, she called Child Welfare Services and inquired if they were aware of a newborn baby girl living in neglect. When the person she talked to asked for clarification, Mrs. Grimes described the situation, no mother and a half-cocked father who consorted with unsavory characters on a daily basis, and, again, no mother, with a father she deemed utterly incapable of taking care of a baby and gave them the names of the parties involved. She was then told by said person that no complaints concerning the father and daughter had been lodged and was told nothing could be done unless there was.

"I *am* complaining!" she responded. "Why do you think I'm calling. Do you think a child should be brought up in those circumstances?"

"Are you a relative?" she was asked, and when she said "no," the response was, "Then what is your interest in this matter?"

"As I said," she replied, "I'm a concerned citizen."

"I'm sorry," she was told, "if you aren't family and we aren't aware of any untoward circumstances, there is nothing further we can do. Is there anything else we can help you with?"

"You haven't helped me at all!" Bobbie spat into the phone, then slammed it down.

Again, she disclosed nothing of this to her husband, so imagine his surprise as well as chagrin when he was ambushed with a blow-by-blow account of this little tidbit courtesy of Mrs. Watkins, the local Hedda Hopper, while at the donut shop that morning. Small town gossip is a real thing, of that Deputy Grimes was well aware, having dealt with the ramifications of it many times, but this was incomprehensible to him. He didn't dare accuse her of this without the facts and had no idea where Mrs. Watkins got her information from (it could have come from anywhere but was usually pretty reliable), but he did have some contacts at Town Hall who'd be able to confirm it, and they did, not long after, that very afternoon in fact. She had lodged a complaint with Child Welfare Services.

This was the first real bump in the road they'd encountered in their marriage, and he figured it was blowback from the first real setback they'd had, that of not being able to have children. He was only now realizing that the impact it had on his wife had been much greater than he thought. He loved his wife dearly and was aware of how salty she could get when roused, but this was different. He knew that while it had to be dealt with immediately, he'd have to tread very cautiously, even though he deemed it so serious that his marriage and livelihood (if not even his wife's sanity) were now being threatened.

She readily admitted it when he confronted her with it but made no apology. In fact, she said nothing at all, just nodded her head when he asked her if it was true. With her back against the wall, she had a good mind to give him an earful but decided against it. The less she said, the better. She'd keep her own counsel, and this wasn't the end of it by any means.

For his part, he knew she wouldn't let it go but also knew he had to nip this in the bud, and that she had to stop this delusional thinking. Then, just when he felt like he was at the end of his rope, help came out of nowhere in the guise of the Ladies Aid Society at church, a group that met once a month, where they planned visits to local nursing homes as well as to the sick, and held events (raffles, bake sales, bingo and such) to raise money for the Lutheran grade school located several miles away in Edgerton, several villages over.

Also playing a part in this was that very soon after that encounter with Mrs. Watkins, a more current rumor was floating around that Gary Graham had taken a wife ("shotgun, no doubt," Bobbie said acidly), even bought a small rundown house over by the Village cemetery, the "poorer" side of town, though there were really no poor in Wilsonville, just less kept up houses and families. Deputy Grimes, just a touch more impartial than the missus, figured that whether Gary Graham made the unnamed mother an honest woman or he'd up and married someone else was anybody's guess and nobody's business. Besides, either way, being married, having a daughter, and a house, alongside a recent step up jobwise, working for the Electric Company now instead of the DPW, made him think that maybe Gary Graham was settling down for the first time in his life. Good for him, he thought.

" I talked it over with the women at church," Bobbie said a few days later, "and we all decided the Ladies Aid Society should pay a call on Mr. Graham and his new bride, thinking it was the least we could do to be good neighbors. It'll kill two birds with one stone- we'll come bearing housewarming gifts and baby things!"

Not totally believing his wife for the first time in their marriage, knowing she'd never let something go this easily, especially something she was so passionate about, he couldn't help but think she had an ulterior motive, that of getting into the house under false pretenses. He hated thinking that of her, but he was becoming a bit mistrustful after her last escapade. It didn't look good for him either as a husband or an officer of the law to have his wife trying to interfere with another man's family. It was only after talking to the Ladies Aid Society members privately that he reluctantly accepted that everything was aboveboard. Eleven God-fearing ladies weren't capable of such duplicity, were they? Besides, he rationalized to himself, that Gary would be at work, so it would only be the wife with the baby when they got there, so there was no inherent danger things would escalate into a messy encounter.

Still, he couldn't help but anticipate this meeting with some trepidation and was tempted to send one of the rookies along to tail her and watch the house until they came out, but knowing Bobbie would be pretty upset if he did that and she somehow found out about it, he didn't. Besides, he could never justify using police manpower for what amounted to a personal matter. He felt they were already skating on pretty thin ice as a couple and figured he must give her the benefit of the doubt and hope things turned out okay. He also didn't want her to get apprehensive (not that she would), so when the appointed day came, he didn't say much, merely wished her luck and to say hello to the ladies for him (she raised an eyebrow when he said that but nodded), and to let him know how things went.

As it turned out, Gary Graham worked the night shift, but while he was home, he was asleep during their stay.

"We won't keep you long, Mrs. Graham, is it?" was the way Bobbie told it, introducing herself and Mrs. Seitz, Mrs. Heim, Mrs. Spoth, Mrs. Dempsey, and Mrs. Morgan (half the roster of that august group) to her. "Do you mind if we come in? We just wanted to bring by a few things a new family might need—diapers, bottles, wash cloths, diaper pins, baby lotion, formula, and baby clothes- and some canned goods. And if you should need anything more at any time, don't hesitate to call the church. May we see the baby?"

"The baby was asleep, but she let us look in on her for a second. She was very big for a girl, blonde, and an easy baby, according to the woman, though how she would know, having just arrived there, I have no idea," she told me. "Her name is Gracie, a nice enough name, I suppose, though I would have preferred Nora, Emma, or Emily myself."

Her voice broke at that point and Deputy Grimes expected her to start crying, but she kept it together.

"The woman wasn't very forthcoming about herself," she continued, "but seemed adequately attentive to the baby. The place itself was tidy, so no complaints there. She did seem a little off kilter, like she didn't belong, almost like a baby-sitter, and no match for a giant ill-tempered lout who was also a member of that motorcycle gang marauding through town. Something's not right there, I can feel it in my bones," she concluded, "and I'm going to keep my eye on things."

'I'm sure you will,' Deputy Grimes thought grimly to himself. 'And I'm going to keep my eye on you as well.'

As for the motorcycle gang, they hadn't done any marauding in the village lately that he was aware of, and he was fairly certain he'd have known if they did.

What she didn't say, but, knowing her as he did, he was able to surmise anyway, was that even if she didn't see Gary, he'd bet she did everything in her power to get a peek at him.

As time went agonizingly by, she kept tabs on Gracie as best she could, although, as she never tired of pointing out, there was no baptismal announcement in the paper, which she was very anxious about. Paying another visit to the family as a participant in the church's annual membership drive, she quietly urged the mother (if that indeed was what she was) to become a member of the church and enroll her daughter in the Sunday School, all to no avail. Oh, the woman was pleasant enough, though she seemed quite nervous to her, and kept glancing around the living room during the entire conversation, making her wonder if Mr. Graham was lurking about somewhere or if she was afraid of him, although she never got the slightest inkling of his presence during her sporadic visits, which was fine by her. Being a diminutive blonde, Mrs. Grimes shuddered to think what would happen if he ever got angry with her. She wouldn't even consider for a moment the girl might have gotten her distinctive blonde mane from her. That would make her too legit and give Mrs. Grimes no hope of ever putting in a claim on her. Her suspicions as to Mrs. Graham's pedigree were confirmed when she offered no refreshments or inquired if she'd like to see the baby, which she most certainly did, forcing her to ask if she could, even though each time she saw her and noted how much she'd grown it upset her as she realized how quickly the days, nay years, were flying by.

And then it happened. Gracie's mother suddenly disappeared. Whether she absconded, died, or even was killed, she was gone, vanished into thin air. Deputy Grimes was not surprised Bobbie found out (though how he didn't know). In fact, he thought she knew about it before he did (again, how, he didn't know). There was nothing untoward, he assumed, as the Police Department would certainly have been called in if there was any suspicion at all of that. He himself didn't hear it through official channels but at Frank's Barber Shop of all places. No need to act upon it as far as he was concerned, but Bobbie was adamant that something had to be done about it.

"About what?" he asked, her only response being a withering look.

She didn't sleep a wink that night but would not discuss the matter with him or answer him when he asked what was wrong if only to mollify her a bit.

First thing the next morning, she went to Village Lawyer William Burnham to inquire what, if anything, was being done about it. The lawyer (a devout Catholic) gave her a blank look as if to say, "about what?" but that didn't stop Bobbie, not by a long shot.

"Are you aware of the situation at the Graham house?" she asked, and if he wasn't (and he didn't seem to be), she got him up to speed very quickly.

"A little girl, practically an infant," she said for effect (she was now four), "is living alone with a violent father who did who knows what to his wife or whatever she was. And you're not aware of that?"

She was dead serious about it, and that concerned Deputy Grimes even more than any possibility of foul play, which he didn't think was the case at all. It seemed more and more she was drastically overreacting and was liable to go off the deep end. And again, he was suspicious of her ulterior motives, but he finally got her to admit what her end game was: to get custody of Gracie or, at the very least, get unrestricted visitation rights. When she said this, he became very worried, as it seemed his worst suspicions were coming true. He didn't let on how worried he was, he merely asked her calmly and coolly if she'd run any of her adoption idea by William Burnham.

She said no, and had a few choice words for the Village Lawyer, "booby" being the least benign. Deputy Grimes was a bit relieved at this, as that meant she was not willing to go that far, at least yet, or she would have without the merest hesitation. Hopefully, she was realizing it was a lost cause and that she didn't have a leg left to stand on. In the end, he believed he'd managed to talk her down from that high limb on which she was precariously perched. This was evinced by her seeming acquiescence (and Bobbie never easily acquiesced) at the end of their conversation when she got very quiet and finally said in a defeated voice, "At the very least, there needs to be some sort of female presence in the house, if only to cook and clean and make sure the poor child gets to school on time."

Deputy Grimes agreed wholeheartedly and said he would look it into further and ensure this was indeed being done.

As she related this to him, the thought 'and I suppose you're volunteering' flashed through his mind, but he didn't dare say it. As mentioned before, it was imperative he give her the benefit of the doubt, and admittedly he had concerns of his own. He knew Bobbie's heart was in the right place, wanting the best for the child. On top of that, of course, bereft of children herself, her heart went out to Gracie.

Meanwhile, Bobbie was thinking she had to find a way to play a part in her life by any means necessary.

CHAPTER 8

Paul Brennan was a kid after Jim Weatherly's own heart. They'd talked many a time over the years about a gamut of things: religion, politics, sports, music, philosophy, the future and the past, and he had a good head on his shoulders. He was way ahead of his time with the hippie vibe (although he kept his hair short), adventurous, leonine with a beard, dressed in Nehru shirts and jeans, wearing beads and sandals, riding his motorcycle across the country, looking very much like the Beat poet Gary Snyder. He'd worked hard at whatever he had done, you could tell that. God bless 'im, Jim thought, with a little bit of nostalgia for the old days. And he had nothing against the hippies either, in many ways they had perpetuated the hobo life he'd led. More power to 'em. He was glad Paul'd gotten out of Wilsonville for many reasons, not the least of which was to broaden his horizons. It pained him a bit when he heard he was back in town, though he had yet to see him, which was unusual, Jim being the ubiquitous character he was, and that they had a past, but he'd just have to wait and see what happened. He had nothing if not time.

Unlike the new generation they were calling "baby boomers", who, once they had an introduction to a different environment than they had grown up in, usually through matriculation at a college, deserted small towns across the country for big city life, seeking fame and fortune, attempting to become "upwardly mobile," the end-all and be-all phrase currently in vogue, in fierce competition with their peers, their ultimate goal a white-collar job and a nice home in the suburbs. Ironically not the Wilsonville suburbs, "upwardly mobile" being the key, and their hometown not, in their minds at least, able to readily facilitate this, although the mass influx of newcomers of their ilk from all over the country seemed to contradict that.

The core members of what would become the Alphas Motorcycle Club, N.A., stayed on in Wilsonville, a couple having taken brief hiatuses elsewhere for college and whatnot, and eventually, along with the others working manual labor jobs, making failed marriages, drinking and fighting, anathemas to the townspeople who once flocked around them to watch their heroics on the gridiron.

They'd been headed that way since the end of high school, all having come from rough childhoods, with no incentive or encouragement to take school seriously, already somehow knowing that their mind-boggling accomplishments on the athletic field would be the zenith in the arc of their lives, and, further, okay with that.

Everyone except Paul Brennan. Although he'd been the one who formed the original fraternity their senior year in high school, he was never seen with them after he'd left and come back. In fact, no one had even seen Paul Brennan in town as far as Deputy Grimes knew. A real mysterious and interesting person with the potential to be a real leader, rumors seemed to abound where he was concerned. In addition to the aforementioned rumors that he was studying to be a doctor, that he'd entered a monastery in Kentucky, that he'd become a demolitions expert and was working in Alaska, and finally, even joined a commune (all plausible scenarios, except that none had ever been substantiated), the most recent rumors Deputy Grimes had heard concerning him were that he'd memorized the Bible, dropped out of school, and become, of all things, a run-of-the-mill born-again Christian, working at the Central Post Office downtown. Be that as it may, the Deputy had yet to see him since his return but figured he'd run into him sooner or later. In fact, he thought he'd better locate him and keep an eye on him. As he recalled, things had a way of happening when Paul Brennan was around.

Gary Graham returned to Wilsonville after his half-year at college a bitter, angry man. He was now big as a house and even more muscle-bound, having been allowed to take full advantage of the U of Nebraska's legendary weight room despite being thrown off the team, the bond between all former and present players being inviolable there, two things that made them such a football powerhouse. He had shaggy dusty-brown hair, a thick beard of the same hue, and a drug and alcohol problem to beat the band. Early on, he'd done some hell-raising with the other members of his motorcycle club (or gang, whichever way you looked at it) but now was seemingly content to stay under the radar, first working at the Wilsonville DPW, then taking a low-key job at the Wilsonville Electronic Company.

Joseph Pierre, as previously mentioned, was pretty much a hermit rarely seen anywhere by anyone after his dad's gas station closed, not that he'd ever been seen all that much, starting in high school. He was rumored to be collecting disability and food stamps (though those few who knew him well highly doubted that), which he, the rumor continued, mostly spent on booze, if the condition of the house he inherited from his dad was any exemplar.

Swede Patrick was now a puffy full-blown alky who looked twice his age, working odd jobs around the village, mainly for his brother's roofing company and hustling pool at the Pool Hall, partial to vodka stingers, up for a fight with any young buck who challenged him, and most times handily victorious, though that was inevitably bound to change, Swede not getting any younger. No matter, Swede would always be game.

There were two other members of the crew, both non-athletes but friends with Paul Brennan since childhood: Gary Zimmer (Sheriff Zimmer's nephew) and Matty Modifarian, a wild man in his own right, making a motley crew of five (not counting Paul Brennan any longer).

That they were all back in town and seemingly laying low was all well and good. Still, the potential for trouble from such high-strung individuals, while not considered imminent, always seemed to be lurking just below the surface, and had finally been duly noted by the proper authorities as a situation that bore watching. Although at times totally out-of-control, they managed to conduct their business outside of town, seemingly further reinforcing the belief some of the town folk (even law enforcement personnel) had that they were not going to be a major worry in Wilsonville. These same proper authorities had been notified each time any of them had been hauled in on various charges of aggravated assault, trespassing, public intoxication, and DWI in nearby villages and towns, but until they began doing these things in their hometown, it made no never mind to them. Overall, admittedly, it wasn't a great situation, and though no one on either end of their shenanigans had as yet come to an untimely end yet, it was still fully expected at any time by anyone who knew them, which made it all the more surprising they seemed to be caught totally unaware when the trouble began.

It seemed there was a new kid in town, who was looking to cause trouble and knew how to find it. The funny thing was he wasn't the new kid in town. He'd lived there most of his life, apparently anonymously, if everyone's shocked reaction when he became a person of interest was any indication. That he'd been away for several years might possibly explain some of this, but no one knowing where he'd lived or that he'd attended Wilsonville High, as well as undoubtedly having passed through the entire Wilsonville School system, didn't.

And this anonymity served him well. Before you knew it, he was in a bar named SpaƆey's, a real hell-hole located in the worst possible place directly across from the high school, buying drinks for the bar in exchange for information about a certain group of guys supposedly only known to him as "The Triple Threat."

They said to a man, "Sure, we know them," going into what to him was tedious detail about their high school heroics and ending with warnings to stay away from them.

Nodding briefly, he asked what their names were and where they were now?

"The only one we regularly see around town, especially in here," one ancient mariner chuckled, "is Swede Patrick, who used to be the star quarterback. If you stick around, you're more than likely to see him for yourself any time now."

Nodding once more, he said, "And the other two?"

Another regular took his turn. "Well, Gary Graham," he said, "the fullback – say, did I tell you he made All-American at Nebraska? – he's a family man now, and works down at the Electric Company on S. Long. Used to work there myself, retired now. A giant, mostly keeps to himself. Has a young daughter, lives on Reiss Street, across from the cemetery."

The previous informant elbowed him and shook his head as if warning him to say no more.

After a long pause, which seemed to mean nothing more was forthcoming, the stranger prompted, "And the third guy, what about him?"

They were all too ready to spill. They were just parched from all that talking and indicated by looking down the bar that another drink for everyone was needed. The stranger smiled and nodded.

"Set 'em up all around, on me," he said.

Immediately after the drinks were brought, another eager beaver chimed in, "That would be Joseph Pierre, the scatback. Not much to say about him. He lives in a house north of here, next town over. No one's seen him in years, not after his dad died and the gas station got sold."

"Say, fella, why you askin'?" another piped in.

"Oh," he said, "I might have a proposition they'd be interested in."

"Like I say," the original respondent said, "stick around. I'm sure Swede will show up eventually."

"Some other time," the stranger said, "I have other business to attend to."

He turned as if to leave but heard a collective "ahem." He knew immediately what they wanted and signaled the bartender for another round, and when he'd paid up, turned around and left.

"Strange fella," one of them said, and they all concurred.

"Wonder what he wanted?" another one said.

"He told us what he wanted!" the senior of the crew said emphatically. "Do I have to repeat it?"

"Well, I think he's trouble, though it's none of my affairs. Let Wilsonville's finest handle it," one said.

They all nodded sagely with precarious grins on their faces and went back to their drinks.

CHAPTER 9

It had been Jim Weatherly's experience that life didn't often go the way we wanted or even planned, but, just as with the barter system, all parties could be accommodated in most instances to everyone's satisfaction if all worked together in good faith. Of course, with modern capitalism, all bets were off, but every now and then, it did Jim's heart good to see the old system work. For a while, at least.

As Gracie's childhood went by, Mrs. Grimes was as good as her word, visiting her whenever she got the chance, and surprisingly Gary Graham seemed to welcome her presence, which made things all the better. Hardly a socialite, Mr. Graham did go out every now and then with the boys at work and knew he had a more than ready and able babysitter whenever he did, although he never abused it. In this way, they got to know each other pretty well, and he could see Mrs. Grimes loved Gracie like a daughter. She'd bring her little gifts, or cakes or pies she made, and clothes every now and then, and saw to it that her daily needs were being met by her father, leaving detailed notes on upcoming events or important milestones in the girl's life, even menu suggestions, often bringing over home cooked meals in her trusty picnic basket. She read to her early on and had Gracie read to her when she learned how. She noticed that Gracie wasn't into girly things, so she kept that to a minimum and was shocked one day when she came over to see that a basketball hoop had been put up on the garage. When Mr. Graham saw the look on her face, he said, "Her idea, not mine." It worried Mrs. Grimes a little, as Gracie was already big for her age and very strong and preferred the company of boys with whom she could ride bikes and play all sorts of games hitherto reserved for boys, and now with the basketball hoop in place, her yard might become a magnet for the neighborhood boys. But no, that was Tony's yard. That would be just dandy, wouldn't it now? Always conscious of her social status (such as it was), her constant thought was, what would the neighbors think?

She was worried she wouldn't fit in with her peers, boys or girls, but Gracie seemed oblivious to all this, dressing in jeans, tee shirts, and sneakers and wheeling out of the yard on her bike, her yellow pigtails flowing behind her, climbing trees, playing sports with the boys, easing up with them at times, but also often coming home bruised and dirty, her jeans torn, sometimes bleeding. But she seemed utterly happy, and, though it certainly wasn't what Mrs. had envisioned and caused her a great deal of concern regarding her future, that's all that mattered, for now. Besides, there was plenty of time for her to grow out of it.

And, even though she accepted the fact that it would never be permanent, she did manage to see Gracie on almost a daily basis, as she lived only a block away, which was the next best thing.

Before she knew it, Gracie was school-aged, and, being a teacher at the local elementary school herself, she was able to keep close tabs on her from kindergarten through 2nd grade. Everything seemed copacetic, as far as her teachers could tell. She was neat and clean, never tardy, and, although shy and reserved, seemed like a good kid. No one knew exactly what her home life was like or who was taking care of her beside her father, who, while from all reports was very reliable at his job, couldn't possibly be dressing her and feeding her so well.

Yet it was obviously being done and done well. Let them speculate all they wanted.

Mrs. Grimes thought, she wasn't about to reveal her role in Gracie's life.

Still, every now and then, she got wind of minor cruelties and mischief being done to Gracie, which she knew she couldn't prevent, as it was a matter of course for anyone who was different, and a part of growing up, no matter what grade level. It still upset her nevertheless, obviously, because she felt very protective of her, though she'd never intervene unless she had to.

It was mostly that she was ostracized by her classmates, boys or girls, the girls because she wasn't interested in their frilly stuff, and the boys because they felt threatened by her, but she had no fear whatsoever of either. Mrs. Grimes did know that nice boy Toby Klein who lived on their street, was a sort of her protector, not that she needed it, and that was somewhat of a relief to her. Even more, she'd heard he was a real friend to her, something she needed more than anything.

Before she knew it, the time had come for Gracie to start 3rd grade, Mrs. Grimes' grade, and she, more than anything else, hoped that both Gracie and Toby would be assigned to her class in the upcoming school year. What a blessing that would be!

To that end, she both stewed and prayed all that summer, hoping they would be assigned to her class, though she had no say in the matter, which was what vexed her the most.

"That darn map they've drawn to decide who is to be assigned to whose class by neighborhood is like a jigsaw puzzle," she complained to her husband, "there's no rhyme or reason to it. And then you have the aggressive parents clamoring for their kid to get what they want. But all the kids can't be in my class," she added half in jest.

And her doubts were soon confirmed: Gracie was assigned to her nemesis Mrs. Egbert's 3rd-grade class, and, even worse, Toby to hers.

They'd been separated. She was fit to be tied. She'd rather they'd have both been assigned to Mrs. Egbert's class; at least they'd be together.

"See, didn't I tell you?" she said to her husband.

All her husband could do was shrug his shoulders and tell her to let it go.

"Besides," he added, "I have a feeling she'll end up in your in your class anyway."He didn't know why he said that; he didn't think he was trying to console her.

He just had a feeling it would, although he obviously didn't have any reason, and he certainly was no fortune teller. Whatever the reason, Mrs. Grimes seemed to perk up when he said it and didn't even raise her eyebrows like she usually did when he came up with one of what she thought were his hair-brained notions.

Mrs. Egbert was the strictest of the three 3rd grade teachers and, as a result, the least

popular. She had the longest tenure and, as such, seemed to have her pick of the litter, so to speak. It could never be proven, of course, although she did seem to have an inordinate number of boys and troubled kids in her class. She ruled with an iron hand and wasn't above hair-pulling or slapping a hand with a ruler, all with seeming impunity and great glee.

She miscalculated badly with Gracie, however, who turned out to be as feisty as her father. It seems there was an altercation on the playground with a boy during recess in the midst of a dodgeball game. Usually, the girls weren't allowed to play games with the boys, and normally they didn't want to. Gracie wanted to. She had been standing on the sideline watching when one of the boys in the center of the dodgeball circle ducked when the ball (thrown way too high) came his way. The kid in the circle who was supposed to catch it stepped out of the way and the ball hit Gracie in the head. Stunned at first, she recovered quickly and, upon hearing the boys' derisive laughter, gripped the ball tightly, fired it at the kid who had stepped out of the way. The boy, attempting to jump in the air to avoid it, had his legs taken out from under him and tumbled hard to the ground. She hadn't meant to do it, it was merely a reflexive action, but unfortunately, Mrs. Egbert didn't see it that way.

Quite a commotion ensued, naturally, and hearing it, Mrs. Egbert marched right over and demanded to know what was going on. All the while, the boy was writhing on the ground in pain, having apparently wrenched his ankle during his fall. All the boys were pointing at Gracie, yelling, "she did it, she did it." Mrs. Egbert went over to question Gracie, who stood there in defiant silence. When Mrs. Egbert saw she'd get nowhere with her, she sent the entire class inside early, which built further animosity toward Gracie.

Mrs. Egbert wasn't about to let this go, however. She deemed Gracie an "incorrigible child," and after several meetings with the administration, it was suggested that Mr. Graham take Gracie out of school and send her over to the Catholic school, where she'd be better served (punished) by the nuns there.

Mr. Graham raised holy hell when he heard that. He was virulently anti-Catholic, which, in itself, wasn't a good thing but was understandable when taking into account the fact that the present County Home had formerly been named the Father Cook Home and had been run by nuns, many of whom could be cruel and punitive, at the time Gary Graham was placed there. Gracie's father, who heretofore had only been marginally involved in Gracie's schooling, demanded that they not only keep her in public school, but that she be taken out of Mrs. Egbert's class.

Mrs. Grimes, on the other hand, was the most even-tempered, patient teacher, who wanted the best for her students, and was known to be the most well-liked, if not beloved, of the third-grade teachers. She would never admit this, of course, but Deputy Grimes heard it over and over again from students and parents alike and, knowing how she felt about children in general, knew it to be true.

Normally the school didn't allow the terms of a child's classroom placement to be dictated, but in this case, they made an exception. At his insistence, an agreement was reached that Gracie be transferred to Mrs. Grimes' class. On top of that, she explained Gracie and Toby's relationship to the principal and guidance counselor, and he was also transferred to Mrs. Grimes' class! Though not one to gloat, she was ecstatic and not a little emotional, feeling that her prayers had finally been answered.

And while at times she found it hard to walk a fine line in regard to her relationship with Gracie as her teacher, she indeed managed to, even going as far as curtailing their extracurricular activities together, which, as far she knew, no one in Wilsonville was aware of. This in itself was surprising, but all the more reason to keep it that way. It would be unfortunate for both her and the poor girl if word got out about that.

But, more importantly, she knew what a crucial year third grade was in a child's education—the most crucial as far as she was concerned—and there were plenty of studies out there to back her up. That's why she chose to teach it. It was during that time kids progressed from learning to read to reading to learn. If they weren't able to make the leap to quick, fluent reading and comprehension, they began to fall behind immediately, rarely to catch up. And she intended to ensure Gracie, as well as all her class, were able to make that leap.

She knew from babysitting Gracie that she wasn't all that fond of books; she'd much rather play with her action figures (Civil War soldiers, cowboys and Indians, U.S. and German World War II soldiers, superheroes, etc.), board games, or put together puzzles. No dolls or books for her, although she did read comic books, always bugging her father for new ones, her favorites being the newly created Supergirl and the long-running Wonder Woman. And while that meant she had it in her to read, Mrs. Grimes knew she needed to do better. She only hoped her being in Mrs. Egbert's class, even if it was only for a month, hadn't left her too far behind.

The very first thing she did was to give Gracie a reading comprehension exercise while the rest of the class did their normal reading assignment. The results were much better than she expected. In fact, she was elated. With a little more encouragement and study, she'd be on a par with even the best students in the class, of which Toby was one. To that end she gave her extra reading to do, knowing she'd mention it to Toby, and he'd volunteer to help her study. And it worked out beautifully, just as she'd hoped it would, her competitive nature making it imperative that she keep up with, if not surpass, her friend.

In the end, it turned out to be the most enjoyable, rewarding, and, unfortunately, swift school year of her career. It was all worth it, though, knowing she sent Gracie on to 4th grade, if still not the most willing, among the top readers in her class.

Around this same time, it became obvious to many that Gracie Graham was nearly Toby Klein's athletic equal, which was saying something because Toby was the top athlete in his grade. While it surprised and intimidated him not a little, he admired her ability and would always invite her to join in any game they were playing if she was around (which she often was, watching the proceedings), much to the chagrin of his friends. But gradually, the shock of this unheard-of practice wore off, and they accepted her as one of them, if only partly because they knew Toby wouldn't have it any other way.

She was a chip off the old block. Her father Gary, as previously mentioned, was a legendary fullback, still talked about whenever the high school football season came around. "They'll never be another Gary Graham," was the consensus of the boys at the barbershop, "they don't make 'em like that anymore. Why, I don't doubt, but even now, he could run through that current crop of namby-pambies we got up to the high school, and he's in his mid-forties," they'd say, cackling like hens.

It didn't hurt that she was bigger than all but a few of the boys, with a sturdy build (big-boned was the euphemism used back then) and a shock of oat-blond hair she wore long but pinned back in a pony or pigtails. She could do it all—run, jump, and throw like a boy—and seemed to have come by it naturally, her father never being around much because he worked such long, odd hours at the Electric Plant.

Sports for girls weren't really a thing back in those days, so she stuck out like a sore thumb, never having really gone along with all the girly-girl stuff the popular girls did, which she was also supposed to enjoy. She was shunned by them and hung around a group of less popular, less pretty girls, who might also be called "tomboys." They were very close, with Gracie being the obvious leader in athletic prowess and a protector against any intimidation or other cruelty from any quarter.

Mrs. Grimes wasn't sure how she felt about this, figuring she'd eventually grow out of it, but it was definitely worrisome. She knew Gracie was a special girl, though she never pushed her in either direction but let her have her head in all things.

She also encouraged that nice neighbor boy Toby Klein's advocacy for Gracie as often and subtly as she could, without seeming to be deferential to either of them, as she knew how disastrous that could be should any of their classmates get wind of it. She thought she'd been quite successful at it thus far, but then the inevitable slipup such delicate maneuvers are prone to occurred.

It seems the main cog in this support entailed that while they were in her class, she attempt to pair the two of them up as often as possible, which was actually more easily accomplished in one respect than one might think (because she had sole control over it), by ensuring they were always next to each other on the class seating chart.

She rotated the desks once a month to promote collegiality, ward off boredom, and nip any bad behavior fomented by proximity to like-minded personalities or any developing conspiracies to be carried out against fellow students in the bud. While the permutations for such an enterprise could be daunting, Mrs. Grimes remedied this by availing herself of the randomness of picking each name out of a hat and writing it in the next open square on the chart. She further refined this by ensuring, as much as possible (it being a mathematical impossibility to guarantee it), that no two pupils sit next to one another other in the succeeding month. All except Toby and Gracie, who, while their desks were moved each month like all the others, always remained together.

With one stroke, this ensured they'd follow one another when they formed lines for anything: assemblies, fire drills, recess, lunch, and school departure. If nothing else, Mrs. Grimes figured such close proximity could not help but facilitate an awareness of each other, a rubbing off on each other, so to speak, if only through osmosis.

There was only one fly in the proverbial ointment. It seems that permutations aside, their classmates began to notice the fact that they were always seated together and, more than that, constant companions in and outside the classroom. Overcompensating by fastidiousness, Mrs. Grimes hadn't accounted for the possibility in children so young that there might already be a natural affinity between them that would have drawn them together regardless of the seating chart, and that she had merely forced the point with her needless intrigue, which, after a while, could not but cause their peers to notice, and ridicule them unmercifully.

Toby and Gracie sitting in a tree, K-I-S-S-I-N-G, first comes love, then comes marriage, then comes Toby in a baby carriage! became a plaint invariably heard where two or three students were gathered together relatively unsupervised, be it on the playground, in the gym, or the rare times the teacher needed to leave the classroom momentarily.

This bothered Toby and Gracie not one bit, or if it did, they didn't show it. They ignored it and, if they heard it, gave no sign. An impartial observer would be embarrassed for the culprits because it was obvious their intended mockery fell on deaf ears. As with most things of this nature, where the risk was greater (in this case much greater) than the reward, it gradually diminished to a trickle and eventually dried up completely, although it was sometimes tried when they were apart from one another. Gracie, when this happened, would get very red-faced but say not a word, and, she being so much bigger and stronger than any of them, discouraged the ringleaders of each particular attempt from pressing the point further in order to get a rise out of her. And Toby, when confronted, also would demonstrate his self-control so eloquently (he too didn't say a word) that the trouble-maker often slunk away with their tail between their legs.

However, this closeness would inevitably have further implications down the line as they grew older, causing jealousy, gossip, and heartache, all with the possibility of either rending or strengthening their relationship for good.

CHAPTER 10

It's amazing how often fate intervened, changing your life completely, for better or worse. Jim Weatherly had seen it time and time again, in his life as well as in others. So, of course, he had always been a very superstitious guy, which made sense given all the vagaries he encountered during his itinerant days on the road. But recently, he had read an aphorism attributed to Jung that said, "until you make the unconscious conscious, it will direct your life and you will call it fate." It seemed appropriate given the duality inherent in western civilization, and it affected him profoundly. Figuring it was never too late for something like this, he embarked on a rigorous course of meditation, as well as indulging now and again in hallucinogenics. As he did so, he found his world becoming more unified and less uncertain, so much so that before he undertook anything, no matter how important, he meditated beforehand, and this always seemed to guide him in a definite direction, whether it was against his will or not. If he went against this, it often didn't turn out well. He supposed this was similar to faith, only faith was in God, and this was faith in your unconscious resources, to put it as simply as possible. Of course, most people weren't aware of this and thus determined their own fate.

As for Mrs. Grimes, her duty over, having shepherded Gracie through 3rd grade and it being the most rewarding year of her career, she decided to retire from teaching. Maybe it was time for her to become the housewife she'd always wanted to be. She even began to think of adopting a child. She was still young enough, though just on the cusp, it was true.

She made this known to the Ladies Aid Society, who said they'd marshal their substantial resources together to make it happen. Sheriff Grimes was dead set against it but figured it would never happen in the first place.

"I don't have time to raise a young kid," he said, "and besides, I'm too old to do all the things a father should, play ball, take him to his baseball and football games, teach him how to ride a bike- all that stuff. My father never did that with me. I had to do it on my own, although I'll admit it was easier back then. Things weren't so regimented and congested. My old man didn't care if I roamed the wide-open spaces around here, and boy did I take advantage of it- hunting, fishing, playing football and baseball with my buddies. I had a blast, and I feel sorry for the kids these days, not having that."

"Yes, dear," Mrs. Grimes said, "I understand, but I'm sure we'll be able to give him all the available opportunities he needs if we work together. Gee, what am I saying *him* for? We might just adopt a girl. What would you think of that?"

Sheriff Grimes didn't respond immediately, although he thought that might be more manageable, figuring Mrs. Grimes would do most of the parenting. Given her relationship with Gracie, she'd probably much rather have a girl than a boy, anyway, he reasoned, not really knowing anything about a mother's heart.

"In that case," he said, "I might agree to it, but only if it's a girl."

Of course, as it turned out, it was a boy, a boy living at the County Home, aged five, who needed to be adopted soon, or he'd age out and remain at the Home until he was eighteen. It took a great deal of doing, Mr. Grimes wanting to wait and see if a girl might become available but was told girls in the foster system were rare, and the ones who were were in an institution halfway across the state, but Mrs. Grimes finally got him to agree to do it, reminding him about the Gary Graham situation, and how much he'd wished someone had taken him in.

"Okay," he said, "but understand me right now," he said, "you're going to have to do most of the parenting. You know how busy I am and the crazy hours I have to work as Sheriff."

"Yes, dear," Mrs. Grimes said, figuring she'd cross that bridge when they came to it, but for now, she was ecstatic.

It didn't go well from the get-go and never got much better as time went on. Looking back on it, it seemed they'd been conned by both Johnny (she thought it was a good sign that his name was the same as Mr. Grimes') and the Home. They'd been thoroughly vetted, and Johnny had stayed with them for a couple of weekends, and they'd seen absolutely no problems.

But problems there were, and they manifested themselves before he even stepped over the threshold of their house for good, chasing their mutt Riley around the yard with a stick, Mr. Grimes having to chase him, catch him, make him throw the stick away, and lead him by the hand into the house. Not a very auspicious beginning.

Thankfully he'd already had the mumps, measles, and chicken pox, but he'd also had rickets when he went to the Home and was thin and sickly, seemingly spending the first year with them in his bedroom in the dark (he'd asked for it to be dark), with one cold after another.

He was so sickly they couldn't send him to begin school in kindergarten, so there went a year of no socialization for a kid who needed it badly. In addition to his various maladies, he also had speech difficulties when he talked at all. He was also unkempt, not having the first clue how to keep himself clean and well-groomed, and his table manners were atrocious. Some of this was understandable, the boy having been given up for adoption at a year old, but the rest of the backward, cretin-like behavior wasn't. In short, he was a very unlovable little boy.

First grade was a disaster. Not a week into the school year, he got into a fight on the playground and stuck a girl in the arm with a pencil. A conference was called, and it was recommended that Johnny be sent to a special school, one with strict discipline, a military school perhaps. The Sheriff was beside himself with embarrassment. Meanwhile, Mrs. Grimes took the principal's advice and shopped around for schools, finally finding a Lutheran school not too far away, where the principal was known for his liberal meting out of corporal punishment.

This turned out to be just the ticket. While there were still some incidents and he was way behind his fellow first-graders in every way (socially, reading, writing, arithmetic), he genuinely seemed to like the school and showed marked improvement going into second grade.

It was that summer Johnny met another six-year-old named Sheila. Where and when was unknown. She lived within walking distance a few streets down, across the street from the cemetery. His parents only found out about her when one day, Mrs. Grimes received a phone call saying Johnny had fallen off a roof and broken his arm. Johnny forever declared he had jumped, not fallen. The roof turned out to be on Sheila's house, a cookie-cutter dwelling, one of many put up after the war — pale yellow, flat-roofed, one story, not quite a ranch, cinderblock stoop and gravel driveway that was going to be replaced or paved over someday but never was or would be unless somebody else moved in.

Her father, one of the town drunks, worked at the DPW, with his main job being caretaker of the cemetery. Not a bad gig, right across the street. He was a volatile man, often screaming at her mother, siblings, and herself. She wasn't afraid of him. He'd eventually drink himself comatose, usually in front of the TV, watching a Yankees game.

Johnny and Sheila both loved the outdoors and being outside as much as they could. When school started, they'd still see each other every day afterwards, Johnny going there, Sheila never coming to his house (she had the cemetery after all), not coming home until the streetlights came on. Johnny's parents were happy he finally had a friend and were more than willing to let him spend as much time there as he wanted. They knew where he was and that he'd be home for supper. It actually proved to be a godsend, Johnny knowing if he didn't get his homework finished, get passing grades, or misbehave, he'd be grounded and couldn't see Sheila.

Johnny wasn't into sports of any kind, and of course, Sheila wasn't either. They'd walk around the cemetery looking at all the gravestones, trying to imagine what the people were like, how they lived. It was cool and shady there.

"If you don't believe in spooks," she'd say, "try living across from a cemetery." On the windiest nights, she'd tell him, they sent up a howl, wailing like banshees, crescendoing into a roar that was unmistakable, arguing and fighting with each other, certainly riled up about something, and on the quietest nights, the hoot of an owl, barking of a dog, or other indeterminate creature sounds, seemed like the cry of an individual soul for its mate, or a lost one crying out in the wilderness, trying to find purchase somewhere. They'd check the next day after a big wind to see if any tombstones had been toppled and walk around looking for new graves that may have been disturbed. It was things like that they did for fun and adventure, mostly for a change, always together. No organized activities for them. While Johnny had never been convinced any of this was true, he promised they'd sleep in there one evening when they were older.

When they reached high school age, they were finally in the same school together. They had constant run-ins with students and teachers alike. They skipped school at times also. They'd walk there together with good intentions, but every once in a while, if it was a nice May day heading towards summer, they'd just look at each other, shrug their shoulders, and veer off on the path that led down to an abandoned factory and some torn up railroad tracks that led to nowhere, where there was plenty to do- great places for hide and seek, many ramparts (crumbling walls) to be conquered, plenty of trees to climb, or lie on the railroad tracks and pretend a train was coming. Once Johnny made the mistake of crawling into a large round vat inside the factory and, because of the smooth walls, couldn't get out for the longest time until Sheila was finally able to get hold of his hand and, with much difficulty, pull him out, almost falling in herself in the process. They weren't scared at all mind you. They looked upon it as a great adventure, one from which they used their wits to escape. They were never worried or scared about the consequences of their actions—Sheila wasn't your typical girl in that or many other ways—knowing they'd be punished, but also knowing they could take whatever was handed out, as long as nobody hit them, and, so far, no one had. As they grew older, they'd find a shade tree on one of the gentle grass-covered hills, which they'd sit under to eat lunch and talk, or, their favorite thing: lying in the tall grass and looking up at the sun trailing across the sky, which they could do for hours. College wasn't in their plans. If they talked about the future, it was about how they'd get out of town as soon as they could and what they'd do: Sheila maybe an actress or a singer, Johnny a cowboy or long-haul truck driver.

It wasn't like Sheila practiced singing or anything, or he'd busted any broncos, but that didn't lessen their resolve to follow their dreams or at least shake the dust of this crazy town off their feet. He could always take one of those semi-truck driver school courses they were always advertising on TV. Besides, Johnny knew Sheila had a pretty voice just from being with her so many years and hearing her sing along with a song on the radio, and from when she sang in the church choir when they were kids. Her favorites were Patsy Cline and Dinah Washington. Johnny wanted to be like the impetuous Rowdy Yates in *Rawhide*, or Big Bill Longley in *The Texan,* although he'd be called Rory Calhoun, a name he loved and associated with the tall, dark and handsome loner. They knew they were a long way off from fulfilling their dreams but were confident that, one way or another, they would.

She hated her name, but when Johnny gave her a recording of Buddy Holly's eponymous song, she came to terms with it. He'd often sing snippets of it to her out of the blue, and she'd roll her eyes, chuck something at him, or lay her head on his shoulder and sigh.

Not that she gave a damn what others thought, it was just something she had to work out in her own head.

"You ever had a song named after you?" she'd say when anyone taunted her about it. "I thought not," she'd conclude, ending the potentially contentious encounter.

It became a moot point when Johnny gradually shortened it to "She," which unwittingly morphed into a regular who's on third routine: who's she? Is she she? She's she? Who does she think she is? etc. Everyone was so busy trying to figure out what was what they didn't have time or the inclination to mock her any longer.

Neither parent was happy with what had transpired so far, but it seemed She's parents didn't care, as, when they'd tried to talk to Mr. and Mrs. Grimes about it, all her father could come up with was, "What's a matter, my girl ain't good enough for you"? Johnny's parents, having tried everything they knew, short of sending him to another school again (the only alternatives being very expensive private schools or the Catholic high school), were at their wit's end. Mrs. Grimes had tried her very best and hated to admit it, but it just wasn't the same as with Gracie. Sheriff Grimes had tried to show him the one thing he thought might establish a bond between them, but Johnny showed absolutely no interest in police work. They did the yardwork together in the summer and the snow-shoveling in the winter, but that was the extent of their time together other than mealtimes. It was very frustrating not to be able to get through to him, or find out what made him tick. They knew little about his early childhood but figured some kind of trauma had occurred, as he remained a cipher to them. And his seeming obsession with Sheila couldn't be healthy, could it? They'd grounded him on numerous occasions for it, but that didn't work either. They'd be back together again practically the moment it was over. While it wasn't a fixed obsession with them, they felt it couldn't help but be noticed in the village, and people would be talking, though no one ever said anything to either of them (yet). One thing they remained united at they were firmly together in their support of Johnny, come what may.

CHAPTER 11

R*amifications ramifications! Had it been a chance meeting, or had it been planned by someone, catching everyone off guard so they behaved other than they normally would? Someone was going to pay at some point, weren't they? They had to, or the universe as they knew it would be disrupted. Hopefully, it would be, even if not in the way or at the time they expected. Hopefully. Until then, they could only wait and deliberate over their libations.*

Shortly after Swede Patrick came in the bar a few days after, the stranger, too, entered. It was eerie, as if he'd been tailing him, not a wise thing to do. A hush grew over the place as he took a seat at the nearest bar stool. He perused the room and nodded at a couple of the men he had talked to the first time he had come there. They looked away.

Unbeknownst to him, Swede Patrick was standing at the opposite end of the bar, talking to a regular next to him, and suddenly pointed at the stranger and the regular nodded. Swede got up and said, "save my seat," then walked (strutted more like) toward the stranger and, upon approaching him, demanded, "I hear ya been askin' questions about me. Who wants to know?"

The bar was mostly empty, and everyone could hear what was said and anticipate what was about to be said and expected the poor man to be cold-cocked soon after. Then the strangest thing happened. The stranger said something in a low voice to Swede, then stuck out his hand, and Swede shook it. Everyone there was amazed and wanted badly to know just what he'd said. But, as he had the other time he was in the place, he called for a round of drinks for the bar, then shook hands again with Swede and again said something to him in a low voice and departed.

As before, everyone was dying to know what the stranger had said, but Swede wasn't one you wanted to clamor around and ask a bunch of questions to, especially about something that was most likely none of your business. But a palpable change had come over him, and the look in his eye was one the younger regulars had never seen there and the older regulars hadn't seen since his high school football days. The fire had definitely been rekindled. That much was clear, though no one could rightly say if that was a good or bad thing for the town of Wilsonville. Like everyone else in town, they'd just have to wait and see. What else could they do?

Tommy Ionion was the stranger's name. Though an elusive character in Wilsonville, he nevertheless suddenly seemed to be in everyone's rearview mirror, so to speak. No one seemed to know when he and his mother first arrived in the town, and many still were never aware they even had.

Yet, when you looked in *The Spectator*, Wilsonville Senior High's yearbook, there he was in black and white, with black horn-rimmed glasses and curly oily hair, longish for the time, a member of Deputy Grimes', Swede Patrick's, Joseph Pierre's, Paul Brennan's, and Gary

Graham's senior class. He even had a nickname, "Onions," which appeared under his name when very few others had one under theirs, so someone must have known him.

For the longest time, Toby Klein had thought Tommy Onions was his real name. Though he delivered newspapers to what was purportedly the house he grew up in, a tumbledown affair resembling a cottage with white wood siding and a green-shingled flat roof, and although he'd often seen a shiny silver and black Harley parked out in front, smelled onions and green peppers through the screen door which someone (he supposed it was his mother) cooked every evening, and heard that same screen door slam, he'd never once seen hide nor hair of either Tommy or her.

He'd heard rumors about them (or the house at least) from previous paperboys, and, at first, wouldn't go near the place, just close enough to sling the paper as near as he could get to the house without, god forbid, hitting it. He'd never had to collect there, thank goodness, as all the previous paperboys had been scared off for no palpable reason that anyone could come up with, forcing the newspaper to ask them to remit their bill through the mail or risk cancellation.

Toby himself had no reason for being afraid, except for the rumors he'd heard and a certain vibe he got from where it was located, the only dwelling in the only back alley in Wilsonville save for Elmer Muck's auto repair garage, where his father took their car when it needed to be fixed, which it often did, with all the miles he put on it. His father, not very forthcoming in the best of circumstances, told him to mind his own business when he asked about the Ionions, which didn't at all satisfy Toby's insatiable curiosity. When he informed his mother of his trepidation about delivering the paper there, she, too, didn't say much, except that she was sure it would be okay and not to bother his father.

After a while he didn't even mind going there. In fact, he looked forward to it, enjoying the smells emanating from the kitchen and, being the positive boy he was, thinking he might just catch a glimpse of them at any time. And while it could be gloomy in the alley on certain days, where, for the most part, little light shown through, except where the sun dappled through the thick trees and foliage there, it was cool on the hottest days, and, for some reason, stimulated his imagination. Which was another reason, probably the main one. He didn't mind going there any longer, even welcomed it, as it gave him the feeling of flirting with danger. He still wasn't allowed to collect there, however, which was probably just as well.

It altered his perspective of Wilsonville entirely, made him think of something out of *Grimm's Fairy Tales*, *Alice in Wonderland*, or even *The Wizard of Oz*, most likely because of all the mysterious rumors propagated by it, and the bucolic setting in a dark grove from which it seemed griffins, ghouls, goblins might set out at any moment, flying over Wilsonville in so thick a gathering that it blotted out the sun overhead. He would much later find its imaginative miasma comparable to that of Hawthorne's story "Rappaccini's Daughter."

And while Deputy Grimes didn't remember him at all from high school and doubted whether any of his football teammates did either, as he had never played any kind of sport they were aware of or had ever been seen around the school halls, although that didn't necessarily mean that much, the others skipped school so often. It was around this time he was informed of some of the problems the motorcycle boys were causing in the vicinity, several of which were very serious, mostly involving B&E, assault, and harassing store owners.

The only names he saw listed in the complaints were Swede and Joseph, never Gary Graham or Paul Brennan. He was relieved to see Gary didn't seem to be involved, as he'd believed him to have settled down quite a while ago, and this seemed to verify it. And if Paul Brennan was in town, he hadn't seen him yet.

He decided to take it upon himself to keep a closer watch on them.

CHAPTER 12

In the web of life, events reaching far into the past can suddenly manifest themselves, throwing the present into a topsy-turvy limbo, events seemingly forgotten completely (though physics tells us nothing is ever really forgotten), emerging into the light of day as though they were just happening. This was not déjà vu, nor was there any reconciliation or regret, but a helplessness devolving into a determination to simply let the chips fall where they may, as there was nothing else one could do.

Then, out of the blue, the shit hit the fan, and events conspired to make Deputy Grimes Sheriff Grimes without one bit of the requisite bootlicking usually involved, which he was god awful at, having had so little practice or inclination.

It all began with an emergency call he got to a flat above the aforementioned bar called SpaƆey's, which itself was well known to the department from the inordinate number of run-of-the-mill calls originating from there, usually involving drunk and disorderly conduct, assault, petty theft, brawls, and destroyed property.

It was also a place which John Grimes personally had rueful memories of during that lost time the summer after he graduated from high school, when, with little or no idea of what the future had in store for him, he idled most of his time away working for the DPW as a short-term summer employee, after which he'd go there to drink and play pool until all hours.

The bar itself was dark and narrow, listed like a ship, usually filled with regulars, and on the night in question, he wanted to bolt as soon as he got in there, especially when they saw who he was with, an old guy named Dudley, who worked as a night watchman around town and would tank up before his shift began. The funny thing was, he wasn't actually with him, he'd just run into him in the parking lot, and they walked in together. Be that as it may, when they entered the place, everyone at the bar turned around as one and said, "Jeezus, look what the cat dragged in."

John Grimes was pretty sure they weren't referring to him, and not only because he was a big boy, but because he was easy-going and didn't have an enemy in the world.

Old Dudley paid them no mind, mumbling to the bartender, "Betty, I'll have a Jenny draft."

Betty, who was also the proprietor, as evidenced by the novelty Wheaties box with her face on it above the top shelf behind her (a little touch of home her patrons had purchased as a token of their affection for her in what was, after all, their home away from home), replied, "Not so quick, buster. You have a tab to settle before you do anything else."

Old Dudley looked hopefully down the row of patrons, but no one was buying. They'd caught his act one too many times.

That didn't faze old Dudley one bit. In fact, he pressed the matter further.

"Come on, Betty, I'm good for it," he said, nonchalantly taking out a non-filter Camel and firing it up, expelling the smoke with a sigh.

"Honey, if you was good for it, we wouldn't be having this conversation," she replied, the barstool occupants erupting in laughter. "Now pay up or get out."

John Grimes, who'd gone to the restroom to take a leak, which was an adventure in itself what with the requisite two inches of water on the floor, wasn't aware there was a problem when he returned. It wouldn't have mattered to him anyway even if there was, he would have still bought old Dudley a beer, which elicited a look of surprise from Betty, and more laughter from the patrons, as well as one for himself.

They walked toward the back, where there was an anteroom, and when they entered, he saw a bunch of guys standing around a pool table watching a game in progress, with Swede Patrick one of the participants.

John Grimes heard the ripple of a murmur seemingly running around the table, and suddenly Swede looked up and, not even looking at him if he'd even seen him, said, "Dudley, you got my money?"

Old Dudley, looking at first like he didn't have a clue what Swede was talking about, replied, "I've been meaning to talk to you about that. I was hoping we could shoot a game—double or nothing. Give me a chance to win it back."

"That ain't how it works, Dudley," Swede said sarcastically, looking at him through gimlet-cracked eyes. "You know that. How 'bout I take it outta your hide?" he said, flexing his brawny bicep, the other guys around the table laughing and gathering around them in a tight circle.

"Hey Swede, it's me, John Grimes. Is there a problem?"

Swede, looking like he had had one too many of his beloved stingers, stared right through him, and said nothing at first, and then managed to slur out, "Aaand this is your bizness hhhow?"

John Grimes replied, "Guess I'll have to make it my business. He said he was good for it. Leave the old guy alone."

It got as silent as the antecedent to the shootout at the O.K. Corral.

Swede spit on the floor.

Things were getting pretty tense. It looked like a brouhaha was imminent when suddenly John felt a tug on his shirt, and old Dudley, seemingly impervious to what was happening, whispered to him, "Can you front me?"

Even though he knew for certain he was making a big mistake, John Grimes wanted to at least give the old guy a chance to earn back his dignity and handed him what he had, a twenty.

Old Dudley perked right up once he had the money in his hand. When he saw Swede had won his game, he held it up in front of him with both hands and waved it back and forth.

"What'll it be?" he said to Swede.

"Eight ball," Swede replied.

"Nah," old Dudley said. "That's a chump's game. Let's make it straight pool, double or nothing. Give us both an even chance. Whatta you got to lose?"

John Grimes couldn't believe the way the old guy was talking to Swede, nor could any of the others, if the incredulous looks on their faces were any indication. He didn't know whether he was way over-confident or just loony enough he might, or at least thought he might actually be able to back up his words.

"Kiss my ass," Swede said. "It's my table, and eight ball it is."

"OK," old Dudley replied, shrugging his narrow shoulders and looking at me with a smirk and raised eyebrows. It was beginning to dawn on John Grimes that this was not good and might only get worse.

Old Dudley went over to the cue rack and spent some time deliberating on which cue to choose. There were only two. Meanwhile, he watched Swede rack the balls and spread talc on his hands. When Dudley had selected his weapon, he rubbed chalk on the tip and said nonchalantly, "I'll break."

'He's either got stones of steel,' John Grimes thought, 'or he's desperate.'

He quickly stepped up to the table and bent over it, his cigarette almost touching the felt, stroked the cue ball solidly, sending the balls scurrying all over the table, smashing into one another as they did so.

'Nice break,' John Grimes thought, 'not a bad start, actually.'

It went quickly downhill from there.

Swede Patrick, not really even that good a pool player, but with such an intimidating presence he didn't need to be, stroked the cue through his thumb and forefinger as he surveyed the table.

Naturally, it came down to old Dudley having to run the rail to sink the eight ball, and he scratched, which set all the spectators to laughing and him to cussing as he handed over John Grimes' twenty to Swede, who turned to his former teammate and said, "Why'd you back a loser like him?"

"Gee, I don't know, Swede," John Grimes said, looking him straight in the eye, "it was a close game, closer than I thought it would be."

"Tell you what I'm gonna do," Swede said, motioning them over to the bar area with a smile that practically cracked his face into tiny pieces. "I'll give you the twenty back, but you gotta spend it before you leave," he said, slapping it down on the bar, where Betty immediately pounced on it and halved it to settle Old Dudley's tab.

"Betty, I want you to make this sawbuck disappear," Swede said when she laid the rest on the bar.

"Last of the big spenders, aren't yez?" Betty laughed, blinking her eyes coquettishly while looking straight at old Dudley.

Old Dudley, of course, was in an expansive mood now that he was fairly certain where his next drink was coming from. He got his Jenny draft, lit up a Camel, and began downplaying his loss in a stage whisper so Swede couldn't hear.

"What'd I tell ya? he simpered. "Eight ball. A sucker's game. I didn't have my own cue either. Besides, I usually make that rail shot with my eyes closed."

John Grimes rolled his eyes and said nothing, nursing the Jenny draft he'd ordered.

"Wish I could play him again," he went on, not noticing John Grimes was no longer listening. "I'd beat him in straight pool, no doubt about it. That's my game." He wriggled his long fingers and observed his nails, which were none too clean.

John Grimes was going to suggest old Dudley start heading for work. He knew Swede was up to something and wouldn't trust him further than he could throw him.

Just then, however, old Dudley reached for the remaining bills on the bar, intending to order another draft. Swede must have anticipated that and before he could do so, called out, "Leave it right there, Dudley. I got my eye on you. That's house money, right Betty? Give my buddies a round of Crown, on Dudley."

"However you wanna play it, Swede," Betty said, laughing and taking a drag on her cigarette, then snatching the bottle off the shelf, her wedding band clicking on it as she did so, setting up half a dozen shot glasses and began pouring, leaving a bead of whiskey on the bar beside each one as she topped it off.

"Grimesy, you gonna join us?" Swede boomed out, looking pointedly at old Dudley.

"No thanks, Swede," John Grimes replied, "I'm in training."

Swede smiled and winked, lifted his shot glass up, nodded at the others, who then tipped their glasses up as one and intoned "sláinte" before downing them.

Old Dudley looked a little nervous now, and began to nurse his draft, realizing there might not be another forthcoming. He was eyeing what was left of the money as well as Swede, who was talking to a woman who'd just come in. He waved Betty over and whispered, "get my friend here and me one last one, and keep the change."

"I'll be sure not to spend it all in one place," Betty replied. "Ya'll come back now real soon, hear?

"Let's drink this quick and get outta here," Dudley said with alacrity. "Chug it. I gotta get to work. We'll go out the back way."

John Grimes did so, with the beer foaming up and spilling all over him. He had a gag reflex that didn't allow him to drink right down like the real drinkers did. He finally managed to kill it and they left as surreptitiously as they could.

The emergency call involved the alleged contribution to the delinquency of a minor, which, upon further investigation, proved to be much worse in many respects. First, there were two minors, male and female, present in a room reeking of marijuana, alcohol, cigarettes, and (if he was not mistaken) sex, and second, it would ultimately turn out to be a county-wide underage pornographic ring.

Upon receiving the call Deputy Grimes hightailed it over to SpaƆey's pronto, gumball blazing and siren blaring. With a call such as this, you never knew what to expect, although it was usually more than the average bar fight (or brawl, be that as it may), this would prove to be a particularly sticky situation.

The door of the room in question (which was actually an apartment, Deputy Grimes realized) was ajar when he entered, which always seemed suspicious, but in this case, amounted to nothing (except that the occupants had forgotten to close the door) when everything was said and done. It was a big place, equal in circumference to the downstairs bar. There was no one in the apartment proper, although he could hear noises coming from a back room whose door was closed. It wasn't locked, he discovered when trying the doorknob, so no need to break it down.

When he entered, he saw two kids who were obviously minors, a dark-haired boy and a wispy-haired blond girl, the girl underneath an adult male engaging in sexual congress with her on a none too clean mattress, with the other minor observing them doing so in an equally ratty about to collapse upholstered chair, smoking what looked to be a big fat doobie. There was drug paraphernalia on a nearby table, so many beer and whiskey bottles layering the floor you could barely open the door, much less successfully navigate the room, as well as an unattended movie camera on a tripod. As it was, Deputy Grimes knocked over several bottles half-full of what at first appeared to be beer but instead was urine.

The occupants barely reacted to his presence, continuing to pursue their respective activities unabated until he commanded them to stop, ordering the two minors to get dressed and the adult to stand up, also get dressed, and put his hands against the wall and spread 'em while he frisked him. It wasn't like Deputy Grimes was a hard ass, but he knew his job and had a knack of assessing a situation quickly and taking swift and appropriate action.

The aforementioned stickiness of the situation occurred shortly after backup arrived, and one of the perps was preliminarily ID'ed. That would be the male adult, who proved to be Gary Zimmer, the Chief's nephew, which startled Deputy Grimes, naturally, not having seen nor heard hide nor hair of him in years. He was immediately led downstairs and put in the backseat of a squad car and driven to the station.

The two allegedly underaged kids could not be identified, having no ID on them, and apparently drugged when questioned, freaking out, asking where they were and what was happening. After consulting with superiors at the station, it was decided the best course of action was to take them to the County Medical Center to be evaluated. Deputy Grimes put in a call for an ambulance, telling them to arrive sans siren and emergency flashers, thinking this would freak them out even further. When the ambulance arrived in stealth-like silence, they were led quietly downstairs to it and driven to the hospital as ordered.

The phone call alerting the authorities had proved to be an anonymous tip that originated from the bar, and Deputy Grimes was ordered to canvass each patron there to gather information and see if he could identify the anonymous tipper before he returned to the station. He wasn't successful in doing so but did gather a significant amount of information regarding the porno ring that had been going on seemingly right under their noses. The most embarrassing part was it was known by everyone, but those who needed to and should have known by now, the intrepid Wilsonville police force, who had in the interim acquired a nickname for themselves, again, unbeknownst to them but to everyone else, especially the younger wits of the town, from whom it had originated, that of the "Wilsonville Jokers."

It goes without saying Deputy Grimes took this one personally, as he admitted to Mrs. Grimes when he discussed it with her later, which he seldom did with other cases, not only because it was against Department policy, but she often tended to only feign interest, though her mind was elsewhere. She listened this time, sensing how upset he was, and did her best to dissuade him.

"How could you have known"? she insisted. "I don't get that."

He couldn't answer that except to say that if he was any kind of police officer, he would have known.

"Everyone else in town seemed to know," he responded. "The department has become a laughingstock and I won't have it."

But not only was Bobby not buying any of it, she also wanted him to go on the offensive. The department was in shambles as far as she was concerned. She'd heard the rumors and the nickname but hadn't had the heart to tell him.

"Sherriff Zimmer is over the hill, let's face it," she said. "It's time for him to hang it up. And that makes it the perfect time for you to make your move. And, of course, his nephew being involved seals it. He'll have to step down."

Did he even want to make a move? There had been no discussion or even rumors of any major departmental changes, and he would have known if there had been. He certainly didn't want to instigate such a thing, even though Bobby rightly pointed out he was next in line seniority-wise, although he wasn't guaranteed the job by any means. She suggested he at least contact the PBA and see what he needed to do should he decide to throw his hat in the ring, as it were if such a change was indeed in the wind. He supposed it would mean a repeat of what he went through to be on the force in the first place but on steroids: meetings with the union, the staff, his fellow officers, the Town Board, further certification and training, and he wasn't sure he was ready for that. It was a touchy situation where his relationship with Chief Zimmer was concerned. A recommendation from Chief Zimmer, which he was pretty certain he'd get, could go either way, either greasing the skids or sabotaging it entirely.

Bobby could be very insistent when she saw the slightest opening in any situation, and she suggested having the Zimmers over for dinner soon, not to feel them out per se, but as a friendly gesture. When she saw her husband bristle at that because they'd never had them over before, and they'd know exactly why they'd been invited, Mrs. Grimes immediately pooh-poohed that.

"What's the harm?" was her argument. "Besides, no one knows that any change is imminent in the first place, and maybe we'll find out from the horse's mouth there just might be. Wouldn't hurt to get a leg up on the competition, now would it?"

In the end Deputy Grimes decided to keep his own counsel regarding that, knowing he had to choose his battles carefully with Mrs. Grimes if he didn't want to get steamrolled into doing something he'd regret later.

But none of this was necessary. Gary Zimmer was indicted on a Thursday, Chief Zimmer stepped down the very next day, and Deputy Grimes was appointed Acting Sheriff in the interim, with the stipulation that he clean up the mess ASAP. Sheriff Grimes took immediate action, requiring his six deputies to go back to The Police Academy for remedial training, as he also did, taking a law enforcement training course, all on their own time. He also gave each deputy a copy of the police manual to take home and study, with the promise of weekly quizzes and the command to follow it to the letter. They also had weekly drills to keep them sharp and shipshape. Sheriff Grimes lost twenty pounds in addition to accomplishing all this. The interim designation lasted six months, and when all his certifications and interviews were completed, he was appointed Sheriff. He felt terrible for Chief Zimmer, but Bobbie Grimes was very proud of her man.

Further investigation by the County Sheriff's Office revealed that Tommy Ionion was the "brains" behind the porno operation, with Swede Patrick being a partner. Before he could be indicted, however, Ionion disappeared.

One night, later that month, as Sheriff Grimes was sitting in the Galaxy restaurant having a cup of coffee, having gone inside to get out of the blizzard that was blanketing Wilsonville, he couldn't help but notice a solitary figure incongruously pedaling a bike down Main Street. Even though it was difficult, almost impossible, to see outside, for some reason he thought it was Paul Brennan, and ran out on Main Street to get a better look, to no avail.

The rider rode with his head down, pedaling through the heavy snow against the wind. Still, what he had seen, a lean rider with short hair and beard, wearing a sheep-herders' coat, made him think it was he. It would make sense for him coming down Main Street from his job. He went outside and got in his car to catch up to him, turning his gumball on when he neared him. He motioned Paul into his car.

"Why are you out in this?" he asked him.

"No other way to get home," Paul said, "taxis and buses aren't running, I would assume. Why'd you pull me over?"

"No real reason," Sheriff Grimes said, "maybe to give you a ride. I'd heard you were home but hadn't seen you, so thought I'd catch up. I'm sure you heard about that porno ring business. A shame we couldn't bring it to trial, Mr. IonionIonion disappearing all of a sudden. I don't suppose you know anything about that?"

"Good riddance," was all Paul would say on the matter, along with, "I believe I will take that ride home if you don't mind."

CHAPTER 13

Just kids looking for adventure, Jim Weatherly knew it was nothing compared to what he'd done in his youth, but the town would frown on it nevertheless, never mind they were one of their own. No one was wise to what happened. They were lucky that way because, although they thought it was just an innocent joyride as far as they were concerned, the uptight town fathers would probably have prosecuted them to the full extent of the law, and their young lives might have been ruined. As Jim knew too well, there was a fine line between success and failure.

Out of the blue on that same day, She asked Johnny, "Do you want to do it?"

Being the sixties, his first thought was, you know, sex. Were they finally going to do it?

He didn't answer right away.

"What?" he finally responded.

"What we talked about," She said.

"Oh, that," Johnny said, "haven't made up my mind yet. Let me think about it. It's not something that needs to be decided right away, is it?"

"Soon enough," She said, "I can't wait forever. If you can't decide, I'll do it myself."

What She wanted was to steal a car and go for a joy ride.

While Johnny was okay with that, he was by nature much more cautious. The time and the situation had to be just right. He was almost settled on old man Kalta's truck. It would be easy to hotwire, although She had her heart set on a car. They'd get what they got and be glad, was his thought. Then again, She could do it herself, he had no doubt about it, but they always did things together and he'd like to keep it that way.

"Sheila! Time for dinner!" her mom called.

"I gotta go, She said, "see you later. Try to figure it out by then."

"Yeah. See you later," he said noncommittally.

Meanwhile, everything was chaos at She's house. Her dad was on a toot and everyone was hiding from him, including her mom, each in their own separate space (there were only two bedrooms and 4 kids, do the math, 2 sets of bunkbeds was all the space they got). Dad finally stumbled into the living room and plopped himself on his chair to watch TV, his tirade directed toward it and the ballgame that was on (the Yankees, who were on the decline, much to She's happiness and his chagrin), which was fine with them, as it took the attention away from them. He'd usually drink himself comatose, which they all waited for so they could go to sleep.

It was chaos at Johnny's house, too, but for a different reason. The news had broken about the pornography ring, and the press was clamoring for a statement from Sheriff Grimes. Johnny was still fussing about which car to boost and noticing that the heat was off, his parents having their hands full with the reporters and some of the villagers who were gathering in front of the house. He briefly thought of using that as an excuse to delay making a decision, but knowing She wanted him to decide by the next day, so he finally just said the hell with it, let's do it tomorrow. He went over to his bedroom window and looked out, and spotting She in her room also and after noticing no one was around gave her the OK sign, which she returned. At least the furor outside took his mind off what he was going to do the next day.

Luckily, neither dad or mom was a problem that day, dad because he was out to the office early, hoping to beat the press there, and mom reading the local paper and watching the local news to get up-to-the-minute details on what was happening.

Johnny decided to wait until the afternoon because things were generally quieter. He had decided to hotwire (he wouldn't admit it was stealing) Mrs. Shannon's car down the street, a single woman with a passel of kids that kept her so busy she hadn't time to notice anything was amiss.

The car, an old Ford heap, was parked right in front of her house rather than in the driveway, which was good because she was less likely to hear anything there, and he could just drive away and not have to back out of the driveway. Of course, they'd be more out in the open on the street, but they'd just have to take their chances. Besides, it wasn't a busy street. Listen to him, hemming and hawing. She and Johnny were going over all this, and She said she didn't care whose car it was and just to get going. Johnny still would have preferred old man Kalta's truck, he was such a mean old man, but he didn't bring it up to She because she had that impatient look in her eye.

The house was the next street down, the second house in. They walked there on the sidewalk rather than the road as they usually would, not wanting to draw any unwanted attention, just two kids out for a stroll. When they got to the car, they both went around to the driver's side and crouched down. Johnny opened the car door, which squeaked a bit, then, after a little bit of a struggle about which wire was which and nervous because She was looking over his shoulder, he got it started by god. She jumped in and slid over to the passenger side, and Johnny hopped in behind the wheel. He drove at a normal speed down the street, looking to get out on the highway that led for miles out of town.

Just as they got on the highway, She saw a sign for a town that said BATESVILLE 35, and she said, "let's go there. I'm dying for some ice cream, and that's farm country if I remember right, so they must have some real ice cream there." So they drove along, She keeping her eye out for staties, and after about a half-hour got off Exit 48 to Batesville. The city wasn't much- City Hall, a couple of gas stations, restaurants, a movie theater, and local businesses lining Main Street, so they blew right through the center of town heading east.

"Let's look for a store that has a sign 'Ice Cream' on it,' She said, "I know there's one out there somewhere. I vaguely remember coming out here when I was a kid. Yes, now I remember, and I had an orange-pineapple ice cream cone, my favorite! What kind are you going to have?"

"Vanilla," Johnny said, and She laughed and said, "Why bother?".

"But I like vanilla," Johnny said, "and I know they're always gonna have it."

"What would you get if they didn't have vanilla?" She asked.

Johnny thought for a moment and said, "Strawberry. First, we have to find a place."

"We will," She said confidently, "just keep driving."

They passed several big farms that had been recently plowed, the soil a rich dark brown. Finally, they reached a little one-horse town with a half dozen houses, a tavern, and a one-pump gas station ("for the one horse," they laughed together).

"There it is!" She said excitedly, "it's just like I remembered it!"

It was a small building with gray-shingle siding (say that twice fast), white trim, and a flat green roof. There was an ice machine on the near side of the place, a water pump (couldn't tell if it was functioning), and what looked to be the lone tree in town, a large maple in the back overspreading the place. And an "Ice Cream" sign.

They piled out of the car and went inside, the screen door closing behind. It was evident right away it was a small country store that catered to its clientele, if all the tins of snoose and beef jerky where the gum and candy would usually be was any indication. They walked over to the ice cream counter and looked through the glass at all the flavors.

"Orange pineapple," She said, grabbing Johnny's arm, "there it is, just like I told you!"

An older man in bib overalls came out from the back and asked if there was something he could get them.

"Is that really orange-pineapple ice cream?" She gushed. "You never see it anywhere. I came out here when I was a little girl, maybe this very same place, and had one and never forgot it. I'll take two big scoops."

"Must have been here. I don't know of any other place around here that sells it," the man said, "and hand-cranked too. My wife makes it."

"Well, it's the best ice cream I've ever had in my young life," She said.

"Why, thank you," he said. "And you, young man?"

Johnny spotted the strawberry ice cream and, while it looked good, thought he'd better stick with vanilla. They were already pressing their luck with the car, was his thought, might as well stay with tried-and-true vanilla and not jinx things.

They paid for their cones and hurried outside to a picnic table to eat them, happy as clams. All the farm smells, the hay, and yes, the manure, smells that repulsed them as kids, were mesmerizing, and they wished they never had to leave, especially with what was looking at them- the long ride home in a car that wasn't theirs.

They reluctantly said their goodbyes and headed back to face the music. Johnny drove strictly the speed limit, and lo and behold, drove right up in front of Mrs. Shannon's house, parked the car, and walked away. They were on pins and needles for a few days, thinking they were going to be caught, but with all the big doings, it never happened, and they got away scot-free. Though it was tempting to let their success go to their heads, they decided they'd better cool it for a while.

CHAPTER 14

Things were happening rapidly in Wilsonville, faster than Jim Weatherly had ever seen before. There was a dull furor tippling through the town but no confusion about the cause and effect. Though it was unprecedentedly bad, at least the solution was right in front of them. Sheriff Grimes was the man to set things right. The villagers trusted him implicitly. They expected a return to normalcy soon, and even when things got worse, their faith in the man continued. They knew he had no control over random events. As long as he addressed them forthrightly and above board, Sheriff Grimes was all right with them.

Now that the dust had settled, Acting Sheriff Grimes didn't know what to think and found himself completely ambivalent about the whole situation, still blaming himself for Chief Zimmer's downfall and feeling he couldn't help being next, and deservedly so, as far as he was concerned. Hadn't he taken it upon himself to watch the Alphas? And hadn't he completely missed the boat on Tommy Ionion, having no clue that he was the mastermind behind the local teen pornography ring? That, for a tidy sum, Mr. Ionion persuaded Swede Patrick to look the other way while he used the quasi-clubhouse above SpaƆey's to do his despicable deeds, with Gary Zimmer merely being the fall-guy, a victim of his illicit appetites? Hadn't he'd been able to carry out his plan for months, with none of the town officials having an inkling as to what was going on? Not that he felt sorry for Gary, not at all. If he felt sorry at all, it was for the blowback that caused Chief Zimmer his job. It just served to show how seedy things could become when politics got mixed into everything. And he was very disappointed in his former football teammate, who showed no remorse for his part in the thing, though he was never charged. No one was. He certainly didn't feel as though he earned his job, especially in the aftermath of the disappearance of Tommy Ionion. No trial or anything.

No, heavy lies the head that wears the crown. In spite of the bang-up job he'd done with his men and the department in general, in spite of being officially appointed Sheriff of the Wilsonville Police Department, he still didn't rest easy.

He became increasingly paranoid about the job, feeling he couldn't slip up in any way and that he'd have to become the bootlicker he'd always dreaded becoming. The thing was, the job wasn't all that stimulating, and he was taking it way too seriously. As a matter of fact, a big selling point for living there was that, in reality, there had only been one murder recorded there in the village's two-hundred-and-fifty-year existence, and the crime rate was mostly nil. It was a great place to live, and it would stay that way if he had anything to say about it. It was his job, after all, literally and figuratively.

It was the political nature of the position he found the most unsavory. He hated sucking up to politicians, knowing he'd have to talk the department up around election time (he was proud of the department, mind you, he just didn't like tooting his own horn), even putting up a few election posters announcing himself as a candidate, but even that wasn't so bad. It was the other stuff he heard about in other village police departments, where the population was larger, there was more at stake, and there was a real competition to get elected to the job. Incumbents, to stay firmly entrenched, would play dirty, starting or spreading rumors about their opponents; conducting a few illegal search and seizures or even some minor B & Es, which, being inside jobs, were solved quickly, redounding to the incumbent's credit; and fudging the crime statistics to make the town or village look good. All through back channels, of course, nothing to really hurt anyone, and all for a good cause—re-election. The Wilsonville movers and shakers knew what his answer would be if he was ever asked to do these or similar things and that he would have a pretty good idea who the parties involved were. No, they'd have to force him out first, and he had a hunch that wouldn't go over too well with the residents.

Yes, he knew how things were in village police departments, why there had even been a big shakeup in one of their "sister" villages named Edgerton recently. Of course, he knew most of the people concerned, but things were different there. It was a much bigger village, even wealthier, which meant a bigger department, more bureaucracy, even more politics, and, eventually, more opportunity for corruption. For the time being, he couldn't envision anything like that happening in Wilsonville, why he'd never had to run against anyone in his life, and knew that if he kept his nose clean and had the backing of the Village Board, he was pretty sure he had the job for as long as he wanted it. Unless things changed drastically, of course, which, in light of what was happening elsewhere, just might. He hated to think that and couldn't for the life of him see what could happen to have that come about. Still, it wouldn't hurt to be more vigilant and mind his p's and q's whenever possible.

To make matters worse, shortly after Sheriff Grimes was officially sworn in, two of the most horrific events in Wilsonville's history occurred. A harbinger of things to come? We shall see.

The first, one of those heart-breaking occurrences that can never be explained, especially given their strong Catholic faith, involved the McGee family, specifically the sons, the McGee brothers. By far the most-gut wrenching experience (it wasn't even a case) he'd ever have was what happened to the McGees. By all accounts they were a happy family (no one had ever heard otherwise) of two boys (Pete and Willy), and Mr. and Mrs. McGee (Ralph and Mary) who lived over near the Expressway and attended the Catholic church, their boys attending the school there also.

Pete, the eldest, was truly the apple of his father's eye (though he never let on much, being the strong, silent, WWII veteran he was): an athlete (baseball and basketball), president of his junior class, straight-A student, popular but with his head on straight and a twinkle in his eye, cut down by leukemia in the summer before his senior year, so suddenly that even though his class knew it didn't really sink in until they came back for their senior year and he wasn't there.

Such promise, so many expectations and so much to look forward to, he would have made a perfect priest (it was rumored he was leaning toward it, though with his popularity- more suited to a politician- it was hardly believable) back in the days when that calling was noble, and many eldest sons answered it, snuffed out. Practically all of Wilsonville came to the funeral, or so it seemed, there being so many mourners they had to make special arrangements to accommodate all of them.

His star shone so brightly it completely eclipsed that of his brother Willy, younger by two years, so much so that hardly anyone was aware of him, or so it seemed until Pete was gone. He took his brother's death hard but then shone briefly in his own right, though in the completely opposite direction- drinking, doing drugs, setting the record for most demerits in a school year- with complete impunity because his parents were so devastated by his brother's death.

Slight and fair, where Pete was brawny and dark, he never had a chance. He just could never measure up. It was no one's fault, he was treated and loved equally by his parents, yet the results were so different nothing need be said; it was self-evident. He did best his brother in one thing: when he too was diagnosed with the same disease two years later, whereas Pete succumbed fairly quickly, Willy managed to cling to life with a ferocity no one had ever seen him show with anything else, with a blaze in his eyes that never dulled despite him being nothing but skin and bones at the end.

Thankfully there were almost as many mourners at Willy's funeral as his brother's (although who was counting?) save one- his father- who just couldn't bring himself to attend, despite his wife and the priest pleading with him.

Ralph McGee went off the deep end with the death of Pete, and at first, allowance was made for that among the townsfolk. Give him time to grieve, get it out of his system was the way the accepted wisdom went. Further, god knows they'd probably do the same themselves if it happened to them, many believed. Whereas he'd been a dedicated family man, a reliable journeyman at his electrician's trade (known to have a drink only now and then), he became a permanent fixture on the bar stool at Summer's Grill for a period of three months, often seen (mostly heard) stumbling home to his long-suffering wife at all hours of the morning, howling at the moon.

Gradually he was partially weaned from it, managing to work until noon before taking his first drink. He made up for it on weekends, though. His house, formerly immaculately kept up, became a run-down eyesore. He ranted and raved to anyone around him yet managed to make it to Frank's Barber Shop once a month for his brush cut, the one vestige he maintained of his former self.

He died of a heart attack less than a year later, a blessing many felt. Mrs. McGee moved to another part of the state and the house was finally sold, having been made much more difficult than it should have if a tragedy hadn't happened there.

The second event, while equally disturbing, was not as anathematized by the community, as it was thought the perpetrator, who'd been given several chances to reform, never did and thus could only blame himself (what was left of him) for his ultimate demise. This didn't take away from the protracted, horrific nature of the event, however.

Eric von Schmidt's father ran one of the largest corporate farms in the state. Having subsumed many of the family farms in the area, he was definitely not the most popular person for many a mile, to put it mildly.

Almost equally despised was his only heir Eric, who tooled around in his chrome yellow Corvette, deflowering many of the high school's buxom young maidens with enough traffic violations to paper a room with. He had yet to run afoul of Sheriff Grimes, as most of the infractions had occurred on County roads within a square-mile radius of his house. That he was even on the road (he'd had his license suspended briefly twice) still was a minor miracle and major hazard in itself. Out in the wide-open spaces, there was little opportunity for accidents or human carnage, but when you added alcohol to the mix, now that young Eric had reached his majority, something was bound to occur, and it did, with each incident growing progressively worse.

The first accident was a garden-variety mishap with a tree, from which he received a broken arm and minor lacerations. The second misadventure was an early morning altercation with a semi after a late-night bender. The semi jackknifed after his car ended up under its midsection, crumpling his fiber-glassed beauty like an accordion and, the top having been down at the time, almost decapitating him. This was according to the eyewitness description given by the truck driver. Eric had no memory of it and, as he awoke from a two-day coma, found that he was paralyzed from the waist down, and his right arm had been amputated.

His rehab lasted more than a year, which certainly kept him off the road for the duration, but to give him credit, he seemed to have straightened out his act, was ostensibly off the sauce, and learning the ropes in his father's business.

Then one morning, he woke up and there was a brand spanking new candy apple gray Corvette convertible retrofitted with special brakes, gas pedal, steering wheel, and gearshift, sitting in their circular driveway, which his old man had unaccountably purchased for him. All bets were off from that moment on.

And when the end came, it came quickly, mercifully. Sheriff Grimes heard the call early on a Sunday morning. There had been a horrific accident in the early morning hours on Sherman Drive, north of the village proper. It involved a late model Corvette driven by an obviously handicapped driver on a clear sunny day with no traffic on the road at the time. The convertible top was down and when the car hit the curb, the driver was ejected forty feet, his body finally smashed against a large boulder in a wooded area. His blood/alcohol level was the highest ever recorded in the County. He never came home the night before, according to his old man, and was still up from the previous day. His whereabouts were easily tracked and included several of his favorite watering holes. Live by the sword, die by the sword.

Sheriff Grimes had been aware of the situation, having seen several APBs on von Schmidt over the years, and went to the scene of the accident in an official capacity. By the time he got there, the road was clogged with onlookers who had to be cleared. Sheriff Grimes viewed the body, and what was left of it and went immediately to tell the family. So it seems his Daddy hadn't done him any favors letting him get off so easy after all, as he no doubt had all his life. There's an epidemic of that in Wilsonville, as you'll soon see about one case in particular.

It appeared to him that this Sheriff's business wasn't going to be any picnic, not that he expected it to be, but what happened next would take the measure of any man and alter the lives of many.

CHAPTER 15

Chickens come home to roost, but when the fox is guarding the henhouse, expect nothing but trouble. Jim Weatherly saw it coming from a mile away. The kid was no good from the start, and there was no one to say him nay. The parents were to blame in this case, the mother a recluse and the father living his life through him. They gave the kid everything, and no corporal punishment was forthcoming when what was needed was a good old-fashioned trip to the woodshed. You would have thought the parents would want to uphold the family name, but such was not the case. They had washed their hands of him and he was allowed to do what he pleased. He was very popular with his peers because he had money and a car and much more freedom than any of them had experienced. He was good-looking and fun to be around, but the older he got, the more precarious hanging around him became. And by the age of eighteen, he had already done some bad things, all with impunity. Still, absolutely no one could have seen what came next.

Meanwhile, as could have been predicted, Joey Wilson had turned into a little hellion, antagonizing parents and siblings as well as friends and foes. He didn't discriminate. Oh, he was never seemingly involved in any of the mischief that occurred. He merely had his surrogates carry out the dirty work he orchestrated. It didn't help that his old man was a boob who was nominally the head of the family by default, his reclusive mother having taken to drink early on in the marriage, ostensibly because she quickly realized the colossal mistake she had made, even though there already was a history of alcoholism and insanity on both sides of the family. Having abdicated her parental duties (she did cook dinner, albeit on such an erratic basis, her brood ordered out for pizza delivery, or Chicken Delight— 'Don't Cook Tonight, Call Chicken Delight'—regularly), she was rarely seen out and about. The only drawback to this, as far as Mr. Wilson was concerned, was the delivery charge, but, looking on the bright side, precluded him from giving any sort of tip to the delivery boy. Dysfunction like this usually got worse, not better, and as we shall soon see, it did.

His vexation at his son's miscreance wasn't even a matter of upholding the family name. Mr. Joseph Wilson didn't give a damn about that, which in itself was telling, given the fact that his sole source of income was derived from it. Even more mind-boggling was his reaction to the obvious fact that Joey's behavior indicated an absolute disrespect for him as a father, to which his only response was a slightly bemused smile at times, though more often only a vacant stare. Not only did Mr. Wilson do nothing to discourage this behavior from his son, but he was also seemingly complicit in it, almost as if he agreed with his son's constant disparagement that he was a weak, ineffectual nincompoop and a total failure as a father, and there was nothing he could do about it. Not in so many words, but that's what it amounted to.

How this came about is difficult to surmise, as it certainly goes against the tradition of primogeniture as practiced in this country even to this day. Perhaps his preference for a life of leisure totally unknown to that of his forebears was responsible, or maybe it was the inherent chaos manifested in the family now and again, the result of too much money and time on their hands, or perhaps he actually believed Joey was the apex of the family line (he had the potential to be with his good looks and natural athletic ability) and it would be downhill from then on. He had no real reason for thinking this. He had other children but figured if his number one son didn't have any progeny, it would be the end of the line, and if Joey kept on the path he was headed on, he'd have a harder time staying out of jail, much less producing legitimate offspring.

The real cause, of course, was a moral laxity which allowed him to give in to his son's every demand, even going so far as dictating what was to be served for dinner every evening, this provoked by his unsuspecting mother serving chicken one night, so incensing Joey he picked up the platter and threw it against the wall, demanding "I want steak every night!" His mother and father looked at each other after that display and merely shrugged their shoulders as if to say that was all right with them, even while washing their hands of the incident.

In addition, his father made no bones about who his favorite was, attending every game Joey ever had and helping coach several of his teams to ensure he always got preferential treatment, not that he always needed it, as he was a talented athlete, just not blessed with great foot speed in several positions that called for it, yet being chosen over another boy vying for the same position who did. He also was outfitted with the finest gear for each sport and showed up for every game in a spotless uniform.

Mr. Wilson paid little mind to his other children's activities, completely unaware that his youngest was a fine ice skater in her own right; he was so busy with Joey that he had little or no time or inclination to attend his other children's functions. With each season, Joey's sport was his only focus, why it was practically a full-time job, which time he could, of course, afford as he had no real job. Joey was also allowed to play sports all year round and spent much more time doing this than he did on his homework. He was still able to maintain a C average thanks to a network of friends who allowed him to cheat on tests and copy their homework as if with dispensation.

Things came to a head, however, when Joey and his friends were caught stealing demerit records from the middle school Vice Principal's Office, as well as some money from her desk drawer one Saturday morning in the fall of the sixth-grade year. Not red-handed, mind you, one of his friends ratted him out later, but it finally came out that this time Joey was actually there at the scene of the crime and, as many times before (though never caught), had masterminded it.

It being fall, it was Little League football season, and the theft had taken place on the same morning as one of their games, shortly after, as a matter of fact. It turned out that Joey, whose father owned all the land behind the school (indeed, it was the site of the field their football team played on), somehow had keys to the school, including office keys, and, with the demerits piling up for him and his friends, took that opportunity to remove all the records and burn them in the fields by the sponge factory, also illegal, of course.

The whole team heard about it on Monday when, in spite of not having been in school and rampant speculation concerning his absence, Joey showed up for practice. His father, one of the coaches, was noticeably absent, no doubt busy greasing the skids at the Village Hall, having already taken care of matters at the Police Station and local newspaper. As a result, no charges were filed against any of the wrongdoers, and the incident was kept out of the paper. Ironically, a picture of Joey catching a TD pass was above the article recapping his team's victory that day.

At practice Joey, while not saying anything aloud, strutted around the field smirking and high-fiving his teammates (those that could stand him), ultimately huddling together with them, laughing and talking in hushed tones, until Coach Warner (a former Marine drill sergeant) blew several piercing blasts on his ever-present whistle signaling practice was about to begin.

But it wasn't over yet, not by a long shot. While Joey's mates were suspended for a week and not allowed to participate in any team sports for the duration of the school year, it had been determined that Joey, being the ringleader and the one who had actually stolen the money, would not be welcome back to the school, a shocking turn of events, given his father's influence.

So, between having to enroll his son in a private boy's school the next village over and being forced to cede his land to the school in exchange for not pressing charges (although it was very rare to charge a juvenile with a crime, there were precedents in the county, and the school was willing to prosecute Joey to the full extent of the law, and Mr. Wilson did not want to chance it), all this hashed out in back-room meetings, Joey's misdeeds had cost the old man a pretty penny. Did that change things? Only for the worse. As Joey was still his fair-haired boy and, in spite of everything, still given free rein to do as he pleased, things could only escalate as time went on.

As obtuse as Mr. Wilson was (which was incredibly), he was even vainer, and putting this vanity to good use, he still managed to get his pound of flesh, stipulating that the land could only be ceded to the school on one condition: that the football field on it be named after him. As much as the school abhorred the thought, they knew they'd never have another chance to possess this extremely valuable property and capitulated, erecting the JOSPEH WILSON FIELD sign above the new scoreboard he'd also "thrown in" before the last home game of the year, with the requisite pomp and BS attendant on such a momentous occasion.

The scoreboard never worked properly, exhibiting so many non-working light bulbs it was often difficult to ascertain the opponent, score, quarter, and time remaining, in spite of Mr. Wilson's good faith efforts to have it fixed in time for each upcoming season. But as long as his name remained above it, it couldn't be replaced.

When push came to shove, however, and it was time for Joey to begin high school, and the private school's athletic program being what it was- a local joke- Mr. Wilson insisted his son be allowed back in the Wilsonville public school system. He'd paid his dues, and they would be getting the best local player around to boot. The deal was finally done with the stipulation that one minor infraction and he was gone, and that old man Wilson would have that scoreboard replaced, a cheap enough price to pay as far as he was concerned, even though it still rankled him that his son had been expelled in the first place. But, knowing he still had plenty of cards to play, he'd let bygones be bygones for now. And he also knew he'd need them, as Joey wasn't about to forgo his shenanigans any time soon.

CHAPTER 16

And then Johnny and She heard about Woodstock. They were in a local corner store purchasing oversize slushies when they heard an ad on the radio for a music festival to be held in the middle of August in downstate New York, the exact location yet to be determined.

"A frisbee and a few bucks is all you need," the disc jockey announced.

It also mentioned arts and crafts displays, games, music and camping, but She wasn't listening anymore.

"You know we have to go to this," She said. "We are fucking going! As far as I'm concerned, I'm already there."

While Johnny nodded enthusiastically, his own genuine and well-meant enthusiasm was tempered by his wondering how they were going to get there. That was for starters, and a million other questions would have come into his head, but he didn't let them, not wanting to dim She's eagerness, if that was possible.

"Sounds good," Johnny merely said.

"Sounds good?" She asked incredulously, "It's the chance of a lifetime! A road trip at the end of the summer, to hear music and party? What more could you ask for?"

"You're right," Johnny said, let's go."

"Oh, do you mean it?" She said. "We're really going?"

"If everything works out, we're really going," Johnny said.

Johnny didn't know why he agreed so readily, but She did that to him. It seems he's a bit of a stick in the mud, according to her, because she always initiates things, comes up with ideas for things to do. They complement each other that way, and sometimes his judiciousness comes in handy, like that time at the Falls when they went there with their church group, and someone brought a bottle of Tango along, and although he told her not to, She took part, then climbed over the fence overlooking the Falls, and he pulled her back, but not before the Park Rangers saw it and came over to question them. Their pastor managed to smooth things over, but Johnny thought they were going to detain them. She was unrepentant, but he thought even she was scared after what she did because she sobered up quickly.

As to how and when they were going to get to Woodstock, Johnny began planning as soon as he figured it out. He remembered their church's annual youth group had a weeklong stay at a Camp out in the boonies with all kinds of activities (most of which they skipped), but mostly just freedom to do whatever they wanted. It went from Saturday to Saturday, and the Woodstock festival would be during that weekend. There would be a big farewell party on Friday, and Johnny figured that would be a good time to slip away. He knew it would be kind of dicey, but he didn't see any other way. No way they could leave from their houses. They'd know something was up. He had to iron out the details as they came up. One was that they'd just have to leave what they brought for the week and hope the camp officials would send it home. It was very nerve-wracking, but She was on board in a big way.

In the meantime, it was back to their respective boring jobs, She working at the hairdresser, Johnny stocking shelves at the local supermarket. Exciting, huh? Actually, Johnny didn't mind his job all that much. He just didn't want to do it for the rest of his life. He especially enjoyed helping unload the produce trucks in the back, where he didn't have to be around anyone. He hated stocking shelves around a lot of people. They were in your way, you were in theirs', and then there was the dreaded cleanup on Aisle 9, to which whoever was closest had to respond. Also, you had people constantly asking you where things were, and, if you were conscientious like Johnny, you walked them right over to the spot where the desired item was. And they were supposed to put out every item, even if it was dented or there was one slightly soft potato in a sack. He hated that, and always put the damaged stock in the very back row, even if it cost him a lot more time rearranging everything. He was good at his job, though, and was highly thought of there.

She, as you might imagine, not so much. Her mother kept reminding her she had a marketable skill she could use for the rest of her life. She never said anything, but she didn't think so, not in a million years. She didn't like the smell, the hair all over the place, trying to sell a certain new product or have their hair done a more expensive way. And the gossip, as soon as they sat in a chair, it started- did you hear so and so had died, to which other people chimed in, "oh, I thought he or she already was." Then there were the rumored affairs, a divorcee's new beau, or some woman's delinquent kid. She didn't mean to be unkind, but she especially hated doing old ladies' hair, trying to cover up their mostly bald pates, and what was with the blue hair? Plus, wondering if a particularly doddering customer might be in for her last trip. And the women She worked with were much older than she, always talking about their problems, which she could hardly empathize with. Who cared if so and so's hubby stayed out too late, or got too drunk, or paid more attention to another woman than they did them?

She didn't give a rat's ass and was tired of the whole thing. Another reason they had to go to Woodstock.

It wasn't like they were freaks or hippies or anything. They had no idea that was what it would turn out to be. They were just a couple of teenagers from a small town wanting to have a good time and figured Woodstock was their one chance. They didn't hear anything about it from anyone else around town, so they didn't tell a soul, figuring the less, the merrier. No one needed to know anything other than they were away for a week at camp. They'd find out soon enough when they went missing by Friday night, but they'd worry about that after. No way they were going to miss what would probably be the biggest party of the year.

One could say they were music freaks, though, with pretty vast as well as eclectic record collections, considering they had to sneak every album they bought in their respective houses and only listen to them when no one was home and when they gradually found out who was going to be there, they knew it was going to be big. Hendrix, Ten Years After, The Who, Johnny Winter, Canned Heat, Creedence, and Joplin (She idolized her and that cinched it- she'd do anything to see her). They knew better than to even hope Johnny's favorite group Moby Grape would be there. They'd gotten in all that trouble early on, had been rumored to have broken up, but came out with that kickass album 'Moby Grape '69', the soundtrack to their summer that year. And while Joan Baez was going to be there, and that was great, She's other favorite Joni Mitchell wasn't. Oh well, they could only hope they'd somehow be surprise guests, knowing that happened quite a lot at these things.

The next step was getting their tickets. They'd heard another announcement on the radio telling them where to send for them in NYC, and once they got the money, they sent away for them ASAP. $13 for Saturday and Sunday was over half a weekly paycheck, but they would have paid ten times that much for all that music. They'd already seen Hendrix the year before, sneaking out during a snowstorm to take a bus downtown to see him, their very first live concert, and they were hooked. Their parents never found out about that one, and while they undoubtedly would this time, they didn't care. It would be worth whatever punishment they got. When they got the money together, they got a money order, sent it off, and had the tickets in their hot little hands the next week! Now all they had to do was wait another month for the festival.

As previously mentioned, this was a crazy town, with all kinds of characters, winners and losers. Take Jim Weatherly, who in Johnny's opinion, was the smartest guy in town. You could ask him anything, and he'd give you an answer, sometimes right away, sometimes having to think very deliberately until he came up with something. Ask him how many rods in a mile, how long a fortnight was, how the moon affected the water's tides, names of stars and constellations, where Timbuktu was, and he'd answer right away. It was mostly the advice questions he took the longest with, but he'd never given him bad advice, and he'd regret many a time he didn't take it. He was a mechanic over at Muck's garage, tall and lanky, and though he was around grease, oil, and grime, you'd never know it. How he stayed so clean, no one knew. And he could fix not only cars but pretty much anything. If you had trouble with your plumbing, phone, and appliance, you could call Jim, and he'd come over after work and take a look. He was also a world-class fisherman who tied his own flies and an expert hunter. He'd never married, though Johnny thought he'd have made a great father and often wished he was his. She agreed. It was probably a lonely life, living above the garage by himself, but you wouldn't know it. He was always smiling and glad to help a body out, and he was not only the smartest but the most well-liked guy in town. No one ever had a bad word to say about him.

He was Johnny's sounding board with many things, and he wasn't real enthused about their plans to go to Woodstock.

"How are you going to get there?" was the first thing he asked.

"Hitchhike," Johnny said.

"I suppose," he said, "I've hitched cross-country several times, and it seems everybody's doing it these days. Still, you have to be careful. Where are you going to stay?"

"In a tent in sleeping bags like the rest of the people there will probably be doing," Johnny said.

"That should be OK, but you have to watch who your neighbors are, and there are going to be a lot of drugs and alcohol being passed around."

"Why do you think we're going?" Johnny said and then quickly added, "I'm kidding."

"You'll have to watch that stuff. You guys are neophytes and could be led astray or get some bad drugs,' Jim said. "What are you going to eat?"

"The posters said there would be food there. And we'll take our own stuff to munch on," Johnny said.

"Make sure you have plenty of water. That's important," he added.

As the summer wore on, Jim got more on board with it. He didn't like the fact that they weren't telling their parents but understood why. He also said if things got out of hand and their parents were talking about telling the police or forming search parties when they didn't come home with the rest of the kids, he'd have to tell them where they were.

It seemed impossible others wouldn't find out, it being such a small town, but their parents interacted with so few people they weren't worried about them finding out, and before they knew it, it was time to go to camp. They'd done it so often it wasn't a big deal to get ready. Stuff a few jeans, tee shirts, and several changes of underwear into suitcases, and they were all set. That was one of the beauties of summer. You could travel light. This time they added a backpack to put all their Woodstock gear (tent, canteens, and ponchos) in, as well as lash their sleeping bags to the bottom of them, and She's father asked why the backpack and the sleeping bags? They thought they were busted, but Johnny came through for once, making up something about the older kids got to camp out one night on the beach after the huge bonfire they had every year.

"Where'd you get the tent and canteens,"? he asked.

"Oh, those are from my Boy Scout days, gotta be prepared," Johnny laughed.

She and Johnny looked at each other.

"Phew," they said under their breath.

Soon everything was packed into She's dad's old Ford station wagon, and off they went. Jim was standing in front of the repair shop and gave them an open-palmed wave, looking so beatific they wouldn't have been surprised if he was wearing a Nehru jacket and love beads.

The ride was about an hour, but they were so filled with anticipation they arrived in no time at all. They parked in the gravel parking lot across the road and got their stuff out of the back. Normally whoever's father drove would accompany them to the registration line, wait until they were registered, and escort them to their assigned cabin, but She begged and pleaded with her dad to not come with them this year, as it was their last, and it was embarrassing. Johnny couldn't believe She was talking to her father like that and was shocked when he readily agreed. They grabbed their stuff, crossed the road, and got in line to register at the Administration cabin.

They were afforded the luxury of being able to watch all the kids as they came in, observing how each and every one of them couldn't wait to get away from their parents. There were two guys there they recalled from previous years, a hippy-dippy type nicknamed Amby (Johnny guessed it was short for Ambitious, which he wasn't) popular with all the girls, who went most of the week shirtless, which showed off the beaded necklace he wore like a lei. The other guy was his friend Willy Fitz, a seemingly shy Peter Noone look-alike, also much in demand by those of the female persuasion. They were also there without their parents, in fact, in all the years they'd been going there, they had never been with their parents, and they acted so carefreely he doubted they even had any.

The only bad thing about the camp was the boys and girls were separated, the girls staying all the way on the other end of the campgrounds. The boy's cabins were all named after Indian tribes or the girl's after famous women. Johnny was assigned the Shoshone cabin and She the Pocahontas cabin.

"Dirty Water" (Standells) was big that summer, as was "Black is Black" (Los Lobos), "Summer in the City," (Lovin' Spoonful), and a song they heard for the first time and were blown away by, "You're Gonna Miss Me," (13th Floor Elevators) which, although they rarely ever heard it again, would thereafter consider it the greatest, most elusive, rock song of all time.

She and Johnny might have to go their separate ways at night, but they had promised they would spend all their waking hours together as much as possible.

Days at Camp Pioneer were very regimented. Up at sunrise, optional shower in a cement block building outfitted with ten open showers, each with their own wooden slatted platform to stand on, making the hundred-yard trek with your towel and dop kit in your bathrobe, be it a hot or cool morning, hoping to get there before anyone else (Johnny would never have waited in line) and shower as quickly as possible, then breakfast in the long dining room abutting the industrial-strength kitchen, though eating in public was a problem for both of them, having to sit at long wooden tables with Formica tops along with everybody else, and never the same people, as it was first come first serve. As long as they were together, it didn't matter. Unwilling to eat in front of other people, they made due with copious cartons of milk, lining the empties up in front of them, amazing everyone at how much they'd consumed, or maybe escaping with a few wrapped sandwiches or hoping for an outdoor barbecue for dinner where they wouldn't be cooped up and could eat freely, this supplemented by candy, pop (cream soda), ice cream cones, and chips at the Snack Bar. There was daily church in the chapel in the mosquito-infested (especially at night) woods among pine trees after breakfast, then back to their cabins to clean up and make their beds for inspection, after which some form of recreation (volleyball on a large court near the chapel in the woods was a favorite), lunch, in the early afternoon arts and crafts (which She enjoyed and which Johnny hated except for making boondoggles, which he tolerated), afterwards a trip to the Snack Bar and then back to their cabins to rest or do whatever they wanted during their brief free time before dinner as long as they didn't leave their cabins or make noise. After dinner Bible study then a brief service at the chapel (mosquitoes eating them alive), where they sang campfire hymns and spirituals, then finally back to their cabins with lights out at nine-thirty.

It was at these times any hanky-panky going on would occur. If you listened carefully, you could hear cabin doors in either camp close quietly on campers going to meet at a predetermined location with their chosen one, usually the small wooded area before the Administration building. I imagined nothing more went on than making out, although older guys like Amby intimated if not outright bragged otherwise. Every once in a while, some unfortunate slob got caught sneaking out or in the act of doing so and was either grounded or sent home, hardly a deterrent to a hormone-raging adolescent. During those times it became increasingly difficult for She and Johnny to maintain their platonic relationship. They were kidded that they were like brother and sister, and some of the guys tried to horn in on her, but She would have nothing of it. They eventually kissed, if only to shut them up, and found they enjoyed it, but not too much, as it was too mushy. It seemed as though they might even want to go further, but not around anyone.

Through all this was their anticipation of Friday, wondering if they would get caught, but otherwise still determined to go through with it no matter what. It was difficult at times not to mention it to someone, but they didn't and made sure no one was around when they talked about it. They'd look in their backpacks every now and then to remind themselves what they were doing (as if they really needed reminding) and to make sure everything was safe and sound in there.

On Thursday, they got quite a scare, as a group of boys got busted making a beer run at a store down the road, but it wasn't like they had a crack security force watching over them. It was because somebody snitched. And the grand finale, the daylong fair followed by the beach bonfire and the older kids sleeping on the beach, all the counselors participated in, and their guards would surely be down.

They were big on naps at the camp, and, sure enough, there was one scheduled even on that day. Even if you didn't nap, you were expected to remain quietly in your cabin. It was a time when everyone took refuge from the brutal midday heat and of reverie as well in anticipation of that afternoon and evening's festivities, all in all making it the perfect time to make their escape. They even changed their plans: they wouldn't come back after the nap break instead of going just before the fair ended, which would give them more daylight, even though they were taking a chance on being seen, but the woods were so thick past the administration building, they just had to make sure they weren't spotted. They'd leave when the other kids were going back to the fair, hopefully slipping away unnoticed, and even if they were, no one would tell on them because, even though they weren't really part of it, it was a pretty tight group.

They hung back until everyone was gone, then grabbed their backpacks and met as planned in the little woods next to the administration building, and, after making sure they were ready, and no one had seen them, headed into the thicket behind it. They were moving as quietly as possible, even though there was no one around when they heard a sudden rustling over to their right. As they peered through the dense tree cover, they saw flashes of white, and when they moved closer, saw it was two guys on top of two girls humping their brains out, and when they got even closer, saw it was Amby and Willy Fitz! Tempting as it was to interrupt them, they knew they needed to get a move on and turned away reluctantly from the desperately carnal scene.

CHAPTER 17

Jim Weatherly saw the wistful look indelibly etched on Gracie's face and it made him wonder how it was all going to turn out for her. Why would he wonder this about a girl her age, with so much potential and so much life ahead of her? Because he'd seen that look before, on the hobos, nay bums, he'd seen and known in his travels all those years on the road, their lives seemingly ended, doomed to try to get ahead of the untold imaginings or the real traumatic events that had ended their lives as they knew them, lives in which they would play out the string and die alone, unaccounted for, to be buried in a nameless pauper's grave. Could her situation be that dire at her young age? Thankfully he didn't believe that and even knew with a certain prescience he possessed that despite some rough years ahead, she would eventually endure and find a modicum of peace, if not happiness, in her life. In spite of his penchant for premonitions, however, he could have had no idea of what was about to happen to her.

As the years went by, Gracie and Toby's relationship could be described as ambiguous at best. While obviously a girl and unquestionably pretty in her own way, she didn't warrant the usual male deference about being the "weaker sex" because she wasn't, yet she wasn't exactly like a boy in temperament either, being very sensitive, with a lingering, just below the surface sadness the primary manifestation of this. The cause of this sadness was undoubtedly the result of not being able to fit in, of being betwixt and between any social niche available to her. In short, she had no context.

She couldn't be Toby's "best" friend at the time because boys and girls just didn't hang around that much at that age (part of the unwritten "code") and because Jeff Nelson already claimed that unofficial distinction, but they did have a "special" relationship, where many things (as is usually only with boys) between them didn't necessarily need to be expressed or demonstrated (although they often could be, with a mere eye roll), these "things" being implicitly understood by each of them in equal measure.

They had spent a lot of time together over the years, albeit mostly with a third-party present, but as they grew older, they saw more and more of each other unaccompanied. In fact, they had gone to both the sophomore and junior prom together, which proliferated the usual gossip in school regarding them (mostly that it was just weird), while their (Toby's actually, Gracie didn't seem to have any) friends were so used to it, they thought nothing of it. But lately, even others had noticed a shift in the relationship, and although they said nothing, it seemed to them to be getting a bit one-sided, with Toby wanting to get closer while Gracie grew seemingly more ambivalent.

And they would have been right, although, similarly, Toby would have never said anything to these others about it, partially because he was so confused, he didn't know what to think. He had no way of knowing if it was the same way for Gracie, perhaps even more difficult, which it was. Was she a tomboy or just a girl? She felt more comfortable as the former but realized it could go either way. It was ultimately up to her. At the same time, she realized she was changing physically but still resisted making herself look any more feminine than she had to. She was a couple of inches taller than Toby, too, and although he didn't seem to mind, it made her even more self-conscious than she already was. She at least had someone she could talk to about it, although it was certainly not her dad. It was Mrs. Grimes, who, despite her old-fashioned notions (or maybe even because), at least listened to her and gave her pointers on how to look more lady-like (not *too*, though), picking out clothes for her, giving her sensible grooming tips, and was very helpful regarding her relationship with Toby, of which she made no bones about the fact she greatly approved.

"You like each other, always have," she'd say, "that's the most important thing. As you're getting older, things are bound to change, but don't worry about it too much. Enjoy it for what it is, and be thankful. Not all boys are as nice as Toby if you catch my drift. You could do a lot worse. Besides, you're both too young to be serious."

Gracie did indeed understand, but things certainly hadn't progressed that far in her relationship with Toby to even think of any permanence concerning it, and she wasn't sure if they ever would or if she even wanted them to.

But, through no fault of her own, there were aspects of Gracie's life Mrs. Grimes could never begin to understand, simply because she was from a different generation. And Gracie could never begin to talk about these things, as she couldn't articulate them herself yet, even if she had wanted to. In short, her burden was double-fold, that of reconciling her identity as a female and as an athlete and the effect this had on her relationship with Toby.

Prior to this, Toby had made every attempt to include her in all his unofficial sports activities, and that was all well and good, but the older they got, the more organized his sports activities became, and thus she was completely shut out unless she wanted to play tennis, which she didn't, or softball, which she did, and which served to maintain her competitive edge, and in which she excelled. But that wasn't her first love, basketball was. While no trailblazer, she began to question the fairness of New York not introducing girls' basketball as a high school sport like other states had, talking to gym teachers and administrators alike, who dismissed her immediately, end of discussion. Further, not only did she want to play high school basketball, she wanted to play *boys'* high school basketball, which was totally out of the question, even to this day. Instead, she was relegated to playing in an AAU league, where again, she dominated much older women.

By the same token, Toby was not one to rock the boat. While they had never talked about it, Toby knew about Gracie's real aspirations, although he never let on that he did, even though he also knew it was affecting their relationship. He had been on schoolboys' basketball teams from junior high on and was now a starting guard on the Wilsonville varsity, and, while he'd championed Gracie's playing with the boys from the get go, this was an entirely different matter. He had no doubt Gracie could compete with the best of them, including Joey Wilson, the purported star of the team, which was going to be a lousy one mostly because of, not in spite of him, ball hog that he was.

Truth be told, Toby was becoming more and more conflicted about the whole situation, not being able to admit to himself how he'd feel if Gracie was given a chance to compete and proved herself to be better than all of them. He'd played enough one-on-one to know she very well could be, and a part of him didn't want that to happen, knowing it would destroy the order of things.

Instead of it all being the good, clean fun it had been up until now, there was a great deal of tension between them, and, while for Gracie, it was irreconcilable, for Toby, it only meant they might not be going to the senior prom together.

Right around this time, a summer day in between their junior and senior years, Toby and Gracie were shooting hoops on a court at a local park run by the Wilsonville Recreational Center. While there were many pickup games played there in the cool of the evening, it was usually empty during the morning hours and the high heat of the afternoon, so empty you could hear the reverberation of the ball hitting the metal backboard or the clank when a shot "swished" through the bizarre chain metal nets, a cost-cutting measure implemented by the Village Board that was very unpopular with the many citizens who used the three parks there.

Whether consciously or not, Toby and Gracie played there on an almost daily basis from mid-morning to late afternoon, this with Toby often returning to participate in an evening pickup game. Whether Gracie knew this or not (she did), neither she nor Toby ever mentioned it, and why would they? It was a matter of course during the summer. She'd have loved to have played in these games, or at least been asked to, but she wasn't going to beg.

That afternoon started like any other but soon changed so radically it would alter the course of each of their lives irrevocably. It was a late August summer day, with school about to begin in a couple of weeks. Whether they were aware of it or not, Joey Wilson, courtesy of his father, was overseer of the parks, a summer job he was neither qualified for nor was, as with most things handed to him by his father, particularly conscientious about, often calling it a day after an early morning visit to each of the parks before they opened. After that, he and his acolytes (a group of young boys who worshiped him and followed him around like he was the Pied Piper) spent the rest of the day sunning themselves on the concrete deck surrounding the outdoor pool at Rec Center, not to return to the parks until well after they were closed each evening. This was common knowledge, he didn't even try to hide it, but nothing was ever said or done, each park having its own summer staff and things running smoothly despite him.

It was never entirely clear why he and his crew decided to show up at that particular park on that particular afternoon, but rumor had it he had heard tell of Toby and Gracie's daily shootarounds there and came to see for himself.

Whatever the reason, their purpose was to ridicule the two. As mentioned before, Toby was on the team and had known Joey off and on over the years and, while he tolerated him, saw him for what he was, a spoiled brat and a bully. Gracie had never met him but knew all about him from everything Tony had told her over the years. Likewise, Joey, who seemed to have his finger in a lot of pies, knew all about her.

Joey, his impressive tan contrasted by his tennis whites, got out of the red Skylark with the white convertible top his old man had purchased for him (he being the one of the few kids in school with a new car), donned his sunglasses, and sauntered toward the court, his minions piling out of the car and trailing after.

"Kleiny," he called out (he had nicknames for everyone), taking off his sunglasses. "So, what I hear is true. You *are* playing with a chick. Now, why would you do that? How're you going to get any better? You should be playing with guys- me, for instance. Or maybe it makes you feel better beating a girl."

His sycophants all guffawed loudly in unison behind him, not one of them an individual in their own right, merely followers, their only strength in numbers.

Toby was about to defend her by saying she was better than Joey thought, but before he could say anything heard Gracie speak up, saying, "I'll challenge you to a game of 1-on-1, H-O-R-S-E, you name it, any time you want."

There was total silence until Joey turned around to his followers and said, "You hear that shit? This chick thinks she can beat me."

They all began pointing at her, laughing at the absurdity of it.

"I didn't say I could beat you," Gracie continued, "although I'm pretty sure I can."

"Not today, dear," Joey laughed, "I wouldn't waste my time. And you, Kleiny, wait 'til the guys hear about this." Shaking his head, he turned on his heel, almost colliding with one of his disciples. "Come on, let's go!" he said and strode away.

But Gracie wasn't finished. "Whenever you're ready, just let me know. I'll be here," she said.

If Joey heard, he didn't let on, but, driving away, he honked the horn and stuck out his middle finger.

"Well, there's your answer, I guess," Toby said nervously. When Gracie didn't respond, Toby said, "You're not really thinking of playing him, are you?"

"Wouldn't have said it if I wasn't," Gracie replied and launched a nearly half-court shot that went straight through the hoop, chinking like snow tire chains in winter as it did so.

CHAPTER 18

Of course, Jim knew everything came to an end at some point, whether affixed or not. That was life, a series of beginnings and endings, but the key was to be as ready as you can be toward what comes your way. Have a plan. Most kids' lives are fairly circumscribed, and they plan ahead or are made to. For most, it meant going to college (if only to avoid the draft), working in their father's business, or learning a trade. But for some who were stuck in limbo for a myriad of reasons: a parent's death, a debilitating illness or accident, or some just wanting to stay at home and live off their parent's largesse, there was seemingly no place to be. It was a very lonely spot to be in, and the survival instinct kicks in, sometimes for the good (seldom as this was), but mostly you were on your own, sink or swim, making decisions you would never make under normal circumstances just to get by. For the most part, these kids' futures were on hold, if not already blighted on the vine, requiring great fortitude to carry on. You were entering the prime of your life with nowhere to go. Now some may have no sympathy ("I had no one to help me" is the usual mantra), and everyone's circumstances differ, as do their coping mechanisms. It isn't too long before some kids fall through the cracks in the system, as they say, due to some untoward circumstances. Then they are totally alone, or in an institution, with no help forthcoming, and what will happen to them then? One does not want to be around their former friends under these conditions, it is best to approach total strangers, or someone from church, a neighbor, but when there is no aid being tendered, it can be a pretty scary time until you somehow get your feet on the ground. And the toll it takes (!), making you old before your time. Jim had seen it many times, where a kid out on the road looked twice his age. And for girls? Forget about it. It was ever more difficult, if not impossible.

Gracie needed to figure something out and quick. Her future was at stake, after all, and she knew she wasn't going to get any help from anyone else, so she had to do it herself. Right before her very eyes, her father had dwindled down to a shadow of his former self (which took a lot of doing) and didn't have much longer to live. Pancreatic cancer will do that to you. She was spending most of her spare time ministering to him as it was, and she felt everyone was moving on without her, getting ready for college and whatnot.

Sure, Mrs. Grimes helped her out on a daily basis, doing the things she couldn't or didn't like to do: bringing home-cooked meals over, the usual straightening up and cleaning, laundry, but Gracie didn't feel like she could go on much longer like this.

Everyone was moving on? Who was everyone? She just meant, in general, that she didn't have any friends except Toby. And he was going to college, would be leaving shortly, somewhere in Michigan. She supposed she could have gone to the local juco and taken a few courses had she really wanted, but, as in everything else, she was ambivalent. And resentful. Very resentful. While her father hadn't discouraged her from going to college, he hadn't exactly encouraged her. And she didn't really know why, maybe because of the money (they had very little, and now her father was on permanent disability, and that would end soon, she only hoped it wouldn't end before he died), but most probably because he was sick. It couldn't be because she was a girl. Her father had never treated her like that. He'd found out early on she could do as well as any boy at anything she wanted. And Mrs. Grimes had encouraged her, offered to help her out with the applications and fees, so she really only had herself to blame. When it really came down to it, the only reason she would have wanted to go to college was to play basketball, and the only way she could have afforded it was to get a full scholarship to do so.

And it shouldn't have even been a question. All things being equal, she was as good an athlete as her father had been, and he had gotten a full ride for football, hadn't he? And promptly pissed it away fighting, gambling, drinking, and doing drugs. It just wasn't fair. She knew she was whining if only to herself, but it wasn't. Fair that is.

Forget it, she thought. I'm going to take Toby up on his offer and go camping for the weekend. Nothing exotic, or, out of necessity now, far away, having to stay close by her father, just in some woods on the end of the village. It was posted, but she'd never been rousted all the times she had gone there because Sheriff Grimes wouldn't allow it. He was good like that. It was the last vestige from the uncivilized past of Wilsonville, her favorite spot by far in the village, and so convenient, as you had to go south for miles and miles before you found anything remotely like it anywhere else, and she'd keep going back there as long as she lived in Wilsonville. It didn't matter to her (or to Sheriff Grimes, apparently) that it was Joseph Wilson's land. She knew he'd sell it off in a heartbeat if he got the right offer for it, so someone might as well get some enjoyment from it, and it might as well be her.

It was a large wooded area of approximately a thousand acres abutting the edge of Elliott Creek on the south end, its perimeter bounded to the north by the at the time longest (thirty-five miles) straight road in the world, according to the Guinness Book of Records, three-quarters of a mile from the village proper. Developers, as well as the village itself (who coveted it as a theme park, always seeking another revenue stream), had been trying for years to get their hands on it, but Mr. Wilson wouldn't budge on Bill Burnham's usually sage advice. It wouldn't be long until Wilsonville's population exploded, he told him, and then it would be the prime area for commercial development (i.e., malls), every other acre having already been overdeveloped, so he must wait for just the right moment (i.e., until he told him) to sell and the sky would be the limit.

And since Toby would be leaving for school soon, they only had a few weekends left to camp out together, as they did most weekends, ostensibly to pick up all the refuse left there by illegal campers and teenage kids during the week, although a greater solitude (with or without Toby) she found while there she had yet to experience. She'd been appalled to find that graffiti had been spray-painted on some of the bigger boulders scattered around the area. When she informed Sheriff Grimes of this, he said he was well aware of the problem but powerless to do anything about it. It seemed that Mr. Wilson was responsible for maintenance of the area, and he supposedly had a full-time permanent crew to do so, but either they weren't doing a good job, or he was being hoodwinked, probably a combination of the two. The old-growth forest itself was still very much pristine, as no vehicles of any sort had ever been allowed there, although there were several well-worn trails scattered throughout. There was even wildlife still to be found: deer, fox, raccoons, and myriad frogs, snakes, and the like, and a few hunters had been arrested for trespassing over the years.

It was rumored to contain an Indian burial ground and regarded as sacred by a tribe whose reservation wasn't far away, and, while no one had seen any evidence of it (the burial ground), the place had an eeriness about it at night, mostly caused by the blackness from the thick tree canopy, that kept most amateurs away. It was Gracie's favorite place in the world, however. So what if it was jeeringly dubbed "Wilson' Folly"? All the better, as far as she was concerned, the old man Wilson had no clue she had ever been there, let alone practically every weekend year-round, or that anyone would have the least interest in recreating there.

She and Toby had finally agreed that it was best if they were "just friends." It was a painful decision (especially for Toby), and it was a touch-and-go situation for a while when they wondered if they could even remain friends, again, on Toby's part. Gracie would have been devastated if she'd lost her only real friend, and, in the end, Toby finally realized that he would be, too. To seal the deal, they went to the Senior Prom together and had a wonderful time, unbothered by the rampant speculation about the nature of their relationship. It was nobody's business, plain and simple.

Then at the last minute, Toby cancelled the camping trip, deciding he'd better attend the college's orientation that weekend. Though Gracie was very disappointed, she understood, and it certainly wouldn't deter her from camping out by herself. She arranged for Mrs. Grimes to check in on her dad while she was gone, then set off walking (she walked everywhere on sturdy unshaven legs, which didn't show much because of her blond hair), her backpack filled with camping implements and sleeping bag lashed to the bottom of it. It wasn't far, nothing in Wilsonville was and would take her a half-hour at most.

Sheriff Grimes was tooling around in his brand-new police car, a blue and white with yellow trim 1965 Ford Galaxie, an updated version of the same car Sheriff Taylor and Barney Fife drove into the ground on The Andy Griffith Show, one of his favorite TV programs. Not that he expected to learn anything valuable about policing on it, it being more about the milk of human kindness, but it was interesting how they handled certain situations, and Andy's relationship with Barney fascinated him.

Then suddenly, he got the call on the radio that changed almost everybody's life in Wilsonville from that day forward.

Just after receiving it, he saw Deputy Rains' car parked at the custard stand on Main Street. He was thinking he'd find out if he'd heard it too, maybe bust his chops a little about stopping for ice cream, but now he was all business.

Deputy Rains intercepted him before he even got out of the car, so Sheriff Grimes assumed he'd heard the call too, but no.

"Sheriff, I was just going to radio you," he said, "I saw a bunch of kids hanging around the ballfield by the Electric Company, and when I got closer to check it out, they vanished."

They'd been investigating some "mischief" going on in the woods leading down to the creek for the past month but had no leads, and though this might be one, it wasn't top priority any longer.

"Deputy Rains, forget that for now. I assume you didn't hear the bulletin that just came across the radio?"

"No," Deputy Rains replied, "I radioed in a 10-7 B (the deputy was big on seldom used radio codes) to get a hamburger and a shake for lunch. What's up?"

"I see that," Sheriff Grimes said, "but you better finish it quick. I just now got a 10-65 (he knew that would get his attention) we have to look into pronto."

Falling all over himself at hearing this, Deputy Rains responded, "No Sheriff, I didn't hear it. As I said, I was on a 10-7 B ..."

Sheriff Grimes interrupted him before he could finish, "Get back to the station, ASAP. Dispatcher Brown will fill you in. Radio me for further instructions. I'm gonna head out to Elliott Creek by the castle."

"Can't you tell me what it's about first?" Deputy Rains asked. "So's I know what's going on?"

"Just get back to the station," Sheriff Grimes responded tersely. "I want everyone on high alert."

"10-4, Sheriff," Deputy Rains said breathlessly, saluting him. "10-4," he repeated when the Sheriff didn't salute him back.

Before he drove away, Sheriff Grimes watched his deputy get in his car and drive off in a hurry, the strawberry milkshake that was still on the roof of his car falling and splashing all over his windshield.

'Poor guy, so high-strung,' Sheriff Grimes thought. 'It's not stopping him, though,' Sheriff Grimes noted wryly when he saw him turn on his windshield wipers and speed off without missing a beat.

Gracie Graham was missing. Mrs. Grimes had called the station when she hadn't returned by Monday afternoon. She gave them as much information as she knew: Gracie had set out on foot up Main Street around 1 PM on Friday, loaded down with her camping equipment (including a tent, cooking implements, and fishing gear) and supplies in a large backpack, headed for Wilson's woods. She said she'd be back on Monday afternoon at the latest. It was common knowledge she went practically every weekend year-round, usually with Toby Klein, but he'd cancelled at the last minute because of a college orientation he'd attended over the weekend. He'd just stopped by to see Gracie and see how her weekend had gone and was surprised to find she hadn't returned as yet. He'd reassured Mrs. Grimes there was nothing to be alarmed about and was sure he'd meet up with her as he set out to their usual campsite, where he was pretty certain she'd gone.

Mrs. Grimes called the station shortly after he left, having had a bad feeling about it and not wanting Toby to get mixed up in whatever was happening with her, which she, of course hoped was nothing. But she was sure there was something happening, and it wasn't anything good, and they must hurry. She'd never been late like this before because she had her father to look after. It just wasn't like her, she'd always been reliable about that.

Before he set out on a wild goose chase, which was the first thing he thought it might be when he heard Mrs. Grimes was the caller who'd reported it, he thought he'd swing by the ball diamond on S. Long and see if those kids were still there. Kill two birds with one stone, see what they were up to and if they'd seen or heard anything at all. He knew Gracie had a mind of her own, could have gone off anywhere to do god knows what. He doubted anything serious had happened. He just didn't have that feeling in his gut that usually said something had. Hell, she just might have decided to finish up her weekend by taking the long way around back into the village, and she and Toby (who'd returned by then and was probably out looking for her) might emerge together, and all would be well. That's what he hoped, at least. That was any lawman's method. Start out simple and gradually work up to the next possibility if no clues were discernible at that point.

When he got to the ball diamond, however, not a soul was there, although you could tell the way the pitcher's mound, the batter's box, and the base paths were scuffed up. Quite a few kids had been there earlier. There was a familiar, well-worn path just past right field that led into the woods a way before it disappeared into the thick underbrush, making the going tough for anyone, much less an out-of-shape middle-aged man such as he was. He and later generations of kids after him had used it, although back then it had been forbidden, which of course had made it all the more enticing, forbidden because it had been the scene of the aforementioned lone murder in the village's history thirty or so years before Sheriff Grimes had been born. A little boy had been lured into the woods by a monster at that very spot and murdered not much further away. The police said a couple had heard his cries of anguish but had arrived too late to save him. They found the perpetrator, an itinerant laborer passing through, and he was summarily executed, but it took the village a long time to recover from it.

He walked a little way up the path, which too looked like it had been recently trodden over by more than one person, but seeing or hearing nothing, he thought to himself, 'guess we're going to have to do this the hard way'. Not that he now thought anything serious had happened; he didn't. He just wanted to locate her and reassure the village (he was sure the word that she was "missing" had spread by now) that everything was under control and there was no need to panic.

Seeing enough to know there was something worth pursuing, he turned around to go back to his patrol car. Just as he emerged from the path out into the open, he spotted a lone figure walking through the driveway of the Electric Company. When he got closer, he saw it was old Dudley, the jack-of-all-trades, as well as night watchman at the DPW. Must be headed to work, he thought. Might as well ask him if he's seen, heard, or knew anything, although he hesitated. Old Dudley was such a loony bird. 'Oh well,' he said to himself, 'any port in a storm, got to cover all the bases.'

"Hey Dudley!" he yelled fairly loudly, "is that you?"

The old man must not have heard him, so he yelled again, and this time he stopped walking, hesitated, then turned around.

Sheriff Grimes walked up to him and returned Dudley's nod with his own.

"What can I do for you, Sheriff?" he asked. "Just heading into work, minding my own business. You know me, just your average law-abiding citizen."

Ignoring his banter, Sheriff Grimes got right down to business.

"I was wondering if you'd seen any kids here earlier," he asked, "less than a half-hour ago, it was."

"Sure did," he said. "Just neighbor kids playing ball. Then a bunch of older kids arrived, seemed pretty hopped up, this bunch did and drove the kids off."

"Did you see where they went?"

"The kids? Just got on their bikes and took off," he said.

"What about the older kids," he asked, "did you recognize any of them?"

"Yeah," Dudley said, "one of them was old man Wilson' son, pulled up in his fancy red car, and all these other kids jumped out of it."

Sheriff Grimes looked around but didn't see any sign of the car, which he was very familiar with.

"Where'd they go?" he asked.

"The whole bunch of them ran up the path into the woods. Wilson didn't go with them. He just got in his car and drove off."

'This is getting more interesting by the minute,' Sheriff Grimes thought. 'Definitely worth looking into.' It was just then he remembered the castle. 'The castle,' he said to himself. 'That's where they are. I just know it! I'd better radio on ahead and have the boys meet me there.'

CHAPTER 19

400,000 people Jim Weatherly heard. Amazing! Good for those kids: peace, love and understanding, and great music. Though he'd never been in a crowd that big (85,000 in Cleveland for a Yankees-Indians doubleheader was the most), he had an understanding of how that must be. People everywhere, nowhere to turn, some continuing to bump into you, or stride right through your campsite. Packed in like sardines, but at least they were outside, not packed into a railroad car on a hot day – boy was it ripe in there! You had to be pretty self-confident in a situation like that, or you'd be lost in the crowd. Jealousies and fights of all kinds were probably happening, one guy thinking another guy was after his old lady, which he probably was. A lot of hanky-panky going on there, no doubt. Drugs and booze too. He'd heard it was a quagmire there, but what could have been a disaster wasn't. Overall, the behavior was good, people helping one another. It gave him hope for this generation, he knew his generation could never have done something like this. They didn't even tolerate it. Never trust anyone over thirty was their mantra for good reason. He hoped Johnny and She were having a good time but had a feeling they weren't – Johnny at least.

They moved through the woods until they were almost past the boundary of the camp parking lot across the road, where the stand of trees ended, and they had to emerge out onto Route 5 and begin hitching. They walked a little down the road until they were out of sight of the camp and stopped to begin. Before they did, however, She reached down in her backpack and pulled out a sign she'd made on one of the craft days that read, in dayglo letters with flowers bordering them: **WOODSTOCK!** Now they were ready! They figured they had a five-hour trip ahead of them, and that was in the unlikely condition they got one ride all the way there.

These were the days before Lake Erie became so polluted it was unswimmable, and there was a lot of beachfront property and several bars that catered to partygoers from the city, and since it was Friday, there should be plenty of traffic. And there was, but it was mostly young kids who were already drinking and would toss their empty beer cans at them or slow down as if to give them a ride and then speed up when they got close, laughing their asses off as if they were the only ones who had that idea. She and Johnny knew they needed to get to the Thruway entrance about five miles away, and then they would be home free if someone was going their way.

And what do you know, two rides, one from a farmer.

"Where's Woodstock?" he asked, to which I answered, "it's not a place. It's a music festival."

"You mean you don't know where you're going?"

"Of course we do," Johnny said, "it's somewhere in the Catskills, at a place called White Lake."

"And you think it's safe, you and a young girl out on the road, not knowing how you'll get there?"

Luckily they reached a fork in the road, where he let them out, and not more than five minutes later, they were picked up by a young kid who looked to be a farm boy himself, who took them to the entrance of the Thruway.

"Good luck," he said, "wish I was going."

"Hey, why don't you come?" She piped in, much to Johnny's chagrin, showing she thought the opposite of him on some things when she continued, "you're certainly welcome. The more, the merrier, I say."

"Can't, I got chores to do," he said, dourly, much to his relief.

Once at the entrance to the Thruway, they stood for a while as there wasn't much traffic in the area, and were beginning to get a little discouraged after an hour with nothing, when suddenly they spotted a truck jouncing along toward them with a couple of kids in the open back. The truck stopped immediately, and someone in the front passenger side rolled down the window and said, "Woodstock? Hop in!" They immediately did so, throwing their backpacks in the back and following after them.

There were two other people in the back who looked to be about their age, though much more hippy-dippy than them, the guy with longish hair tied back with a headband, wearing carpenter jeans, no shirt, and sandals, the girl with a long peasant dress with beads around her neck and head as well. They were from the city of Buffalo, which they claimed, despite She and Johnny's experience there, to be a "happening place," both students at the University, which probably explained why.

She and Ari hit it off immediately, while Wesley and Johnny not so much, mostly because Wesley kept ogling She for the first ten minutes until Ari visibly kicked him and he stopped. It turned out he was something of a bigwig in something called SDS, while Ari, originally from the big city (NYC), was a regular person, surprisingly much more of an enthusiastic girly-girl than She. She knew a lot about White Lake, where the festival was being held, as her parents had a summer place nearby.

"All farm country and wide-open spaces, beautiful and quiet, with not a lick of anything to do around there. Should be a great place for a concert, though," she said, "with the surrounding hills making for a great amphitheater."

Ari and She bonded over their love of Janis Joplin and disappointment that Joni Mitchell wasn't going to be there. She even broke into a rendition of "Piece of My Heart," which even Johnny was amazed at, and Ari was tremendously enthused about, assuring her she had the goods and would definitely make it big someday. All this from one song, but Johnny had to admit, it did get his hopes up. Now all he had to do was his part, which was to figure out exactly what he wanted to do, which wasn't looking too promising at the moment. Except to get any kind of job he could to support She while she tried to find a gig.

But Johnny was getting way ahead of himself at that point, and determined to forget all that, stop worrying, and have a good time. Wesley ("call me Wes") ameliorated his initial intense dislike of him when he pulled a big fat doobie out of his pocket, lit it, then passed it to him. Johnny thought it was a cigarette, which made the two girls laugh, and red-faced Johnny took as big a toke as he could and, almost choking on it, passed it on to She, who refused it, as did Ari.

The truck them jostled a bit, but the breeze it created was a great relief from the broiling sun. They soon stopped at a rest stop for a bathroom break and for a snack to assuage their munchies and a drink to slake their thirst. It turned out Ari and Wes didn't know the inhabitants of the truck, so they all introduced themselves. Abby and Gail turned out to be the real deal, members of a Western New York commune in a place called Zoar Valley, they were told, which She and Johnny had heard of but never visited. They seemed like nice enough, laid-back people.

Soon they were back on the road again and halfway there, according to Ari. Johnny was stoned out of his gourd, not moving and staring. Things went pretty smoothly until they got off the Thruway onto 17B, where it seemed there was a five-mile backup of cars at a standstill, which, while annoying, they had to stick out until they got closer than ten miles from the place, which is where they were now. Gradually they inched along until they came to a complete stop, with cars strewn along the road and surrounding fields like a junkyard. They got out and waited for Abby to park the car and then began to join the myriad throng on the long trek to White Lake.

They decided to stay together as they pressed through the swarm of people coming and going (many people, discouraged because they had been told the concert was a no-go, were heading back to where they came from), a myriad of cars abandoned on the side of the road, which all made for tough going, but, with strength in numbers, they slowly made their way forward. It was just about sundown, and they were dead on their feet, but after a good hour, they began to see some clearing up ahead. They veered right toward some hills and, finding one relatively unpopulated, headed up it.

"Just temporary, or maybe we can bivouac here, start out early in the morning to get nearer the stage," Abby said, which they couldn't see in the gloaming but knew was there because the large towers holding sound equipment were nearby.

She and Johnny thought they'd walk around for a bit but turned back almost immediately for fear of getting lost, the hill they were on was filling up so rapidly. When they returned, Abby and Gail had gotten their big-ass tent up, with plenty of room for six people. Ari and Wes were nowhere to be found, but from the looks and wry smiles on Gail and Abby's faces, they got the distinct impression they were off somewhere getting intimate.

When they awoke Saturday morning after a good night's sleep had by all the hill was packed so tightly they could hardly move. It seemed impossible it could have filled up so quickly, but it had, and they could still see the lava-like surge of humanity filling up every nook and cranny in the area. Ari and Wes were all over each other like a bum on a baloney sandwich immediately until Abby told them to take it outside. They made some peanut butter and honey sandwiches, the bread toasted in the freshly-banked fire next to the coffee pot, which they generously shared with them. Then they left them to tidy up and set up some more of their camping equipment for what they thought would be a leisurely stroll through the crowd, but it quickly became stiflingly maze-like until they finally managed to zig-zag way out to the periphery of the crowd and headed toward the stage, eager to get themselves placed when the music began that afternoon.

At first, he wasn't all that enamored with the first two acts, finding them both boring, although the crowd really dug them. Country Joe and the Fish's goofing became a lot more palatable once you joined in the fun, which he would never have done if he'd been straight (he'd smoked again), and Santana's interminable guitar solos weren't as noticeable once they got into the rhythm sections, which were very groovy, and moved things along quite nicely. John Sebastian was a lightweight (except for "Darlin' Be Home Soon") without the Lovin' Spoonful, but the next two acts, The Incredible String Band and Canned Heat, were wonderfully diametrically opposed, although he really could have done without Canned Heat's interminable blues and improvised boogies he was unfamiliar with, although they knocked it out of the park with "Goin' Up the Country" and "On the Road Again." Then Leslie West and Mountain continued the raunch, although they disappointingly omitted "Mississippi Queen" from their set.

Next came back the goof vibe with The Dead and their myriad Deadheads. It got really crowded then, and when the rain hit, they had no problem splitting and heading back to camp. It was pouring and lightning and the sudden wind howling like a banshee and somehow, She and Johnny got separated, an easy thing under the best of conditions, what with all the people packed in together like sardines, let alone the instant chaos that ensued after the rain came pouring down in buckets, everyone scurrying for somewhere- anywhere – to get in out of it. The rain continued despite the fact the Deadheads started their own Fish cheer, "Fuck the rain! Fuck the rain! Fuck the rain!" It didn't help, but they were enjoying it, going with the flow, so to speak.

Johnny finally managed to make it back to the tent and assumed

She was behind him, as she always was, but she was nowhere to be seen. His tent mates dissuaded him from going back out to look for her, remonstrating with him that then they would both be lost, and drenched to boot, and they were sure she had found a place to get in out of the rain, reassuring him not to worry, everyone was so nice there, and whoever she was with would take care of her. That was the point for Johnny- they were *too* nice, someone would/could be taking advantage of her. A deep black mood suddenly enveloped him, insane jealousy the like of which he'd never felt before. He became convinced that at that very moment, she was cheating on him (not that they'd ever discussed being a thing, he just assumed they had an understanding) and during the whole time he was hearing Joe Cocker wailing out, "With a Little Help From My Friends," his voice refracted through the downpour, waging a good battle with the thunder, the sound system crackling- normally such a jaunty hopeful song, and an unbelievable rendering of it he normally would have appreciated the hell out of- ruined for him forever after he was so miserable. He couldn't shake the awful feeling of dread over what he was certain was taking place, but, in spite of (or maybe because of) everything, he fell asleep.

When he woke up late Sunday morning, there was She talking to Abby and Gail in the tent as if nothing at all had happened. Johnny knew She saw him out of the corner of her eye but gave no sign of recognition or greeting. That's not a good sign, he thought, and he (so unlike him to be forceful and demonstrative) went over to her, grabbed her by the arm, and led her over to a slight opening. The sun by then was shining brightly, the water from the previous evening suspiring steamily into the air, making the humidity even more palpable. Not giving She a chance to respond, Johnny poured out all the accusatory invective he could muster, that she had cheated on him, that he should have been her first, he always thought he would be. She's face showed no expression, she just pivoted and walked away, throwing back over her shoulder, "I'm tired.",

He didn't follow her, he was beside himself, one open wound, positive she had cheated on him, and appalled at the seeming coldness that had come over her, which in his mind confirmed it. The festival was all over as far as he was concerned. He wandered around in a daze, accepting the food, drink, and drugs handed to him as he wended his way; he knew not where through the crowd, finally realizing he was headed toward the stage where Jefferson Airplane were performing, as Grace Slick's siren voice lured him on. He sat there the whole day transfixed by the music of Ten Years After, The Who (who were to his taste very disappointing - too much "Tommy" and a shortened version of "My Generation" minus Keith Moon's drum solo, which is what he really wanted to witness), and Creedence (especially "I Put a Spell on You"). Though he was totally lost in the music, every now and then he'd find himself wondering where She was, why she wasn't there listening with him, and what She had been doing when Janis came on right after Joe Cocker the night before.

Then he felt her presence as she tentatively put her hand on his back just as The Band set began, but he was angry and stomped away and headed back up the hill, determined to have his way with the first woman he saw who seemed amenable. He spotted one who looked totally gone, her top askew, swaying to the music, a joint in her hand, alone as far as he could see. Before he knew it, they were kissing, and she was begging him to ball her, asking him where his old lady was. He said he didn't know, but how about they make it right here, but just as quickly realizing he could never do something like that in public, much less his first time, and walked away, gradually finding his way back to the tent, and, angry again as well as frustrated as he was by then, went to sleep after summarily dismissing questions about if he'd seen She, who was looking for him.

When he awoke to Jimi playing "The Star-Spangled Banner," two things became immediately evident: the place was practically deserted (where could all those people have gone so quickly?) except for the sea of detritus left behind on the ground, and She was asleep next to him. Gail came over to tell them they were getting ready to split and they'd be glad to give them a ride back to Buffalo. Up to that point they hadn't really thought how they'd get back; they'd just assumed with them. They gathered up their belongings and began the long trek back to the truck, from which it seemed ages ago they'd left by the side of the road.

They were definitely different people after Woodstock, for better and for worse. She wouldn't talk about the night in question except to say she'd seen and heard Janis up close and personal. Johnny had become very querulous and extremely put upon around her. What had happened to them? It had all been so innocent before and now this. They were apart from each other for a month, a punishment imposed on them by their parents (luckily, Jim had held up his end of the bargain by telling them the very Friday they left where they were going, which had prevented them from having APBs issued for them), but after a month or so things got back to normal, as their respective parents ungrounded them with the strict warning never to try anything like that again.

Not long after they got back together, She even told him all about that Saturday night, and it assuaged all his doubts, making him feel like a fool. It had all been above board, what with She running into Ari out of the blue (who would figure, out of all the people there, she'd run into her), who persuaded her to go to the back of the stage area and just as they got there, the wind, thunder and lightning all crescendoed to make it a dangerous situation. Suddenly they heard a female voice say, "come on in here." They looked to see the voice was coming from a nearby tent and made for it. The tent turned out to be for the performers and the voice they had heard was none other than Janis Joplin's!

She could tell they were awestruck and said, "what'll it be, ladies?" brandishing her ubiquitous bottle of Jack in one hand and a joint in the other. They each took a swig and a toke and began gushing about how much they liked her, and then Ari blurted out how She did a fantastic takeoff on her songs and She was mortified and shook her head, but Janis was eager to hear her, but She demurred until Janis suggested, "how about if you just sing it in your own natural voice, would that be better?"

And so She began singing "Summertime" (one of her favorites and the one that felt most natural to her), and soon she was lost in her singing, pouring her heart out in a virtuoso threnody rendition, knowing while she was doing it she'd never sung better, and by the time she finished several onlookers were also listening.

"Bravo!" Janis said when she was finished, "good on you, girl," clapping her hands enthusiastically. "In fact," she continued, "I'll be right back." She returned moments later with a card in her hand, which she handed to her. "Here's my agent's card. Give him a call sometime when you're ready and see if he'll take you on or if he knows someone further east that can help you. It pays to know someone if you want to get a start. Believe me, I know. I came outta nowhere and am lucky to be where I am. Of course, you gotta believe in yourself. That's the biggest thing."

The storm had passed rapidly, and although it was going to take some time to get things set back up, it was Janis' turn to perform. "Whyn't you girls watch from the stage?" She suggested. Ari and She were thunderstruck and mesmerized the entire performance. She feeling like she learned so much watching and listening to her from that vantage point. When it was all over, they were both exhausted, but Janis was ready to go. She invited them backstage and, though they stayed for a little while, had to leave. It was just all too much, an experience they'd never forget.

"All right," Janis said, reluctant to see them go, "go if you must, but She I expect to hear your name again before all is said and done." Janis signed her name on the back of the agent's card, which was almost like a personal recommendation!

Now that high school was over and they had reached their majority, it was obvious they had to get out of this backwater town. Unfortunately, Johnny's father had marched him up to the Town Hall to register for the draft three days after his eighteenth birthday, and since he had no plans for college and since he wasn't married, he was classified 1A. All the more reason to get out of town as far as he was concerned. But they needed a plan. He could go anywhere and do anything but with She, it was different. She was determined to be a singer, and they had to figure out how to make that happen. In the end, they'd decided they'd head to the city one of these days.

CHAPTER 20

Though Jim Weatherly couldn't have foreseen what would happen, he wasn't all that surprised. Remember, this was a man who'd seen it all and was no dummy. If he'd thought about Joey Wilson all that much, he might have seen it as one possible outcome. It's what happens when a poor little rich kid gets everything he wants and has a tantrum when he doesn't until he does. Only this time, he took his tantrum to a public forum and took it out on the wrong person, a person who was having a tough time of it and had no sympathy for the richest kid in town. A little overkill, perhaps, but it was what it was. She was threatened and reacted the only way she could at the time. Rather than be angry, Jim was sad for the little town and all its inhabitants, who doubtless had no prior experience with anything so ghastly, but also proud that public sentiment was on the right side, despite public pressure deeming it to be otherwise. It wasn't all that common that someone (especially someone from money) paid for a lifetime of bad behavior with their life, but there it is.

Elliott Creek meanders west for 45 miles from its origin near Derry State Park, turns sharply north past the county airport on the outskirts of Wilsonville and bisects the village proper where it flows under Main Street, then continues on through several other villages until it empties into the Niagara River. As previously mentioned, the creek formed the southwestern boundary of "Wilson's Folly," with Mr. Wilson having built a house practically on its banks further west. About halfway in between his house and his woods, there was an island, and on the island, there was a castle.

A castle in Wilsonville! Sheriff Grimes had never gotten over that from the time he first heard about it as a young child. Old Man Oxnard built it. Seems he was from Germany and was homesick, so he decided to build a medieval castle similar to one that was in his hometown. A meticulous mason, he constructed it on a one-acre island in Elliott Creek just four blocks south of Main Street. Because the island was marshy and overgrown, it was necessary to fill and raise it. The creek had a natural sandstone outcropping he excavated to comprise some of the material out of which the castle was built, the rest being mostly fossil rock that was dredged up and shipped in from all parts of the state. You could almost say it rose right out of the water. An oasis, he called it, smack dab in the middle of the creek. Trees were planted, and the walls of the castle, towers, and moat were constructed. It took him twenty-five years to finally complete it, but he died before he ever lived in it, and, with most of his clan having also died or moved away, the property was abandoned. Sheriff Grimes remembered that just before he had entered the service, there had been a fire that swept through the castle, destroying almost everything but the walls. Since then, it'd been deserted and was crumbling to the ground in places while other parts looked pretty solid still.

Townspeople talked about restoring or razing it every now and then, but no one put up the money to do so. Mr. Wilson himself had thought about restoring it at one point but backed down after Mr. Burnham threatened to quit if he did, so there must not have been any money to be earned from it. And there it sat, now pretty much the town's dumping ground. Who'd want to live there anyway? It was a wreck ready to collapse at any time.

Oh, Sheriff Grimes had heard the rumors since he was a kid about all the goings-on there over the years. Everyone had: trysts, fights, stabbings, drinking, drug-running, rapes, drownings, strange noises and disappearances, even murder. But it was all talk, legend, myth, what have you, especially murder. He'd have known or found out about and investigated any unusual activity over the years, or he didn't deserve to wear the badge anymore. He'd checked the past records, too, and just as he thought, many of these things had been reported, followed up on, and found baseless. As far as he knew, there hadn't been any activity there since last winter when he rousted a couple of vagrants who'd set up camp inside.

Sheriff Grimes pulled off the road almost up to the creek's edge, got out of the patrol car, put his binoculars around his neck, and grabbed his walkie-talkie. He walked along the creek bank a way and, just where the thick underbrush (formerly known as a thicket) began, realized he didn't have far to go to reach the castle. The creek was even almost hidden at that point, with all kinds of vines and branches that formed an arch over the creek at various points. Here the going actually was kind of tough, and carrying the walkie-talkie didn't help. He'd forgotten about the foliage, which got thicker each year, and the creek bank eroding more and more, so there was barely any place to walk. 'As soon as this is over, I've got to get in shape,' he thought, 'this is ridiculous.'

As he neared the spot where the path ended by a huge oak, he heard the faint sound of voices echoing in and out of the trees, and the closer he came, the more distinct they got. He stopped and looked at the castle, trying to detect any movement around there but saw nothing. He could still hear the voices, actually being able to discern individual ones, but none he recognized.

Suddenly he slipped off his perch and started sliding towards the creek, pushing stones and dirt that made quite a splash when they hit the water.

"Shit!" he exclaimed, "feels like I broke it," meaning his ankle, which he had twisted badly when his foot got snagged in a root of the oak tree. 'A painful way to stop my momentum,' Sheriff Grimes thought ruefully, 'but if I hadn't done that, I might have gone right into the creek.'

There was complete silence. Sheriff Grimes had steadied himself and didn't think whoever was there had seen or heard him, just the splashing of the rocks into the water. He grabbed his walkie-talkie, which had fallen next to him, and, crouching down as far as he could, radioed as quietly as he could into the station, requesting a couple of deputies, a bullhorn, and a long, heavy-duty rope be dispatched to the castle on Elliott Creek as quickly as possible.

Just then, Deputy Rains broke in to tell him he was on his way. "I'm bringing Cutter," he said.

"I want you to organize things, make like it's a routine training exercise, minus the full body armor," Sheriff Grimes said, grimacing wryly.

"What's going on out there?" Deputy Rains wanted to know.

"I'll tell you when you get here. You know my 10-20, don't you? And no sirens! Be as quiet as possible. I'll hold down the fort until you get here. 10-4?"

"Sure, Sheriff, by the castle," Deputy Rains replied.

"10-4 then," Sheriff Grimes said.

"10-4, Sheriff."

Sheriff Grimes could tell Deputy Rains was raring to go. He imagined he hadn't even saluted anyone after that last 10-4. He'd been looking for some action for a while, and now it was here. The sheriff just hoped he wouldn't get too gung-ho and blow their cover. 'This will be a true test of his ability to follow orders,' he thought.

Unbeknownst to the sheriff the individuals belonging to the voices were well aware of his presence. They didn't know who or what it was but had heard some strange noises, so, to be extra cautious, they retreated to the castle, leaving two of them as lookouts.

Not much the sheriff could do now but sit and wait until help arrived. He didn't know what to make of the situation. It could be nothing, but he had a feeling something was going on in that castle. He hoped not. He scanned the scene with his binoculars. It all seemed harmless, he rationalized, maybe a vagrancy or trespassing charge.

Just then, he heard the men arrive and waited for them to locate him.

"Geez," Deputy Rains said when he saw him, "what happened to your ankle? It looks pretty busted up. We better get you some first aid."

'Observant little devil,' Sheriff Grimes fumed but said nothing except, "Never mind about that, I have a missing person report on Gracie Graham. There was some suspicious activity over by the ball diamond, and I believe Joey Wilson and some kids who hang around him headed this way. Don't know if the two are related but thought I'd check it out and think I'm on to something. There were definitely some individuals out there, and I think they retreated inside the castle when they heard me."

Technically, a person wasn't missing until twenty-four hours had elapsed, but since his wife had called it in, he knew it was legit and had to follow up on it.

"Gracie was camping over the weekend out on Wilson's land," he continued, "east of here a bit, in fairly rugged territory. She was due home this morning and never showed. My wife called it in. I don't know if you know it or not, but her dad is very sick, and she's been taking care of him pretty much by herself. My wife went over there to give her some relief for the weekend, but there's no way she'd not show up to take care of her dad. Besides, he could go at any time. Her friend Toby Klein knows where she camped and is out looking for her. I'm hoping to hear from him that he found her and she's OK. In the meantime, I came here to check things out and thought it was Wilson and his hangers-on I heard. And I have a funny feeling Gracie may be in the castle with them."

"What do you think's going on in there?" Deputy Rains asked.

"I don't rightly know," Sheriff Grimes answered, "but I intend to find out. I want you to spread out and reconnoiter for a bit," Sheriff Grimes said. "I definitely heard voices, but what they're doing in there, I don't know."

"Why don't we just ask them?" Deputy Rains said, brandishing the bullhorn.

"No, no!" Sheriff Grimes said, trying to keep his voice down, "do as I told you, now. Spread out and watch. It may be nothing, and I don't want to scare innocent bystanders if at all possible. I want you both in position on the lookout. Deputy Rains, I want you on the other side of the creek, so we have them surrounded somewhat. Take the patrol car up Oakgrove and hurry. Park it right across from us, and be as quiet as possible."

"10-4," Deputy Rains said, saluting.

Sheriff Grimes gave him a half-hearted salute and told him to get going.

"Cutter," he said, "I want you farther down the bank, so you're kitty-corner to the other side of the castle. I don't know how familiar with the area you are, but you'll have to get back up to the road and walk a way, then, when you think you're at the right spot, look for an opening to the creek. There should be one if I remember correctly, but if not, you'll have to make one. Better bring your gloves just in case, there are some thick brambles all along there. Let me know when you're in position."

"Yessir," Cutter said.

They were all in place within five minutes, all of them checking in on their radios, and now the waiting began. They were looking and listening for the slightest movement or sound. They waited for some time and heard or saw nothing.

"What do you think's really goin' on in there?" Deputy Rains repeated.

"Damned if I know," Sheriff Grimes replied. "It's probably just a bunch of kids hanging around together. And what kind of a question is that? We're supposed to find out what's going on, not play guessing games. Now pipe down on that squawk box."

They waited a few more minutes, and then Sheriff Grimes radioed them both. "Cutter and I will head toward the castle, Deputy. Nothing seems to be happening, and we can't be waiting around all day. Whatever this is, we gotta nip it in the bud. We'll move steady and cautiously to the objective when I give the command. Deputy Rains, hold your position in case someone tries to escape. I repeat, hold your position until I tell you otherwise."

They had scarcely moved from their perches when they were stopped in their tracks by a blood-curdling scream.

'Now there's a sound,' Sheriff Grimes thought grimly. "Stay where you are, men, until I can look around," he said. "Not long, mind you. We gotta move, and quickly, but wait for my signal."

He got out his binoculars and perused the castle area. Seeing nothing, he barked out the order for Cutter to move. Suddenly he heard a rustling sound and Toby Klein's head suddenly popped up over one of the castle's crumbling battlements. You could have knocked the sheriff over with a feather. His head was bleeding and bandaged with a blue bandana, and he looked very pale. Sheriff Grimes motioned for him to stay put, not quite sure what to do next. He scoped Deputy Rains with his binoculars and could see he was straining at the leash, ready to see some action.

Toby was only half a football field away, and when Sheriff Grimes asked him if he could come to him, he said he might need some help, as he thought his leg was broken.

"Cutter," he radioed, 'get to my car and bring the rope with you. Can you swim?"

"Well enough, I suppose, don't think I'd drown if that's what you mean."

"Good enough," replied the sheriff, then immediately cut off to Deputy Rains. "Deputy, hold your position until I give the order to move and keep a lookout for any signs of activity in the castle. It's vital that you do that."

Deputy Rains looked confused and none too happy. As soon as he heard the scream, he was all for rushing the castle and hauling those damn kids out by the scruff of their necks. This wasn't at all what he had in mind, and they were wasting valuable time (he hadn't seen Toby appear) but knew from the sound of the sheriff's voice he meant business.

Sheriff Grimes' ankle was really aching and swollen now. When Cutter arrived on the scene, he did most of the pulling once he had swum out to Toby and tied the rope around him, as gently as possible but at the same time with some alacrity. The sheriff needed to find out what Toby knew and make their move accordingly.

They got Toby as comfortable as possible under the conditions, but Sheriff Grimes could tell he was hurting.

"I need you to tell me as simply as possible what's going on in that castle," Sheriff Grimes said.

"We got a bad apple in there, Sheriff, and he's got Gracie," Toby said, after some hesitation, his face blanched with worry and pain.

"What's his name, son?" Sheriff Grimes responded.

"You're not gonna believe this, Sheriff," Toby said, "but it's Joey Wilson. Just when you think you know someone, I never thought he was capable of this."

"Capable of what? How many are there in the castle, Toby? Come on, spill it. Time is of the essence," the sheriff said, growing testier by the minute.

Again, Toby hesitated, then said, "I hate to say it, but I think he raped Gracie. There are four others with him, those young guys that hang around with him all the time, and that's what they said. A couple of them are pretty big," he continued ruefully. "I tried to get in there, but they knocked me down the stairs, then dragged me out and threw me where you saw me. Please hurry and get her, sheriff, before anything else happens."

"We're going right now," the sheriff responded. "You sit tight until we can get someone out here to get you to a hospital. Two more questions: where in the castle are they, and did you hear a scream?"

"It's not like I'm going anywhere," Toby said ruefully. "They're at the very top of the castle, right under the belfry. I keep thinking they're gonna throw her off. Yeah, I heard the scream but couldn't tell who it was. It didn't sound like any of them. Or Gracie, thank goodness," he added.

"You did good, son," Sheriff Grimes said. "Now, let us do our job. We'll be back ASAP and get you some first aid."

Just as he turned around, he saw Deputy Rains' shadow flit across the wall of the castle.

"Damn him," Sheriff Grimes said, "I'll have his ass after this is done."

The sheriff paused and, as he did, conjured up all kinds of scenarios but still had no idea how this was going to end. He didn't even know if the Wilson kid was armed, which would complicate things further. The best-case scenario that no one would be hurt, already looked to be wishful thinking.

"You ready to go, Cutter?" the sheriff asked. "I don't know how much help I'm gonna be with this bum ankle, but I'm a pretty good swimmer even with it, and I gotta be there when we get the sonofabitch. Tie this rope around us just to be safe. Think you can hold up your end?"

"No doubt in my mind, sir," Cutter said, "whatever it takes."

Sheriff Grimes liked this kid already.

"OK, let's move out as quietly as possible. I'd like to get the drop on them if we can. Draw your weapon only as a last resort. Don't forget, in spite of everything, those are just kids in there."

They had clear sailing entering the castle as far as they could tell, seeing no one and hearing nothing. Just an ominous silence. 'It can't be this easy,' Sheriff Grimes said to himself, 'something's going to happen.'

They saw nor heard any sign of Rains. They would find out later he had rounded up the accomplices, which the Sheriff commended him for, reminding himself to ball him out later for abandoning his post.

"Let's hit the stairs,' the sheriff said to Cutter as softly as he could, "try not to make any noise. And stay alert. We have no idea what we're walking into." He motioned to the stairs, indicating that Cutter should go first.

Just then they heard footsteps, but couldn't tell where they were coming from because of the echo in the high-vaulted stairs, followed by a scream identical to the one they'd heard earlier, then a scurrying sound the sheriff couldn't identify until he realized it was one or more persons running. The closer the footsteps got, the sheriff realized it was now only one person, perhaps running away from danger or escaping after committing a crime. They had been paused on the stairs the entire time all this transpired. Suddenly the sheriff espied Gracie coursing down the corridor brandishing a knife, her disheveled oaten hair streaming around her, looking not unlike a Viking.

Sheriff Grimes and Cutter, on seeing her, appalled by her appearance, went toward her to offer assistance, not imagining what horror made her look like she did.

"Gracie," the sheriff began, but Gracie stopped him.

"You're too late, sheriff. Thankfully, I can take care of myself," she said. "I had to do it," she continued, jerking her head back down the hallway. "It was him or me. I've never felt better in my life," she said, wiping her bloodied hands on her jeans. "Ever."

CHAPTER 21

The town was abuzz, of course, nothing close to this had ever happened in Wilsonville before. It was a black day, and they supposed it would be a black mark on the town. Things like this just weren't supposed to happen here. Jim Weatherly wondered what the fallout from this would be. He expected there would be some, it was unavoidable, but he hoped there would be no rush to judgement until the facts became known, that there would be no punitive reactions beforehand, or that Mr. Wilson would buy himself his pound of flesh. Whatever the outcome, he knew two things for sure: Gracie's life would never be the same again, and ultimately Wilson would be taken down a peg or two.

As Sheriff Grimes pulled into the Wilsonville PD early on the morning after the bombshell Grand Jury investigation was over, the press (such as it was) was outside waiting for him. He composed himself before getting out of the police cruiser, just as Mrs. Grimes had instructed. Deep breaths in and out, she'd said, count them, and make sure you end on an even one. He had his own ritual every morning before he went in the station. He'd stand in the lot, listening to and smelling the creek that flowed nearby and through a viaduct under Main Street. But he knew he wouldn't be able to observe it that day because of the relative commotion.

He was surprised and grateful to see Jim Donovan, owner and Chief Editor of the Wilsonville Voice, as well as an old friend and drinking buddy among them, most likely there to observe. He'd keep them in line, he smiled to himself before getting out of the silver grey and blue police cruiser.

"Sheriff Grimes! Sheriff Grimes! Any comment on the Grand Jury findings yesterday?" this posed by a young female reporter who looked like she was fresh out of the journalism school at the University.

Liking to keep his answers brief, he looked over at Jim before he responded. "I'm just glad it's over."

"Sheriff! Sheriff!" Lenny, the old beat reporter who'd done "The Blotter" column in the Voice for years, followed up with, "Yes, but what do you think about the findings"?

"Well, Lenny, everything was well-run and above board. That's all you can ask for," the Sheriff responded.

"But, but..." the cub reporter tried to interject before the Sheriff short-circuited her.

"It's all a damn shame for everyone concerned. That's all I'm going to say about it."

Though it looked like he was shielding his face from the sun, he was really hiding it from the two cameras pointed at him before he snuck in the side door of the PD – his PD.

He'd had a good mind to not even come in that day but knew it was expected of him, what with all the reporters and what not, and he was never one to shirk his duties.

What a harrowing day yesterday had been. He'd never experienced anything like it and didn't ever want to again. As he told the reporters, there were no winners. Sure, Gracie had been completely exonerated of any wrongdoing, but he knew she couldn't live in the town any longer. That was tough enough, but then on top of this, her Dad died. Thankfully he was never told what had happened out there in the castle.

Bobby was as upset as he'd ever seen her.

"You can't just let her leave," she said, crying all the while, and Bobby was not a crier. "Where will she go, what will she do? She'll have nobody. She can live with us until she gets on her feet."

The sheriff had no dog in this fight, and he knew he was treading on thin ice as it was. But he had to be rational about the situation. He calmly pointed out that Gracie was no longer a minor, that she could do what she wanted, and, having talked to her, knew she wouldn't stay in Wilsonville one day longer than she had to. She told him she'd probably move a few villages over, get some kind of job, probably waitressing. She had a little money to tide her over, money from her dad's life insurance, so she wasn't worried about that.

That mollified Bobby a teeny bit, but she still had her back up. The sheriff tried to reason with her, telling her it was for the best and that she had to let go, that they could visit her often."

"Hmmmph," she said, with a shake of her head, and walked away.

And, of course, one person was dead. 'No great loss,' the sheriff thought before catching himself. He hadn't wanted him to die, he didn't want anyone to die, but he'd brought it on himself. He was no good. Of course, he was surprised how many stab wounds Gracie had inflicted on him, a baker's dozen, but some of those were defensive wounds.

"I lost it," she told her attorney, a public defender named Dick Roche (who never divulged this information that amounted to a confession), "I just kept stabbing and stabbing, not even knowing if I was hitting anything or not. Then I had to push him off me."

She was.

"I was angry and scared," she continued, "angry because I knew the reason he was doing what he was doing because I'd beaten him in both a game of H-O-R-S-E and one-on one, and scared because he got the drop on me. He didn't rape me, though, at least."

It was clear that she was in denial.

Joseph Wilson was beside himself. Not only had he lost his first-born, but she'd also got off scot-free. He didn't believe for one second his boy had done the things he was accused of. And she was a cold-blooded killer. William Burnham, who was with him at the hearing, advised him to cool it. It was an open-and-shut case as far as he was concerned, and he had no credible witnesses to vouch for Joey. He was powerless, tapped out as far as favors he could call in (he was now on the deficit side of that ledger), and so strapped for cash he couldn't wield his threats of charging exorbitant fees for the privilege of developing his land.

It had affected Toby Klein in a big way. Blaming himself for what had happened to Gracie (he shouldn't have cancelled the camping trip, he should have been able to rescue Gracie), he was a wreck. Having lost most of his considerable equanimity, he'd dropped out of school, at least for the time being, taking back his old job at the drug store. His father had deserted the family several years ago, so there was that extra burden of worry about his mother's fragile mental health and her drinking. Still, Toby, ever the positive one despite his straitened circumstances, figured this could be a blessing in disguise. He wouldn't be away from college, leaving his mother all by herself, and so could look after her on a daily basis.

The details printed in the Wilsonville Voice in the aftermath of the crime and the pursuant Grand Jury Investigation were sketchy at best, disingenuous at the least, leaving more questions than answers, with no mention of motive or the boys who helped Joey perpetrate said crime, as they were underage (in years only), no real backstory, no mention of Toby Klein's valiant if unsuccessful attempt at preventing the crime, but they still managed to be salacious enough to keep the town's interest while the story ran.

It managed to, while not absolving Joey of the crime, cast aspersions on Gracie's character: the copious number of stab wounds could only be characterized as overkill that suggested an abnormal amount of pent-up rage that might make her a powder keg ready to explode at any moment. Why was she camping unaccompanied and while her father was at death's door? There was even meretricious speculation among the village gossips of a tryst gone wrong, Gracie standing to gain a great deal in such an affair, either through blackmail or even becoming a member of the family and sharing in their copious wealth.

Sheriff and Mrs. Grimes were livid upon reading this. They knew better. He was surprised at Jim Donovan allowing his cub reporter to write such innuendo when it was obvious she had no real story. Shame on Jim for pandering to his boss Gavin Stevens in an attempt to sell papers. Of course, Joseph Wilson owned the paper, so there was that too. Anything to get his fair-haired boy off the hook by deflecting blame. And it certainly hadn't helped Gracie's cause.

"This stinks to high heaven," Bobby Grimes said to the Sheriff. "What are you going to do about it? I have a good mind to write a letter to that rag. They probably won't print it, but I just might do it anyway."

There wasn't much Sheriff Grimes could say to that except to tell Bobby that she must know he felt the same way, but it was out of his hands. Freedom of the press and all that. And he hoped she'd rethink writing that letter, or at least let him read it before she sent it in."

"I don't want your sympathy, sheriff," she responded. "I wish you'd stand up to these people once in a while or get off the force." She then stomped away.

Sheriff Grimes shook his head. Again, nothing much he could say. 'Heavy is the head that wears the sheriff's crown,' he thought instead, feeling a little sorry for himself and dreading the upcoming weekend. Just when he'd felt a bit of relief at the whole debacle finally being over, although he knew very well it would never be over. And he'd help

Gracie as much as he could without Bobby knowing. He knew influential people over to Edgerton who could help her out and, at the very least, keep an eye out for her.

Sheriff Grimes knew the backstory, of course. Toby Klein had laid it out in all its particulars before the Grand Jury. There were no mitigating circumstances. Joey Wilson was a bad actor plain and simple. He was getting back at Gracie for having been embarrassed by her in a H-O-R-S-E contest and a one-on-one game, not a week before. It seems he had gaslighted her not long before that at a local playground where she and Toby had been shooting hoops. Not one to back down, in fact, more than willing to take it up immediately, she had challenged him then and there to these contests and he had laughed it off, he and his cohorts. But then, in the ensuing week, he found out that people in town knew about her challenge and were intimating that he might be intimidated, which he again laughed off. The truth was that, while he wasn't at all intimidated, he was a little uncertain about the outcome, and until he could be guaranteed a victory, he wouldn't give her the satisfaction. He mentioned this to no one, of course. He knew he hadn't picked up a basketball since the season ended. He'd gained fifteen pounds and had been employing a steady course of drugs and alcohol in the interim. Still, that wasn't enough to make him lose to a girl, was it? Was it? As long as he had that little seed of doubt, he'd try to avoid it as much as possible, buy a little time to get in shape, get his touchback. Then it would be no contest. But his acolytes, not knowing he had any doubts, kept bending his ear about the rumors and bolstered his confidence that he would destroy her, it would be absolutely no contest from the get-go. When he continued to demur, they, who had never had the temerity to question any thought, word, or deed of his, encouraged him in the least intrusive way to play her and get it over with. He got angry at that, his authority being questioned, and threw caution to the wind.

"Fuck it!" he said, "bring it on!"

The group cheered him lustily, secretly relieved. "You'll kick her ass!" they said, fully on board again.

"Set it up!" Joey said to them.

Needless to say, it didn't end well for Joey in any way, shape, or form.

In better shape than Joey on his best day, Gracie was in the best shape of her life, having played basketball every day that summer—one-on-one and shootarounds with Toby, pickup games at night, AAU games (albeit the women's division)—Gracie's dance card was full all right. She even had an inch on Joey, could definitely outjump him, and her BMI compared to his? Forget about it. There was no doubt in her mind she was going to win, just as Joey was equally sure. Word had gotten around town (of course it had), and quite a bit of money was being bet, the majority of it on Joey. Some guys even bet on the H-O-R-S-E contest, hoping to parlay them into an even bigger score.

When the day of the contest, a Friday afternoon, came, there were more people lining the court than at a high school varsity game. It was perhaps telling that none of Joey's family was there. Gracie's either, but to be fair, there is no way her dad would have missed it if he wasn't gravely ill. They didn't tell him about that either, knowing he would have insisted on trying to get out of bed to go see his daughter play. They appointed a local "legend," Teddy "The Hacker" Wronker, to oversee the games to ensure everything was above board. This didn't bode well for Gracie, as he was apt to allow any rough stuff, as long as it wasn't egregious.

They were about to toss a coin to determine who went first in H-O-R-S-E, but Joey patronizingly deferred by saying, "Ladies first," and bowing. That sent a ripple of laughter through the crowd.

That was his first mistake. Gracie brought the house down with her very first shot, taking off from the foul line looking for all the world like she was going to dunk it, even though that was not allowed, à la Sidney Wicks, who had illegally dunked the ball after a sluggish UCLA start in the championship game against Jacksonville last spring, knowing it was illegal, drawing a technical foul, but pumping up his team so much it was no contest from that point on. She pulled up at the last minute, still over the rim, and dropped the ball through the hoop with a finger roll worthy of Wilt the Stilt.

Joey made the shot, but it was disallowed because Gracie had called "above the rim" when she named her shot. Joey, used to getting his own way, was not pleased and began a game-long pout. That was "H" for Joey.

The rest of the game was even, but Gracie, having gone first, was the winner. While Joey was a sharpshooter, making most of his shots from what would today be 3-point distance, which Gracie couldn't match, though she gave a good account of herself, Gracie used a lot of trick shots, including one behind the basket that had to be a swish, a couple of layups, one with the ball passed through her legs and around her back, the other passing the ball under her leg and shooting it while it was still under her leg (that got the crowd buzzing all right), with her final make being a sky hook swish which Joey missed badly. Game over. Joey tried to play to the crowd afterwards, pointing out the shots Gracie took would never be taken in a game, whereas his all were legitimate in-game shots. People either laughed at him or booed him, but most of them beat a hasty retreat to the bar down the street, the local bookies' hangout, to change their bet on the one-on-one game.

When the bookies asked why they were changing their bets, each man said, "Joey looks beat already."

The game itself was anti-climactic. Joey never had a chance. Gracie was stronger and faster than him and could outjump him. All she needed to do was post him up and shoot that little hook shot she had finished off the game of H-O-R-S-E with. It might as well have been Alcindor's sky hook for all intents and purposes. And Joey, for his part, could barely get a shot off. She stuck so close to him, as close as white on rice. And she even rejected some, and if he missed, there would be no put back for him. Gracie made sure of that, blocking him off the boards and outrebounding him. Joey kept calling fouls on her, which the Hacker disallowed every time, although it did pause the game and allow Joey, who was winded and sweating like a pig, a brief rest. The crowd was stunned. Joey's acolytes, who'd been raucously cheering for him prior to the game while deriding Gracie at the same time, even whispering a few veiled threats at her whenever she got close enough to them to be out of earshot, were speechless.

Toby was getting very nervous, wishing Gracie hadn't humiliated Joey so badly, which he could tell was clearly her intent. The final score was 21-15, but not nearly as close as it looked. Gracie had stopped playing Joey so close and gave him several long jumpers that he drained to make the score respectable. The disgruntled crowd walked off, some of them pretty pissed at having lost money on what at the time seemed pretty easy money. Joey, disgraced, beat a hasty retreat, surrounded by his posse, who were embarrassed by and for him.

In the end, it had seemed a pretty hollow victory for Gracie, who didn't feel nearly as vindicated as she thought she would. She had at least hoped there would somehow be a couple of college scouts from the University at the game, but there didn't appear to be, as she'd never heard from anyone afterward. And, although Toby said nothing, he had an ominous feeling there would be some kind of repercussion redounding from this debacle.

Sheriff Grimes felt so bad for Toby Klein. The kid just had to let it go, it wasn't his fault, and he couldn't have prevented it even if had been there. He knew how these things worked. Those boys had worked themselves into a fevered pitch, and four on one weren't very good odds no matter who the one was. They'd been hopped up on bennies and had a real blood lust. They'd been arrested on possession and had given up their supplier, none other than Joey Wilson. The boys were someone else's problem now, with they (having pled down to a misdemeanor in exchange for their testimony against Joey) and their families having hightailed it out of town with the strong encouragement of Sheriff Grimes.

The sheriff was only glad Gary Graham hadn't known (thankfully, he had passed the day before this happened, while Gracie was still camping) what had happened to his daughter as he swore he would have risen like a phoenix from his death bed, transformed into the Gary Graham of old, and taken Joey and his crew apart piece by piece.

Sheriff Grimes had tried to reassure Toby that he had done Gracie and the town a great service by witnessing before the Grand Jury, it couldn't have been an easy thing to do, but he had done it and done it bravely. But Toby wasn't buying any of it. It was his fault, he should have been there for Gracie. He did find a little comfort in learning that as far as he knew, no rape had occurred, that Gracie had prevented it all by herself, which didn't really surprise him. And now she had been banished and his future itself looked pretty bleak.

The whole affair was so disheartening, and the fact that it had taken place in his hometown and on his watch made it doubly so for Sheriff Grimes. Although it seemed to have been carefully planned and carried out, there was still a great deal of serendipity involved. That Gracie and Toby camped every weekend was no secret, but it was unclear how Joey had realized she would be camping alone that fateful weekend. And where had the knife come from? It was a badass Case Bowie Knife and a hefty model at that. He was awaiting lab results on the prints they'd lifted from the knife handle, not that it mattered much at that point.

Of course, he felt worse for Gracie, Sheriff Grimes did. It was just a terrible situation. As bad as he knew Joey to be, he never thought he had that in him. And his old man was a disgrace, whining about his fate, not owning up to what had happened, which was the reason Joey had gotten to be the way he was in the first place. He highly doubted the crime had been that calculated. He saw it more as a crime of opportunity. Oh, he had no doubt Joey had bad intentions, but he didn't think he set out to rape her, and he certainly didn't know it would escalate so quickly. Once again, he had badly misjudged his opponent, a miscalculation that cost him his life. She had humiliated him in a stupid game that neither should have taken that seriously. He was almost more shocked that Gracie had beaten Joey than he was that she killed him. A nasty business, he shuddered each time he was reminded of it. He was OK with the Town Board, though. They'd given him a vote of confidence immediately after the Grand Jury Investigation was completed.

He was still trying to piece the events leading up to the killing using mostly Toby's version of those events, as Gracie was no help at all, refusing to talk about the killing and in denial of the rape, all understandable, but it didn't make his job any easier. Adding to that frustration was the more he got into it, the more he realized that the knife and its owner were the missing link. The only sense he could make of it was that although Joey knew in general (it was common knowledge, remember), she went camping on weekends, it was usually with Toby (also common knowledge). Was he planning on attacking her whether or not Toby was there or had someone tipped him off? He remembered those boys having been seen at the ball diamond by old Dudley before they took off into the woods. He wondered if there had been anyone else there who might have tipped them off and provided them with a weapon. If so, they were definitely a person of interest and needed to be found and brought in for questioning ASAP.

Until then his hands were tied. He'd just have to wait for results, this for a man who hated waiting.

GRACIE TELLS HER STORY

It was my camping out back in those days that got me into trouble through no fault of my own. It was common knowledge I camped out every weekend, rain, sleet, or snow. And that I usually didn't camp alone, I camped with a boy named Toby Klein, who I'd known since first grade. That particular weekend, however, the penultimate weekend before Labor Day, Toby begged off because at the last minute, he decided to go to his college freshman orientation in Michigan. I was pretty upset, not that I showed it. Maybe it was best, a clean break, probably not being able to see him until Thanksgiving, things between us, which hadn't been too good lately, might be calmed down by then. We'd been pulling apart from each other bit by bit, ever since the Senior Prom. The only reason we even went to the prom in the first place was to show everybody. Gossip, would they? We'd give them what they wanted. We'd endured it since forever, and as far as I was concerned, we'd be friends forever, but if he wanted more (and I never was sure about that, as he never came right out and said it, but I got the distinct feeling he did), I couldn't give him that, not at that point, maybe never. He was moving on (though he denied it), and my dad was dying, so I was at a real crossroads, about to be bereft of pretty much everything I'd known and loved. Sure, there was Sheriff Grimes and his wife, I could always count on them for support, but I knew they were in favor of me living a conventional life, settling down and raising a family (that was more Mrs. Grimes), and I knew she definitely had favored Toby as a permanent partner, she had pretty much thrown us together since we were kids, but I just didn't have it in me. I didn't want any partner, truth be told, being content to live on my own, especially after what happened shortly after we graduated high school.

I knew I was different from the other girls, if only from my size. I loved to play sports, especially basketball. My father was a great high school and college football player, making All-American as a fullback until he got kicked off the team for almost killing (unintentionally, he just didn't know his own strength, the man could bend iron bars, came by it naturally, never lifted a weight in his life until he got to college) a man in a bar fight. Story of his life, which went precipitously downhill after that, poor man.

That's how I came by my athletic ability and my strength as well. Like my dad, I could play any sport from the get go without any practice or prior experience. That's just how it was. I was a natural athlete, like Jim Thorpe, Jimmy Brown, and Babe Didrikson Zaharias. Not that I'm putting myself in their class, mind you, but I could have been pretty damn good if given a chance. Who knows how far I could have gone? I'm very bitter about it, can't you tell?

And I could beat the school boys and later the high school boys. It was unheard of back in the day, not so much now, though there are still many barriers to hurdle. It was all about the male ego. I had no competition among the girls, it was too easy, and I wasn't allowed to play with the boys, at least in an organized setting. Do you know how frustrating it is to know how good you are and not be able to prove it? Well I proved it to Joey Wilson and look what it got me and look what it got him.

In keeping with that, Toby Klein used to think he had to protect me, which may have been true when we were much younger if only to facilitate my entrée into the boy's world, but not after a certain point, let's say 6th grade. I gradually began to resent it more and more after that and became so disillusioned that my best friend in all the world didn't think I could fend for myself. That's what pulled us apart and led to so many ambivalent feelings between us. And now he feels guilty because he wasn't there to protect me from what happened. It's practically ruined his life, a young man who showed so much promise. How do you think that made me feel? It was another reason I had to leave town.

I was preoccupied that whole weekend, what with my dad being on his death bed and Toby leaving for college. Still, everything was normal on the camping trip. I'd even caught a couple of fish each day (bass) in Elliott Creek for my dinner. I slept well and was certainly not nervous, at least until Sunday night, my last night there. I'd heard an owl hooting for some time and saw some bats flying overhead, which, while not all that unusual, unsettled me for some reason, and I slept fitfully. The next day, as I was packing up to leave, I thought I heard some unusual noises, but after scanning the area, I decided it was nothing, maybe an animal or something. I was bent over, just about to hoist my backpack on my back, when someone tackled me from behind, and a hood was put over my head. I struggled like crazy, but it was two against one and the two had completely overpowered me. My hands were tied behind my back. I was gagged and blindfolded and led away, where I did not know. No one had uttered a sound except me, I had screamed my bloody head off before they gagged me, but no one was going to hear me in those woods. I could tell more people had joined the party, and soon I was thrown into the trunk of a vehicle, which drove away, destination unknown. Still not a peep from anyone to tell how many were there or to identify any of the voices. We soon arrived at our destination, wherever that was. As soon as I got inside, I knew where I was- Old Man

Oxnard's Castle. Just then I heard a voice echoing down the hall or stairs. I wasn't sure which, and I knew immediately who it was. Joey Wilson.

"Bring her up here. What took you so long?" he said. "Hello Gracie, it's payback time."

Then, using my powers of deduction, I figured out by then who it was that had abducted me: Joey's gang of underage surrogates.

They began to drag me up the stairs as I kicked, squirmed, and let out muffled screams the entire time. They, in turn, were pretty rough with me and I got knocked around quite a bit, barking my knees and elbows against the stone wall of the stairway and the stairs when I fell on them a couple of times when they couldn't hold me.

"Be careful!" Joey admonished. "I want her to be able to enjoy what I have planned for her."

When we reached the top of the stairs, Joey commanded, "in there!" and I was taken inside a room and thrown down on what had to be the most disgusting, evil-smelling, moldy mattress I'd experienced in my limited number of years. I was on automatic, didn't utter a sound, just ready to spring into action the moment I got the chance.

Then they made their fatal mistakes: first, they untied me, pinning my hands against the mattress so Joey could straddle me and take over; second, they left me alone with him; and, third, they didn't search me for a weapon. I won't even mention a fourth about the male ego. I believe I made my case about that a while ago.

A couple of them had yanked my shorts and underwear down.

"It's just you and me now, Gracie, one on one, *mano a mano*," Joey spit at me, "we'll see who wins this time."

I hadn't expected this. Maybe a good old-fashioned ass-whipping or a scare, but not this. I froze for an instant, enough time for him to almost enter me, then I exploded. I bucked him off of me and got my trusty case knife I always brought with me on camping trips out from my boot just in time as he came for my throat and gutted him like a fish. He was, for all intents and purposes, dead, with his guts hanging out and a shocked look on his face, unless he got immediate help, but I wasn't going to allow that. I stabbed him for what I thought was a couple of times more and could tell he was already dead. I was shocked when I found out later how many times I had actually stabbed him. A bit of overkill, I know, but as I said, I was on automatic and angry, the rage having built up over my life about to go to shit, and then this, the ultimate insult.

Then I got up, took the gag and blindfold off, straightened myself out, and walked out the door, still brandishing my knife in case his flunkies were still there. But the corridor was empty and I didn't see anyone until I was about to go downstairs and saw Sheriff Grimes and a deputy about to come up. I dropped the knife and it clattered down the stairs towards them, and then said what they said I said.

After being taken into custody until everything was sorted out, I was then taken to the hospital for a thorough checkup as a precautionary measure.

Because the kid I killed was from a prominent Wilsonville family, they tried to get me for manslaughter, but, thanks to a court-appointed lawyer Mr. Roche, I was spared. In fact, after the inquest, it never even went to trial, although the evidence gathered did go before a Grand Jury. Why, I don't know, probably to cover their asses. Sheriff Grimes was big on that. It wasn't necessary, and I think Toby having to do most of the testifying destroyed him. Those were dark days indeed, Toby feeling like he was responsible for my being raped because he hadn't gone camping with me that fateful weekend. I know he loved me and wanted to protect me, but I didn't need it. I've always been able to fend for myself and prove it to everyone. And I love him too, but not in the same way. We were practically inseparable when boys and girls being pals wasn't cool. I'm sure he took a lot of grief for it. Then my dad dying when I wasn't there, though I had no way of knowing it at the time.

What kind of God allows that? I regret having to kill Joey, but not the fact that he died. He was a piece of shit and got what was coming to him, but even he didn't deserve to die that way, no matter what he'd done. Then finally, having to pretty much start my whole life over again in a strange town where I knew no one.

After the Grand Jury testimony leaked out, I think most of the townspeople understood why I had done what I'd done and didn't hold it against me, but I knew they felt uncomfortable around me, knowing I was capable of such violence. The swells could never imagine one of their own was capable of doing what Joey did and wanted nothing more to do with me, not that they ever had that much to do with me anyway. If I hadn't had the Grimes's, I don't know what I'd have done. Even though my dad had been sick for a while with pancreatic cancer, an automatic death sentence, I still will never get over the way he looked in his coffin, his face blasted beyond recognition, this behemoth of a man all skin and bones. I should have had the coffin closed. Too numb to think of that, I suppose. I didn't even have time to grieve properly, as I had to leave town ASAP before I was ridden out on a rail. Wilsonville would never be the same for me. Too bad, it was never what everyone thought it was in the first place. I found that out early on the hard way.

And on top of that, there was the civil suit lodged against me. It seems it was the only recourse Mr. Wilson had to bring the case to trial, which seemed like it might drag on forever, further frazzling my last nerve. Then suddenly, the judge dismissed it as frivolous and quashed all the evidence and eyewitness testimony, which was minimal. I was now free to get on with my life, such as it was, somewhere else.

It wasn't always that way, believe me. For the longest time it seemed I was the center of attention in Wilsonville. It started in grade school and continued on through the rest of my school days. I never seemed to fit in anywhere there. Either the girls hated me or were jealous of me, and early on, the boys were resentful of me then lusted after me the older they got, all of it ending up in that castle.

I hated it- couldn't wait to get away. I've always been a big girl (inherited that from my dad) with blonde hair (courtesy of my mom), so I stuck out like a sore thumb. That's partly why I've come back, to see if, after everything died down, I could live in peace. A vindication of sorts. And after all, as I said before, it had the only natural area within walking distance, and if I couldn't find it there, I'd have to leave for good, go somewhere else and start all over again. And I didn't want to do that, not again, at least not in this country. Been there, done that. It was here I'd make my stand- for now. But I know eventually, I will need to get out of here and out of this country, once and for all.

In spite of his reputation (and it was a fearsome one), my dad was a good guy. It wasn't his fault he was so huge. He was born that way. What was he supposed to do? In spite of all the rumors, he wasn't ever a violent man, and had never purposely hurt anyone. It's just that he was so big sometimes it was unavoidable. When he hit somebody, they stayed hit.

As I said, I had a tough childhood, but it wasn't because of my dad. Still, my childhood was nothing compared to his, having lived in foster homes until he was adopted by a woman who turned out to be a sadistic alcoholic and a mostly absent traveling salesman father, who ultimately abandoned him after his mother was institutionalized after having several psychotic breaks and episodes, and finally to be diagnosed as schizophrenic, as a result being declared a danger to herself and my dad, after which, with no one to care for him, he was also institutionalized, being sent to live at the County Home.

On the contrary, he tried to make things as nice as he could for me. It wasn't his fault my mom died of breast cancer when I was a little girl. Some people get all the shit it seems, and our family did for certain, one thing after another.

Yes, my mom. I know the accepted version was that it was uncertain who my mother was, but that's not true and so unjust, if not plain spiteful. While it was true, they never married, that doesn't change the fact that she was my mother. I don't remember much about her- my dad never talked about her- but I know they loved each other very much, and she helped turn his life around. I've seen pictures of her, of course, but a picture never does a person justice and is most certainly no substitute.

When she got sick, she went away for treatment, somewhere in Arizona, I think it was, as I say, my dad never talked about it. But I did somehow know that much, from where I don't know. In addition, she's not buried here, but in her hometown outside of Cleveland, I came to find out later after doing some research on my own. I should go there someday before I leave the country once and for all.

My dad did the best he could. He could have given me up for adoption after my mother died, but it never once crossed his mind. I remember things being hectic for a while after her death, and I had a whole bunch of care-takers who I later found out were various "old ladies" of the guys in his motorcycle club. They were rough-edged and somewhat crude, but they had my best interests at heart, had been good friends with my mom, and definitely did right by me. Hey, look how I turned out, right?

Speaking of motorcycle clubs, the only constants I remember from my childhood seemed to be the loud revving of motorcycle engines and the smell of motor oil and gasoline. It got so I could fall asleep even with all the racket, and I enjoy those smells even today. It all reminds me of spring, my favorite season. When I heard those sounds and smelled those smells, I knew the long winter was over. Soon the boys would have their bikes tuned up, itching to be back out roaring over the county roads.

And the town folk always turning up their noses at the motorcycle boys, dismissing them as unwashed thugs and their women even worse. I can tell you I was there, and it was all BS. Sure they had their rowdy ways, but they had hearts of gold. All except Swede Patrick, as it turned out.

It was the scions of the well-to-do families who were the real problem, always were and always would be as far as I'm concerned. Ask Sheriff Grimes. Who do you think raped me? With no remorse and thinking, I was enjoying it! He found out soon enough I wasn't. Speaking of remorse, I felt nothing when I killed that SOB Joe Jr., even though I didn't mean to, still don't today. It was him or me, although I don't think I was in any danger of being killed. Angry, yes, you bet I was, but not so depraved as to have enjoyed it, in spite of what I was told I said afterward.

I don't much believe in labels, too confining, but my court-appointed therapist diagnosed me as having something called "Gross Stress Reaction", and in the course of treating me, I was finally able to see and thus admit I had been raped by Joey Wilson. It took a very long time for that to happen. Funny how that works. While my therapist told me I was in denial, it wasn't that at all. I simply couldn't remember it! If you don't think that's possible, why don't you try it yourself sometime and get back to me?

It cooked my goose in this town, though. After the inquiry in the aftermath of my rape, I fled (I'm exaggerating, it wasn't like I was a fugitive or anything) across a couple of town lines to Edgerville, where, even though it was a mere ten miles away, no one knew me. I had nothing or no one left in Wilsonville anyway, what with my dad's passing, and the rape would never have happened if he had been well. God no. He would have squashed Joey and his minions just like the little bugs they were.

In spite of everything it was tough to up and leave that abruptly. Even though life had been very traumatic, it was all I had known. But at least being in new surroundings made trying to forget recent events a little easier, though, of course, I knew I would never erase those memories completely.

Still, I was angry. I could at least have gone to college but instead was left to fend for myself, although, to be honest, I wasn't all that keen on going to college anyway. It seems whenever I'm feeling sorry for myself, I dredge up things from the past (ergo, why I'll never erase those memories), and this was definitely one I obsessed about. I thought about my peers at school who had graduated and were now in college, probably having the time of their lives- partying, going to football and basketball games- at the very least, away from here. And what did I do instead? Got myself raped!

If Title IX had been legislated back then, I would have been their poster child. I could have gone to any school I wanted. I coulda been Ann Myers before Ann Myers. The story of my life: the one talent I had I couldn't use because women couldn't participate in sanctioned college sports back then. Naturally, I convinced myself I had been on the cusp of fame and fortune, even though I see now that wasn't necessarily so. I could have bombed, gotten injured, flunked out, any number of things, but if I had one thing going for me, it was supreme confidence in myself. Still do, as a matter of fact, although I've tamped down my aspirations. Now they have the WNBA, which I know I could have played in, or the Olympics even. But, being on my own, with no guidance, except for Mrs. Grimes, of course, she wanted me to get a job, work for a while, then get married and have children, like she wished she'd been able to do. While I love her dearly and would never want to hurt her, that was out of the question, and, though I never said as much, I think she eventually got the point, although I'm sure it was a heartache. That must have been difficult for her, I realize now, *déjà vu* all over again, but I had to live my life. It was the only way I would survive, I knew instinctively.

The one thing I was sure of was my athletic ability. I couldn't get any competition with the girls, so I had to play with the boys, which, while all well and good, led to attempted extracurricular activities in the guise of fouling or close guarding me when they were actually trying to cop a feel, getting one of my sharp elbows in the puss for their efforts, yet still not dissuaded, coming back for more, with the same result, and potentially entangling alliances, which were not gonna happen.

And it went downhill from there. Now on my own, I had to parley my natural beauty into modest financial security, and this led to other things, things I did to be able to survive, and instead almost ended up dead what with all the illegal substances I took, which I sometimes wish I was.

At first, things were okay in my new place, what with my dad's life insurance and what I earned as a waitress at a local greasy spoon, but it didn't last long and then got to a point that I was barely able to pay the rent, especially when tips weren't exactly flowing into the new girl in town.

In addition, the rent on a place I could barely afford was a dive, an apartment above the only laundromat in town, a 24-hour one to boot. It was stifling in the summer and somehow freezing in the winter, and all the chemical smells, and who knew who would show up at all hours, and the noise, and the sickening perfumy smell of laundry detergent. Plus, equipment was always breaking down and the customer would get pissed off and loud and finally yell up at me, in spite of all the signs prohibiting this and instructing them to call the owner at a certain number. But worst of all was on the frequent days, no one who was supposed to be there came in at all. Apparently, the owner hired an unusual number of poor employees. Then the shit would hit the fan, especially on weekends, when I would be called from downstairs to help unjam a machine, report a broken one, or make change. There even seemed to be a lot of sex being had in there if my ears weren't deceiving me.

I would either call the owner or the police, depending on how dire the situation was. I had to get out of there, but how? Without much money, I'd come to find, you had very few options.

Edgerville wasn't all that different from Wilsonville, except that nobody knew me, which kind of surprised me, as I'd played some AAU basketball and softball games there, and, most of all, there was no readily available green space, which was major. Oh, like in any relatively affluent community, there were all kinds of playgrounds, ball diamonds, and basketball courts, and most of these were located in a so-called park, but it was no park as far as I was concerned. In fact, it was almost identical to the cookie-cutter "park" where Toby and I shot hoops on summer afternoons and where I played one-on-one with Joey Wilson on that fateful day. If you're going to call it a park, at least let it have some trees and water like Olmstead Park in Buffalo, or Central Park in New York, both designed by FLO.

That should have been a sign to pass go ASAP, and leave the area entirely, but something kept me here. I don't know what and am still trying to figure it out. Heck, as I said, my mom's not even buried here, and I couldn't visit my dad's grave because- well, you know. I regret every day not getting the hell out of there, and now I know it was because I was too afraid to take a chance, had no confidence in my ability to make it on my own, and was concentrated on barely surviving.

I wasn't too successful with that, and then things really went south. I ended up doing things I never in my life thought I would do.

It wasn't until I was hit with several drug and alcohol-related charges, as well as prostitution that I really hit rock bottom. Luckily, I was able to plead out as a first-time offender, but I was remanded to a dependency treatment facility in Buffalo named Brian Lane for a period of six months. It was there I got my life together, became sober, and figured out a direction for myself. After a few successful weeks, I was allowed supervised outings, and it was during one of those outings at City Hall, while looking through Civil Service job listings, that I saw one for a Librarian and decided that's what I wanted to be. I enrolled at the University night school for a semester immediately upon being released and was later accepted in the day school; my grades had been that good. My lawyer, Dick Roche, the same one who'd represented me back in Wilsonville, gave me a job as a file clerk in his office, giving me just enough to support myself and pay for school. I finished in two years with three semesters a year, took the Librarian's Civil Service exam, and got a job right back in Edgerville not six months later. I have no doubt getting sober and becoming a librarian saved my life, and I've never looked back.

Who am I kidding? I liked Jake, but I couldn't let it be anything more, couldn't let him know about my past, that I'd been raped in that castle, even though I'd killed the bastard afterwards. A dozen stab wounds, blood everywhere. I lost it.

I would have let Jake know anything else he wanted but not that, never that. Again, who am I kidding? I also could never tell him what happened after I arrived in Edgerville, destitute and suicidal, doing favors of all kinds for the rich philanderers around here. Pillars of the community. What a laugh. And I'm sure Jake must have known some of it, things being the way they are in small towns, where nobody's business was everybody's. And while he never let on, I could see it in his eyes, the questions, the doubts. And then there was that book business.

So I had to let him go, and I had to do it irrevocably. It was the only way. Break his heart, so he'd never want me back. Let him know the truth about me, except for that one thing.

Jake is necessarily part of the story, one of the two men (besides my father, the other the aforementioned Toby Klein-poor Toby that is- who I'll talk more about later) I have looked to for support and understanding, if not necessarily love. Jake was the one man I suppose I could have married if something dreadful happened, like an unwanted pregnancy, if not settle down with, but it wouldn't have been fair to him, as I wasn't the settling down kind of woman, and neither was the basis for a good marriage. I think he realized that in the end, though it didn't make it any easier for him when I left. And thankfully, he never asked me to marry or live with him, as I think he was on the verge of doing more than once.

I know I gave it everything I had, but it probably was a mistake to get started with him in the first place but by then, it was too late; I was too far in emotionally, and it all got mixed up with that damn book. I may be flattering myself, but I think even he'd admit he couldn't have gotten as far as he did with it without me, both for my research and encouragement and for stealing the goddam book he wrote about, without which he'd have been up shit's creek without a paddle. And that's what got us together in the first place- that book.

I didn't have to plan the theft all that carefully. In fact, I'd rationalized it wasn't really theft. A client needed it, and if it wasn't being used (which I was sure it most definitely wasn't), it was my duty to get it. No different than any other book thief. No one would miss it, and I'd return it soon. I ascertained the call number and location of the book, made my way boldly up to the stacks on the 4th floor of the University library, located the volume in question, and, when I found it without much trouble at all thought the caper was going to be a piece of cake, until, seeing the size of it, despaired of getting it out unnoticed. Not to worry, though, I said to myself, taking a deep breath to compose myself. Eyeballing first the volume and then my satchel, it looked like it would easily fit. It was a good thing I didn't bring my purse instead. No way would it have fit in there even though I never carried much in it, just my glasses case, some tissues, and my house key. I slipped the book into my satchel, then hefted the bag to my shoulder and, looking straight ahead, proceeded down the back stairway and through the nearly empty library (it being between spring and summer sessions) and, avoiding the Circulation Desk altogether, stepped through the back entrance with alacrity into a beautiful sunlit summer day!

It began totally on the up and up, strictly professional in my capacity as a librarian, but as you no doubt know how such things go, the more time we spent together, the more inevitable it was something would happen between us. He had no baggage as far as I knew, except maybe an excessive shyness, which I completely understood, having a large dose of it myself. I think for some reason, we played off one another, in the sense that, as I was understandably reticent about my past, he saw that as a signal that he shouldn't ask, and, by the same token, while I think that naturally, we both wanted to know about each other's, I couldn't ask him about his because I was never going to tell him about mine for fear I'd scare him away. Even in spite of this, I think we developed feelings for each other, the extent of which I'm not sure of, including mine.

I do think that somewhere along the line, he found out about some things, it being inevitable in a small town where people will talk. How did I know this? At one point we didn't see much of each other. I think it was when he embarked on his book project, which we both tacitly understood was going to take up a great deal of his time for the foreseeable future. I was fine with this, in fact, considered it an opportune time for a break, as we both sensed the barriers between us were gradually coming down, and we both, being preternaturally cautious, didn't want to rush things.

In short, I didn't hear from him for a month until he came into the library and told me he'd finished reading the book and now needed to begin making the list of references he wanted to research, which he figured would take him another week, and then he'd probably need me to help him track down sources he needed and help him find others if he couldn't find the answers from the ones he'd already consulted, and would that be okay?

I laughed and reassured him it was more than ok, that that had actually been the plan all along, hadn't it? He smiled shyly and said, "I just don't want you to think I'm taking you for granted."

So, when he was finished with his list of almost more than 700 plus references (!) and a five-page synopsis that filled an old accounting ledger he had from his father (first ever mention of him aside from acknowledging he did indeed have a father and mother). It looked something like this:

Words
doughty
acclivity
lighter
imposts
geophagus
fret
carboy
cuirassed
remontant
declivity
incipient
grandee
magot
midden
inhumed
disapprobation
pusillanimous
jalousies
insipience
autofructiferous
organdy
paretic
beadledom
febrile
cacodaemonic
cucumiform
supralapsarian
sedulous

crucifer
diffracted
syndicus
recourses
consentaneous
inspissated
imbrication
circumspice
volitive
carnation
vilipended
abscissa
ordinate
tailsheets
paraselene
alterant
lugubrious
plenary
playa
withershins
immured
mastic
eserine
foramina
glamour
pelagian
nostology
hebetude
bathysiderodromophobia
palimpsests
charish
superciliary
hapteron

rasceta
panoplied
caparisoned
hierophants
portcullis
strabismic
consentaneous
epiphenomena
novocord
flexures
screws
pleached
gnathic
costive
cephatic
discountenanced
boveda
cocido
juerga
taliped
energumenical
ghoum
fundament
merkins
continent
vasodilating
debagged
spaved
viguable
umbrage
finaiguing
vivisection
caduceus

hulock
pullulating
stigmata
superficialing
fenestrated
minuterie
lavabo
peripteral
postulates
homunculus
lakhs
cayuga
brachycephalic
ostmotially
moribund
timorous
lemerarious
eructations
odalisque
polychrome
gimbals
innominate
hyperduliacs (117)

Persons, Places, or Things

Malebolge
Adamo da Brescia
Alfonso Liguor
Pope Pius IX
Mordad
Argo

Algeciras
Vela
Carina
Arius
Heteroousian
Homoiousian or Homoousian
Saint Jean Vianney
Don Felipe V
Menander
Sierra de Guadarrama
Antaeus
Mount Lamentation
Saint Edmund's nose
Saint Anthony
Ossian
Theophrastus
Dog Star
Gervase of Tilbury
Al-Shira-al-jamânija
Wathi wathi
Kublai Khan
Tamerlane
Prester John
Heracles
Hawthorn tree
John Huss
King Wenceslaus
Emperor Sigismund
Kyrie eleison
Synod of Dort
robin
Lucifer
wren

Malachi prophecies
bay tree
William Miller
Saint Bonaventura
John Wesley
William Law
Doctor Fell
Saint Clement of Rome
Venerable Orsola Benincasa
St. John's Day
Saint Lawrence
Saint Catherine of Alexandria
Asclepius
John of Bohemia
Pope Innocent VIII
Bacchus
Osiris
Krishna
Buddha
Adonis
Marduk
Balder
Attis
Amphion
Quetzalcoatl
Brahma, Vishnu, and Siva
Mithras
Pelagianism
Manto
Jansenist
Pascal
Margaret Marie Alacoque
Virgin of Lourdes

St. Denis
William Godwin
Monseigneur Ségur
John Cremer
Pope Urban VIII
Cardinal Mazarin
Captain de Mun
Gregory XIII
Empress Theodora
Raymond Lully
Diogenes Laërtius
George Berkeley
Charles Fort
Baruch Spinoza
Johann Gottleib Fichte
Persephone
Origen
Vainiger
Kant
Albertus Magnus
Zosimus
Geber
Phyrro of Elis
Khalid ben Yezid
Hermes Trismegistus
Michael Majer
Theophrastus Bombastus von Hohenheim
Doctor Ehrlich
Swinburne Malthus
Djuana Barnes
Diptera
Saint Wulstan
Aubusson

Cronus
Palinurus
Basil Valentine
Lucius Mummius
Dürer
Somerset Maugham
Francesca de Serrone
Henri Bergson
Sun King
Sir Arthur Eddington
Sir James Jeans
Sir William Rowan Hamilton
Saint Nicolas of Tolentino
Laberius
Lupercalia
Victoria and Albert Hall
Tarahumara Indian
Phillippe Auguste
Leptis Magna
Jesuit Father Anchieta
Saint Peter of Alcántara, Saint Peter Nolasco, Saint Peter Gonzalez
The Gabrielis
Corelli
Cardinal Spellman
Saturnalia
Paul Valéry
Saint Louis
Ennius
Chrysippus
Fermat's last theorem
Caligula
Gresham's law
Agatha of the Cross

Blessed Dodo of Hascha
Blessed Bartolo of San Gimignano
Saint Rose of Lima
Martha Constantine
Zeno
Cleanthes
Mara
Mother Shipton
Averroes
Antiope and the goat
Pasiphaë and the bull
Sir John Mandeville
Piute Indians
Blessed Leo X
Constantine
Nicodemus
Carnelevarium
Mary of Egypt
Thaïs
Kundry
Salome
Saint Irene
Costanza
Valeria Messalina
Marozia
Anaxagoras
Xavier
Philo Judaeus
Aristobulus
Lao Tzu
Alexander VI
Zoroaster
Aldebaran

Arnobius
Saint Bernard
Laodicea
Boreas
Baedeker
Archimedes
Mary Baker Eddy
Saint Gregory
Saint Giles
Cavalieri
Sheol
Pete Mcartney, Fred Biebusch, Big Bill the Queersman
Brockaway
Johnnie the Gent
Salerno
Holy Year
Democritus . . . Aberdites . . . Hippocrates
Gainas
Prince of Kapilavastu
Cesare Borgia
Father Dinet
Schiller
Dale Carnegie
Damon . . . Phintias
Roger Bacon
Kapila
Charles Schwab
Dutch Schultz . . . Capone . . . Two-Gun Crowley
Pola Negri
Old King Akhtoi
Albert, King of the Belgians
Procrustes
Proteus

Theseus
Motherlant
Ibsen
Carnot
Saint-Gaudens
Francesco Manfredini
Thakin Nu
Edna St. Vincent Millay
Goering
Yaddo
Charles Reade
George Borrow
Ischia
Frothingham
Dostoyevsky
Gnosticism
Nietzsche
Heisenberg's Principle of Uncertainty
Sir Thomas Beecham
Robert Maillart
Tolstoy
Sappho
Aristotle
Mauberge
Voltaire
Simon Magus
Rilke
Browning
Einstein
Gertrude Stein
Aldous Huxley
Sigismond Móricz
Géza Gárdonyi

Cécile Tormay
Dezso Kosztolanyi
Sándor Bródy
Demotic
Pázmány
Molnár
Mikszáth
Kerkel
Ganymede
Tuthmosis
Martin Schoongauer
Dryden
Adoration of the Mystic Lamb
Dante
Dis
Vergil
Andrew Jackson Davis
Jules Verne
Sozomen
Paul of Nola
Himerius
Crassus
Saint Clare
Portiuncula
Cleopatra
Nefertiti
Saint Sebastian
Walpurgis
Joseph Conrad
Saint Gertrude
Ioan Alexandru Bratescu-Voinesti
Sam Hall
Stesichorus

Calderón
Saint Simon Stylites
Rosamond Culbertson
Rebecca Reed
Saint Paul the Hermit
Marchioness of Brinvilliers
Viaticum
John Masefield
Saint Hilarion
Blessed Catherine Racconigi . . . Saint Veronica Giuliani . . . Saint Lutgarde of Tongres
Blessed Stefana Quinzani
Poor Clare of Roverto
Boccaccio
Charles Marie René Leconte de Lisle
Ouled-Naïl
Forster
Saint Stephen
Saint Joseph of Copertino
Thomas à Becket
Saint Anthony of Padua
Saint Raphael . . . Saint Auriel
Pissarro
Denys the Carthusian (298)

Written Word

Buffon's Natural History
Foxe's Book of Martyrs
Penetralia; Being Harmonial Answers to Important Questions
Doughty's Travels in Arabia Deserta
Coptic Treatise Contained in the Codex Brucianus

Rosarium Philosophorum
Wyer's *De Prestigiis Daemonum*
Llorente's *Inquisition d'Espagne*
Egyptian *Book of the Dead*
Malleus Maleficarum
Inferno
The Glories of Mary
Theologia Moralis
The National Counterfeit Monthly
Phaedrus, *Fables*
Opus Majus
La Tentation de Saint-Antoine
Osservatore Romano
De Contemptu Mundi
Histoiria di tutte l'Heresie
Christ and the Powers of Darkness
De Locus Infestis, Libellus de Terrificationibus Nocturnisque Tumultibus
Malay Magic
Religions des Peuples Noncivilisés
Le Culte di Dionysos en Attique
Philosophumena
Lexikon der Mythologie
The Glories of Mary
Pistis Sophia
Obras Completas de S Juan de la Cruz . . . Dark Night of the Soul
The Grave of Blair
Breva Guida della Basilica di San Clemente
An Appeal to All Who Doubt or Disbelieve the Truths of the Gospel
The Waste Land
Divine Comedy
Trucs et truqueurs
transition

Antony and Cleopatra
Al Misri
Clementine *Recognitions*
No Orchids for Miss Blandish
Essay towards a New Theory of Vision
Book of the Damned
Skeptical Chemist
The Church and the Papacy
Libro dell' Arte
La Chimie au Moyen Age
Grimorium Verum
Turba Philosophorum
Fabrica of Vesalius
Surgery of Paré
Royal Mummies
The Secret of the Golden Flower
Problems of Mysticism and Its Symbolism
Prometheus and Epimetheus
Cantilena Riplaei
Transcendental Speculations on Apparent Design in the Fate of the Individual
Die Philosophie des Als Ob
Cicero's *Paradoxa*
Remigius' *Demonolatria*
Thus Spoke Zarathustra
A Season in Hell
Paul et Virginie
Four Quartets
Society and Solitude
The Joy of Cooking
á Kempis . . . Imitation of Christ
A la recherche du temps perdu
Justine

Essay on the Principle of Population
The Sound and the Fury
Die Frau nach der man sicht sehnt
On the Trinity
Annotated Mother Goose
Aeneid
Otia Imperialia
De Virginibus Velandis
De Coronâ
De Praescriptione Haereticorum
Walden
Bhagavad-Gita
The Compleat Angler
Through the Looking Glass
Sanctuary
Stromata
Liber Usualis
Loyola's *Spiritual Exercises*
Twelfth Night
Natural HistoryPrince of IndiaMedea
Dead Souls
Beyond Good and Evil
Peer Gynt
De Rerum Natura
Die Geschichte der fränkischen Könige Childeric und Clodovech
Purgatorio
Phaedo
Romeo and Juliet
Triumphal Car of Antimony
Sir John Mandeville . . . *Travels*
The Spanish Tragedy
Liber de Insidiis Daemonium
Sodom; or, The Quintessence of Debauchery

Autobiography (Edward Gibbon)
La Vida es Sueño
Hamlet
Songs of Innocence
Songs of Experience
Letters (Emperor Flavius Claudius Julianus)
Contra Celsum
Doctor Faustus
Adversus Gentes
Nonnus . . . In Sancta Lumina
De Praescriptione Haereticorum
De Errore Profanarum Religionum of Firmicus Maternus
Brothers Karamazov
Kingdom of God
The Possessed
Baedeker's *Babel*
Uncle Tom's Cabin
Counterfeit Detector
National Counterfeit Detector
King Lear
Galen's *Anatomy*
How to Win Friends and Influence People
Ovid's *Metamorphoses*
Homer's *Odyssey*
The idiot
Science and Health
Justen Martyr, *Apology*
A Day with the Pope
Lucius *Golden Ass*
Origin of Species
Seven Pillars of Wisdom
And He Hid Himself
The Cocktail Party

Redemption
The Vertebrate Eye and its Adaptive Radiation
Sonnet to Orpheus
Orion
The Works of Sir John Suckling
The Razor's Edge
The Power of Darkness
Eyeless in Gaza
Azigazi pozitiv filozofia
A Véres költö
De Omni Sanguine Christi Glorificato
Liliom
Szent Peter esernyoje
Everlasting Rest
Histoire des ballons
Hindoo Holiday
The Destructions of the Philosophers
In Tuneric şi Lumină
Jules Verne's Tour of the Moons, Round the World in Eighty Days, Five Weeks in a Balloon (155)

Music

Rock of Ages
The Teddy Bears Picnic
Reformation Symphony
Handel
Palestrina
William Boyce
Henry Purcell
Vivaldi
Couperin

Mozart

Beethoven

Pilgrim Hymnal

Tosca

Mozart's Symphony Number 37, Köchel Listing 444

Don Giovanni

Sleigh Ride

Egmont

Die Fliegende Holländer

Die Ägyptische Helena

Sibelius

The World is Waiting for the Sunrise

Pagliacci

Suite Number One in C Major of Bach

Handel's . . . *Judas Maccabaeus*

Mozart's, *the Concerto Number Seven in F Major*

Enesco's *Third Rumanian Rhapsody*

Claude Debussy, *Claire de lune, Prélude à l'après-midi d'un faune*

The Ring of the Nibelung

Orfeo ed Euridice

In Dreams I Kiss Your Hand

Let's Do It

Return to Sorrento

Twit Twit Twit

Andrea Gabrieli

Giovanni Gabrieli

Misereris omnium

Pavan for a Dead Princess

Onward Christian Soldiers

The Stars and Stripes Forever

Violets

Thunder and Lightning Polka

God of Our Fathers

Adeste Fidelis
Oh for a Faith that Will Not Shrink
Almira
Yes We Have No Bananas
Bruckner
Reformation Symphony
March of the Sardar
Turkish March
Too Much Mustard
Sorcerer's Apprentice
Frère Jacques
Christmas Concerto
The Triumph of Time and Truth
Nearer My God to Thee
The Great Elopement
I Can't Give You Anything But Love
Harmonious Blacksmith
The Gods Go A-Begging
Royal Fireworks Music
Bye Bye Blackbird
On the Sunny Side of the Street
Carmina Burana
Jupiter Symphony
L'Enfant et les Sortilèges
Silent Night
Missa Solemnis
When the Saints Go Marching In
Perfect Day
The Bells of Saint Mary's
Paganini's *Perpetual Motion*
Beautiful Dreamer
Transfigured Night, Schoenberg
Sweet Betsy from Pike

Dinah
La Tani
Jealousy
Red River Valley
Beethoven's duet for viola and cello
Marriage of Figaro
Hark the Herald Angels Sing
Verdi *Aïda* (84)

Art and Artists

George Frederick Watts, *Sir Galahad*
Pieter Breughel
Hieronymous Bosch, *Seven Deadly Sins*
Praxiteles
Jean-Jacques Henner
Roger de la Pasture
Hans Memling
Gheerardt David, *The Flaying of the Unjust Judge*
Edgar Degas
Hubert van Eyck
Jan van Eyck
Jacques Louis David
Millet
Dirk Bouts
Cennino Cennini's *Libro dell' Arte*
Melozzo da Forlì
Picasso's . . . *Night Fishing in Antibes*
Juan Gris
El Greco
Lorenzo di Credi
Francesso Cossa

St. Jerome in Prayer
Lady of the Junipers
Ucello
Léger
Chagall
Soutine
Constable
Modigliani
Cézanne
Turner
Titian
Patinir
Van der Goes
Raphael
Fra Angelico
Dürer
Virgin and Child and Donor
Bronzino
Piero di Cosimo
Annunciation, Tintoretto
Murillo
Michelangelo
Velasquez, *Venus and Cupid*
Lipchitz, *Mother and Child*
van Gogh
Ben Shahn
De Chirico
Kollwitz, *Zwei Gefangene Musik hörend*
Saint-Gaudens
Madonna of the Rocks, Leonardo da Vinci
Goya
Dama de Elche
Francisco de Zurbarán

Navarette . . . Juan Fernández
Peter Paul Rubens
Pietà
Laocoön
Hercules, della Robbia (59)

Foreign Phrases

Nihil cavum neque sine signo apud DeumImportacíon illegal de carnes dañadas
El aire de Madrid es tan sutil, que mata a un hombre y no apaga a un candil
Cave, Cave, D^{s} videt
Cave, cave, Dominus videt
mesa de los pecados mortals
Abscondam faciem meam ab eis et considerabo novissima eorum
Très curieux, vos maîtres anciens. Seulement les plus beaux, ce sont les faux
"A mon très aimé frère Lazarus, ce que vous me mander de Petrus l'apostre de notre doux Jesus . . ." "Notre fils Césarion va bien . . .,"
"Il ya tant de saints, ils forment un tel rampart autour de Paris, que les zeppelins ne passeront jamais."
Quántus tremor est futúrus, Quando judex est ventúrus . . .
"I min Tro, I mit Håb og I min Kjærlighed"
Infra dig dominocus
Zwei Brüste wohnen, ach! Im meiner Seele
Religio perperit scelerosa atque impia facta
Obscurum per obscurius, ignotum per ignotius
Varé tava soskei
Ti soffoca il sangue?
Ah! è morto! . . . Or gli perdono! . . . E avanti a lui tremava tutta Roma!

Natalis invicti
Sempre con fè sincera . . . la mia preghiera .. .ai santi tabernacoli salì
Das Unbeschreibliche, hier wird's getan . . . Das ewig-Weibliche
Il y avait une jeune fille de Dijon
Es gibt ein Arbeiter von Linz
Des gens passent. On a des yeux. On les voit
talitha cumi
Musica Donnum Dei
"Werr, wenn ich schriee"
Und wir bewundern es so, weil es gelassen verschmäht . . . uns zu zerstören
qui tollis peccata mundi . . . miserere nobis . . . dona nobis pacem
Fas et Nefas . . . pene passu pari . . . Prodigus non redimit vitium avari . . . Virtus temperantia quadam singulari
Azigazi pozitiv filozofia
A véres költö
Mais cette peinture-là, je veux l'acheter, vous savez, mais le prix! . . . bien sûr que c'est Memlinc, alors, mais le prix qu'il demande, il est fou!
Con permiso, señor . . . conoce Usted el Señor Brown? . . . Nada, nada, gracias
Iført den uovervinnelige rustning
Oui, à vendre à l'amiable, vous savez, au prix d'uyn retable de . . . La force, voyez vous, encore plus la . . . tendresse
On va faire des zigzags
Ah mais oui, mais . . . c'est charmant
Bien entendu, la visage de la Vierge
Après tout, chargé de defender
Et ce vieux moricaud ... où se cache-t-il?
Men den himmelske rustning
son métier
les pieds, voyeuz vous, les pieds de cette armure, il a trébuch vous savez . . . Et sans la lunettes alors . . . Les pieds? Les pieds, voyez vous? Des Bosches, pas vrai? Voyez vous quelle gaucherie allemande . . .

Il faut que je parte, je viens de me rappeler d'une . . . heh heh assignation vous savez, mais le Memlinc, voyez vous, le Memlinc, je veux l'acheter vouz savez . . .
Attention? eh? Qu'est-ce que tu veux, alors! Va donc . . . laisse-moi passer . . .
Il sangue? ti soffoca il sangue? O yes, ecco un artista . . .
Ah oui, qu'il voulait un souvenir, vous savez, un tout petit souvenir de sa vielle connaissance du monde des truqueurs . . .
Bleu de Prusse, alors, ça ne fait rien vous savez, le ciel en bleu de Prusse, retouch simplement vous savez . . .
!Así por la calle pasa quien debe amor!
Hace años que los Prelados de la Iglesia vienen repreniendo la borchornosa . . .
Que ya no se respetan ni la santidad del tempio, ni los misterioso más augustos y sagrados en cuya presencia . . .
Coño! . . . Dios! Válgame Dios!
Cien iguales me quedan
Napok óta nem aludt . . . Hetek óta . . . mindent megprobáltunk. Még amerikai szereket kényszerüsegükben.
Ninscen oka nem aludni
Nézzen rá, nézzen a szemére
Indulgeat tibi Dominus (58)

And he said this wasn't even a complete list, that he surely had missed some, as well as most of the literary allusions he knew, were in there but he couldn't identify. He began using all the resources he could in our library first, and then when he'd exhausted those, asked me to help him find others. This went along for over a month- he'd come in every Saturday and Sunday and work and we'd go out after for something to eat in town (neither of us had a car), usually at the Copper Skittle, which was really the only choice, the other place in town, the

Eagle/Beagle, being too rich for our blood, and too close to the part of my past I never wanted Jake to find out about. I couldn't afford to run into anyone who might recognize me and spill the beans.

Speaking of that, I never found out how Jake found out the things he did about me (I figured it could have been several sources and had an idea who they were) or how much or what they'd told him, but the one thing that made me sure he knew something was the way he was trying to draw me out every chance he got when I mentioned, even vaguely alluded, to anything he suspected was even remotely related to my past.

At first, I shrugged it off as him being in "research mode," which I'd seen before with other patrons, as we bonded during our time together in the eternal and often times elusive quest for just the right book or citation or journal article, similar to transference with a therapist, but I knew that wasn't going to last any significant amount of time and was able to deflect their questions as unprofessional, or even make up an imaginary beau to get them off the scent.

Jake was different, we had an understanding, or at least I thought we did. Up until that point, we'd talked in generalities, nothing at all specific. But we were deeply involved in the huge project he'd undertaken, collaborators, let's say, if I'm flattering myself, so I'd necessarily spent much more time with him than I had with any of the others, procuring books for him, finding leads about others, suggesting sources in our library (mostly the *Encyclopedia Britannica* and the one-volume *OED,* I'm embarrassed to say), but, more importantly, sources in the downtown central library, things like *Lives of the Saints*, *Jerome's Biblical Commentary*, *Fraser's Golden Bough*, Weston's *Ritual and Romance*, more versions of the *Bible* than I never knew existed (Calvin, Douay, RSV, King James, Luther, English, Jewish, Catholic, Jerusalem, Quaker, Tyndale, and Westminster) and many, many other books Jake had listed in his accounting ledger, which I was never privy to, Jake not liking to carry it around town or on public transportation.

My point being this eventually inevitably led to my cardinal rule of not ever seeing a patron after work hours being broken. As I said, this was different, the work we were doing required constant communication of one sort or another, it being labor-intensive as it was. And it was exhilarating to find a rare reference in an obscure book we had no idea existed, mostly by blind luck, following the trail of bibliographies from one work to another.

And interesting! I may have mentioned I was no big reader, but we came across so many interesting books in the process I couldn't help becoming a convert. Among all of them, two stuck out in particular: *Coneybeare's Myth, Magic, and Morals* (which I wouldn't recommend reading to anyone with any doubts whatsoever about their faith, as that book would confirm all of them and perhaps introduce a few more), and what had become my favorite book ever (I'd really never had one before), Fraser's *Golden Bough*, both books appearing several times in the bibliographies of some of the books I'd used. I could read the Golden Bough all day, especially the sections about the rites of spring, and particularly those surrounding (excuse the pun) the Maypole! I liked it so much that, finding the cost of all 11 volumes prohibitive, I purchased the condensed 1-volume edition, which, in itself, was quite a read, but left me wanting much more, so I bit the bullet and eventually purchased the entire set one volume at a time. I'm not sure why I liked it so much, mainly because it made me feel good to know we're not alone, that people from the past and all different countries basically shared self-adapted versions of all these rituals, and that the origins weren't merely frivolous, but had a purpose, a purpose that was shared by the local and worldwide community. Also, and even more important, that everyone fits in somewhere.

Most might not think so, but we found it to be pretty heady stuff, and in the exhilaration of the moment, I agreed to go out for coffee with him one Saturday evening after work. He being shy, myself guarded, not a lot was said at the beginning, just the most embarrassingly usual stuff (weather, jobs, etc.), but we both enjoyed each other's company and became acclimated to one another fairly quickly, so much so that we even broached the subject of our plans for the future. Jake's was, of course, to write the book he was researching and mine the prosaic goal of leaving the country to live in Madame Bovary's country.

Well, that got us warmed up, and when Jake began talking indirectly about the book he wanted to write about the book he was reading, I wholeheartedly (perhaps too enthusiastically when I look back at it) voiced my support for him.

But I'm getting ahead of myself, and before I catch up, let me just start out by saying that, while the beginnings of this enterprise were completely innocent, like anything else that becomes too protracted, things got messy, more so as we went along. Jake hadn't directly sought my support in this, but I figured how he was describing it so enthusiastically and in such detail and that I'd stolen a book (more on that later) made me at least complicit. Instead, I got the impression (again, he never told me directly) that he thought perhaps I was a little too forward (I'm not sure how much he knew about me at that point), and the whole thing got off on the wrong foot. The male ego being as fragile as it is, I saw him pulling back a bit as things played out, although, then again, it might have been both of our preternatural reticence, which I had to sublimate completely to break the first tenet a librarian learns: stealing books is not cool. Who knows our motivations, though? I suppose I may have been the slightest bit intrigued by him and frustrated by not being able to get him the resource he needed (the second tenet a librarian learned), in my case, needing to disregard the first if I was to fulfill the second, which I realized was the most important to me. And doubtless, my ego was at stake: I'd been able to supply most of what he needed up to that point, and I wasn't going to stop now. For some reason I was deathly afraid of disappointing him, probably because he came up with the biggest challenges of my career.

But it was all for nothing, as you'll see, except for the fact that it greatly improved my research skills, and I learned an awful lot. In spite of everything, we still parted as friends, which I am grateful for.

PART TWO

CHAPTER 22

The "Crow's Nest" was a "neighborhood" bar. An endangered species these days, it was Jake's oasis of choice. Not that he drank that much, something owner Studs Merkel often kidded him about.

"If all my regulars were all like you," he'd say, "I'd be broke."

Not that he would be, in fact, again, as he often said, "I need this place like I need a hole in the head."

On a normal weeknight, with a few patrons huddled together at the bar or alone, doing some serious, deliberate drinking, it resembled Van Gogh's painting "The Potato Eaters." Perhaps, after a few drinks had loosened them up, they might talk amongst themselves. Every now and then, when the door opened, and a new patron, customer, or denizen entered, they would get the requisite once-over and be greeted, acknowledged, or ignored.

The reason Studs (Steve was his real name, he got the nickname when he rode with a local motorcycle club, the Alphas, back in the bad old days when everything he wore- his jacket, pants, and boots were studded) didn't need the negligible income his bar brought in was that he was set for life, albeit in the most gruesome of circumstances. One

Sunday he and his wife Jenny were riding in their car out on Rt. 11, on a normal Sunday drive out in the country to get some fresh-squeezed apple cider, Steve now a reformed alcoholic. As they neared the pro football stadium located there, where the game had just ended, a drunken fan plowed head on into them, killing Jenny and crippling him. As is often the case, the driver emerged unscathed. Charged with vehicular manslaughter, he was out of County lockup after serving a year.

It took just about that long for things to be back to relatively normal (physically at least) for Studs. It was touch and go for him, in and out of surgery as well as consciousness, but after several surgeries and months of rehab, he was finally released with a permanent limp as well as a mangled right arm. He refused a cane and learned to use his left hand, soon able to handle the stick almost as good as he had before the accident.

A wrongful death lawsuit was settled fairly rapidly, as such things go, just in time, in fact, for another football season to roll around. Although he now had no worries financially, it went without saying it was small consolation for what he had endured, losing Jenny. He hadn't been able to make it to the funeral and was planning on having a memorial service for her at some later time but just hadn't had the heart for it yet. The Edgerville Cemetery just happened to be on his way to work, and often he went up the hill to her grave under a huge oak tree to commune with her and place wildflowers (her favorite) there. He wasn't sure what he'd do once winter came, but he'd think of something.

You might think that owning a bar and having patrons come in on Sundays and expect to have the football game on would be torture, but for some reason, it wasn't. Sure, every once in a while, he'd get a twinge when at the end, they showed the stadium and the fans pouring out, but although he'd made the football team in high school, he'd never really been invested in it since then. Certainly not like these people, who lived and died with the team. He didn't even have a rooting interest but certainly didn't begrudge them that. Besides, it was good for business. And the patrons (and even those who weren't) who were fans had been awfully supportive of him during that time, and he appreciated it very much.

Not enough to start serving wings, however. His place was strictly a bar. No food except bowls of beer nuts or Chex mix he made himself and, occasionally, popcorn. He could have made a killing serving wings on Sundays, but there was the overhead, and he'd have to hire some extra help, which he was ever loathe to do. Beware of entangling alliances was his motto. Besides, no one could ever take Jenny's place.

If you're gonna be a ditch digger, be a good ditch digger...

Jake Barnabo, who worked for the Edgerville DPW, laughed each time he saw that sign on the wall behind the bar and, hoisting his glass, snickered ruefully to himself. 'I'm doing my damnedest,' he'd think, 'and even if it's only once a week, I make it count.' Studs, the barkeep, put it up there. Seems every time Jake got drunk (which, being a lightweight, was every time), he said it over and over. So all the regulars got a laugh at his expense, but he didn't mind. It often gave him a pass on ever having to buy anyone a drink. He was providing the entertainment, wasn't he? Besides, the sign became quite a conversation piece for anyone new coming in the place, so much so he kidded Studs he should pay him royalties.

It was what his Dad used to say after he'd disappointed him somehow: a bad report card, not making a sports team (he tried out for them all), not doing something which his father had asked him to do that didn't measure up to his father's standards. His Dad, God bless him, long gone now, wasn't a bad guy. In fact, he missed him but was sort of glad he wasn't around to see what a failure he'd become. He was always kind of sad when he disappointed him when he'd say (in addition to the ditch digger remark), with a sigh, if that was the best you could do, it wouldn't bother me, but I know you can do better, you just don't try. He didn't want to disappoint him, and he did try. He just wasn't much good at anything. What made it worse was his dad believing in him when he didn't even believe in himself.

He was a second-generation Italian, which made his father want him to succeed in everything he did, to uphold the family name, to prove they were the equal of any gringo in town. He'd never made it through high school, still had an Italian accent, and still pressed grapes for wine in the basement with his own feet. It didn't mean much to Jake at all. He thought it was too old-fashioned. Jake knew his father had died thinking he was a failure, and it hurt him. He knew he had it in him to be something, but what it was, he didn't know. He felt, though, he was on the cusp of it. He'd thought high school was a joke, finding the material easy (except for geometry). Therefore, he coasted along with Cs with very little effort. Now he'd become an avid reader. He couldn't explain it; it just happened. Well, it hadn't just happened; he'd discovered a book that had changed his life. In spite of not being interested in the things they read in English class, he was constantly on the lookout for unusual, even obscure, books. An older kid who was a great student, who was now at one of the little Ivies, and whom he talked to now and again, had turned him on to poetry, in particular a poet named Lawrence Ferlinghetti, specifically his book *A Coney Island of the Mind*. An Italian! he thought, my pa would have loved that. Well, in one of the poems there was a line that caught his eye, "discus throwers reading *Walden*;" "Walden" was underlined, so he figured it must be a book, and he set out to find it, which he did, at his local library, a place he'd never been before. He couldn't wait to read it and was amazed when he did. The writer had a totally new way of looking at life, and Jake was all for it. He'd never met anyone with whom he practically agreed on everything. Just the name of the towns in that area of Massachusetts, like Billerica and Fairhaven thrilled him, and as he read the book, he could even smell the soaking hickory nuts, the mossy riverbank, and the myriad leaves on the trees surrounding him. He made a promise to go to Walden the first chance he got.

Yet here he was, working for the Village DPW, hauling trash, mowing grass, sweeping up leaves, paving and cleaning streets, plowing and shoveling snow, and yes, like a self-fulfilling prophecy, now and then digging ditches. He knew he could have done better, but here he was. Somebody had to do it, right? Water seeks its own level, and this was where he'd ended up. Most of the guys he worked with mainly seemed content with their lot, in spite of the bitching they constantly did, and it suited him just fine also.

Unlike most young men his age (unless they had a family), he'd managed to save enough money to buy a cottage-sized fixer-upper near a small park not far from his birthplace, a park where he'd played many times in his childhood of which he had fond memories.

Water seeks its own level. Each time he heard or thought that phrase, he had to keep himself from shaking his head and saying to himself, at least I'm not cleaning sewers like the Town Sanitation Dept. guys had to. The shit gang, they called them each time they saw them at one of the greasy spoons or local watering holes, most maliciously, driven by jealousy that they made a lot more than the DPW guys did, even though to a man, the DPW guys knew they couldn't/wouldn't do what they did. Not in a million years. Jake didn't bear them any ill will, though; everyone had to make a living. It just so happened the Town had the money, the manpower, and the equipment necessary to maintain the sewers, which was fine by the Village guys. That substantially extra money they made wasn't worth the stigma of having to clean up their fellow citizen's waste, not by a long shot.

It worked both ways, too, this rancor that dated back to high school, with its caste-like system. Some who had been higher on the totem pole back then were now relegated to cleaning sewers, but at least they were making more money than the others who had been beneath them; some were lower on the totem pole back then and making less money now, but at least were not cleaning sewers; some had been lower on the totem pole and were now cleaning sewers, but making more money than their peers, which in their eyes made them a success; finally, there were those (a much smaller group) who had been highest on the totem pole and were now working for the DPW, making less than their high school counterparts at all levels on the totem pole and aspiring to clean sewers themselves.

These latter were the hard cases. They valued themselves much more highly than the DPW did yet seemed stuck in their lower paying jobs. These were the men Jake drank with and often seemed to be partnered with. Not content with their lot, they were suspicious of anyone who was, i.e., Jake. Most of them had been successful or popular in high school for one reason or another but had now, mostly through no fault of their own, become less than they had aspired to be.

Jake, on the other hand, had never considered that he ever had a social niche, had never aspired to be anything more than he was, which perturbed them no end, as though he were dragging them down. In fact, though he didn't mean to be and didn't see himself as one, he was a cipher to all who knew him. He had no friends, close or otherwise (only Studs could even be considered an acquaintance), no family (except for distant relatives he'd never known), though this wasn't his fault, and seemingly no prospects of it ever changing.

And while Jake drank and worked with these men, his private life (which he guarded very carefully) was his own, and what a surprising life it was.

Unbeknownst to anyone in town but his local librarian (and she would never tell, privacy being all in her profession), as mentioned before, Jake had become an inveterate reader, couldn't get enough, so much so that when the local library couldn't supply him with all the books he needed, this librarian could, being very resourceful that way.

An inveterate reader with a caveat: follow the method. Not having gone to college, never having wanted to, ever since reading *Walden*, he had the desire to read as many books as he could. He wasn't sure where that came from, but there it was. He instinctively knew that to accomplish this, he was going to have to follow an extremely detailed and measured path so as to avoid the temptation to read anything and everything. What was it Thoreau had said? "Read the best books first, or you may not have a chance to read them at all."

The method he came up with was to compile reading lists using Kunitz's *Famous Authors* series, as well as Spiller's American literary survey *Literary History of the United States*, augmented by perusing book reviews in the magazines the library subscribed to: *Atlantic, Harper's, New York Times Book Review, The American Scholar*, even *Time, Life*, and *Look*, though he seldom found books rigorous enough for him there. This was akin to the literary surveys he created on his own that you would find in the college curriculum, except he didn't read much criticism.

He began with individual authors: first Hemingway, next Sinclair Lewis, then Thomas Wolfe (he'd already gleaned *Look Homeward Angel* from a high school reading list and enjoyed it immensely), and finally two individual books cut from the same cloth, *A Spoon River Anthology*, and *Winesburg, Ohio*. It was these latter two that got him interested in regional groups of writers: first the Transcendentalists Emerson, Thoreau, Alcott (Bronson), Very, Channing, Fuller; then on to New England in general, Hawthorne, Melville, Brown, Dickinson; and on to Chicago, Hamlin Garland, Robert Herrick, Henry Blake Fuller, and Theodore Dreiser. He got to the point where he had a book for every season and mood, reading many of these books several times.

And then he got sidetracked. Oh, he still read assiduously, but a peculiar thing began to happen: he got bored to the point that he no longer wanted to discover new books. He just kept reading his favorites (*Walden, Spoon River Anthology, Winesburg, Ohio, Sister Carrie, An American Tragedy, Babbitt, Look Homeward, Angel, Son of the Middle Border, The Sun Also Rises*, and *Moby Dick*) over and over, and had to find a new obsession, which didn't take long.

He remembered in Sunday School how when he used to get bored. He used to count certain letters in Bible passages, mostly vowels- just that, he didn't tally them up or compare frequencies- he just kept counting individual numbers, and it did the trick. Before he knew it, Sunday school was over, and no one was the wiser. It simply looked as if he'd been intently studying his Bible passages to the point of having them memorized.

Then one day he was noodling around in the library's reference area when he saw a huge KJV Red-Letter Edition of the Bible with silver clasps on it sitting on a stand and, piqued, went over to peruse it. As he did so, the memory of his Bible school scheme suddenly came to mind and he decided he'd give it a whirl once again for old time's sake. As he did so, something came to him. He went over to a nearby counter where there were some scrap paper and golf pencils and brought them back to *The Bible.* As he scanned each passage, he began to count the various vowels, but this time instead of merely counting them, he wrote the results down on the scrap paper. He was a fairly quick study, and he began to notice patterns, but what he could do with these patterns, if anything, he wasn't quite certain. For now, he'd get as good a sample as he could by counting as many letters as he could. He decided not to just count vowels, either. He'd somehow known that 'e' was the most prolific letter and 't' the most prolific consonant, so he was definitely going to count them, as well as the other vowels. What else would be worth counting? Typography-wise, the descenders (g, j, q, and y, although y he sometimes would count as both a vowel and a consonant) would seem to be worthwhile to pursue, and finally, he decided the "weird" letters (x and z and throw in q which was also a descender).

It seemed he had what he needed to do whatever he was going to do with them: vowels, 't,' descender, and unusual letters. The more he kept playing around with them, the more he realized what he could do: he could invent a private game for himself, and, even better, it would be based on his favorite sport, baseball. He'd tried to do it with football, but it just didn't work that way, being too clunky, with too many offensive positions to account for, and thus too time-consuming. On top of that, the numbers just did not add up on a consistent basis.

The next thing to do would be to decide which types of books would give him the most bang for his buck, that is, the most letters. Luckily, he was in the reference section to get a representative selection. He got some from each discipline (except math) and noticed immediately the thicker the book, the denser the text, which made sense. Ultimately, he found the best books in the sciences, sociology, and history. Grabbing a stack of them, he was about to take them over to a table in The Reading Room, his favorite place in the library, with its cozy chairs, fireplace, and the thousands of books on the bookshelves lining the walls, when he heard a voice behind him, that was somehow authoritative yet not breaking the universal etiquette of quiet in the library.

When he turned around, he saw it was a very pretty, substantially built young woman with glasses attached to a chain around her neck, and oaten blond hair pulled severely back in a ponytail, wearing a tartan plaid skirt with a decorative pin in it, a white blouse, and, most surprisingly, Keds sneakers on her unusually large feet.

'Well, what have we here?' he thought to himself. 'Not your average Miriam the Librarian, that's for sure. She must be new here because I've been dealing with Audrey all these years, and this certainly ain't her.'

"Sir, I'm very sorry, but reference books can't be taken out of the Reference area," she said.

"Well, that's annoying," he said with a smile on his face, first noticing the name badge she was wearing, "Grace, is it?"

"Yes, sir," she responded, "I'm sorry for the inconvenience, but I'm going to have to ask you to use them at one of the tables in the reference area."

"Certainment," Jake answered, for some reason trying to impress her with one of the few French words he knew, "I wasn't aware."

"Thank you for your cooperation," she responded.

Jake watched as she made her way back to the Reference Desk.

'Well, Grace Graham,' he said to himself, 'looks like we're going to be seeing a lot of each other from here on out if I have any say in the matter.'

He settled himself at the farthest table in the reference area, kitty-corner from the Reference Desk, so he wouldn't be tempted to look her way every five minutes.

'Now, back to the matter at hand,' he said to himself. As he pored over the various volumes, suddenly, things began to coalesce in his mind. It would work! He decided. He knew it would. The books he had were performing so well for his purposes he almost decided to steal them, but, looking toward the new librarian, he decided he'd better not. 'Wouldn't want to get her in trouble for being too lax,' he thought to himself, 'no, we definitely wouldn't want that.'

Instead, he walked around the open stacks in the history, sociology, and science sections and, looking for the thickest ones he could find, after checking them out, made his way home with his quarry. These were books he had no chance of understanding or even interest in reading, wouldn't even try to read, in fact, spreading them around his room in elaborate disarray in miscellaneous piles when he got them home, plucking one of them indiscriminately out of its perch when he felt the urge, which he would then scan in order to play the elaborate static statistical baseball game he was making up in his head as he went along. Surprisingly (or not), he'd decided not to codify this, most likely because it had to do with numbers, which he wasn't very comfortable with, and were subject to randomness, but also because he was worried his brain might atrophy if he didn't fly by the seat of his pants every once in a while.

Might as well hit the ground running and get right into the method: Jake would write down the statistics he'd garnered from qualifying paragraphs, qualifying paragraphs being paragraphs with one or more lines of text, one line being a rookie season or a veteran's final year, two lines for sophomore or injury-shortened season, three lines for a first complete season or an injury-shortened season, four lines for a player's prime ... inexhaustible permutations... including indent and outdents of

¾ lines, ½ lines, ¼ lines, ⅓ and ⅔ lines to augment said injury-shortened season, a slump from a prior season, or a gradual decline in physical abilities. The reverse could also be true, of course, i.e., a gradual increase from prior or early career seasons. Then there are the letters (the aforementioned vowels, descender letters, and infrequent letters such as x, k, q, v and z) from which the statistics are derived; "e", being the most frequent letter, usually designated home runs for a power (cleanup) hitter, unless the home run to rbi ratio is unrealistic (he liked it to be 1:3), then adjustments had to be made, i.e if that guy is a bonafide home run hitter, and there aren't enough RBI per home run (for example, only in rare cases would he want someone to have 40 HR and < 100 RBI, a very rare occurrence in real life) he may go to the next half line and use all the qualifying letters to augment his RBI, except for a catcher, whose ratio he expects to be lower (i.e. because lower in the order means fewer RBI opportunities, and with no footspeed infielders can take their time starting the rally killer, a double play, and can play him pretty straight up, because he's not going to bunt or beat out an infield hit, prolonging an inning), but rarely less than 1:2.5. For a number three hitter (usually the best hitter on the team) it's most desirable to have high numbers across the board, which isn't always possible (he can tell right away which books will be the most desirable for that), but if that's not possible with the book he's using, high batting average (which means 1:4 HR to RBI ratio) usually means less home runs, because batting average always takes precedence for the number three-hitter. The figures can also be adjusted for the position (middle infielders weaker hitters; corner infielders good power, lower batting averages; outfielders good all-around, except for rare low-average hitters; or a CF with low power numbers but a high batting average- a Richie Ashburn type); all this according to what the letter-frequencies showed. Qualifying letters capitalized at the beginning of a sentence take precedence, and stand for home runs, and are the default number unless another letter appears more often, which means that number will be the home run number, which is usually with the letter 'e'.

The RBI plays a crucial part in the overall numbers of a player in this game, so it must be weighed carefully and adjusted one way or another to make the figure look more realistic. Another thing that weighs heavily is the player's prior seasons, which give a better indication of the type of player being represented, give or take a few aberrational seasons (slump, injury, rookie, sophomore slump).

One can usually determine the type of player being represented with a 2-3-line paragraph. Once this is determined, boilerplate calculations can be made to project that player's statistics for the remainder of his career. The dearth of 4-letter lines now and then can throw this (and one's career) out of whack, of course.

Jake could scan a page so adroitly he could project immediately what sort of player he was getting (in that sense, he would have made a fine GM) and could begin to establish that player's place in the realm of the many who'd come before, whether spectacular or mediocre. No marginal players were included as it was felt this would be even more a waste of time than it was already, said waste of time being a moot point because the "game" was so addictive, Jake obviously not being a proponent of Thoreau's wasting time was injuring eternity dictum.

The basic criteria of establishing a player's (paragraph's) potential began with the frequency in which qualifying letters appear in the selected paragraph. The letter "e" being by far the most often used letter in the alphabet, is the gold standard for home runs, and it can be safely assumed that this will be the case in most instances, which speeds up the statistic compilation a great deal. In the rare case, it isn't, or if the player being created isn't projected to be a legitimate slugger, the next most frequent number of letters in the paragraph is used to indicate home runs. All things being equal, the number of "e" (s) is then counted and a mental note is made of it; in addition to the aforementioned exceptions, the only other time the "e" isn't counted initially is if another qualifying letter begins a paragraph, in which case that letter is counted first, again making a mental note of the total, which, for some reason unaccounted for as yet, is difficult to maintain, and has to be repeated using the new qualifying HR letter after all the counting has been done. Then, only after all the other letters have been counted and proven to be less than this initial letter in number is it used to indicate home runs, which is fairly rare, unless, of course, the initial letter is an "E" or, albeit less often, a "T". Any qualifying letter that is capitalized anywhere in the paragraph counts double, and any descender letter that is also an infrequent letter ("q" for instance) counts double, which is also the case for the vowel "y." No letter can count more than double.

After the initial letter counting, be it "e" or another qualifying letter beginning the paragraph, has begun, the counting sequence goes in the following order: a-i-o-descender letters-t-infrequent letters. The sum of these letters represents the number of RBI in a season. If the ratio of home runs to RBI is satisfactory, those numbers are recorded in pencil in the margins or in the spaces at the beginning of indented paragraphs. If not satisfactory, there are several options available, most often that of using the "t", but whatever number makes it closest to that ratio is used, which is determined by recounting the other letters and selecting the one that makes the most sense. It is then time to calculate the batting average, which is usually derived by the HR:RBI ratio in the following manner, which at first glance may seem to be fairly arbitrary, but hopefully, the supplied rationale for each will make sense and will, with diligent application, become second nature.

On to the batting averages calculations. Let's take the three categories of hitter (slugger, best overall player, catcher) and show the paradigm figures for each: slugger, usually batting cleanup (35-39 HR, 90-100 RBI, .250-.300 BA), best overall hitter, usually batting 3rd (20-30 HR, 100-130 RBI, .300-.350 BA), or a slow-footed first baseman or catcher, batting anywhere from 5th to 7th in the order (20-25 HR, 50-75 RBI, .250-.275 BA).

Applying these to a hairy-assed slugger, whose numbers are 35 HR/91 RBI, his BA would be .286, the optimal 1:3 ratio (always using a .300 BA as the benchmark) would make the RBI total 105 (3x35), from which his total falls 14 short (105-91), so you subtract 14 from .300 and the result is .286.

For the best overall hitter with a power line of 24 HR /96 RBI, the BA would be .324 (96-(24 x3 =72)) = 24, so BA is .324. In some cases, depending on prior years or where the player is in his career, it could just be left at 4:1 ratio, making it (96-((24 x 4 = 96)) = 0, so the player's average would be an even .300

Finally, the case of the slow-footed 1B or C with numbers of 27/68, the BA would work out to .260, the result of 27x4=108-68=40-.300=260.

The formula for the above is: (HRx3=x, x-hr=y, y±.300=ba),

Since the above may seem somewhat complicated or, more likely, confusing, the following examples are presented as representative of 1-2-3-and 4-line scenarios, randomly using the author's own work (in parenthesis) to derive the statistics for the purposes of copyright. A detailed explanation of how the results were arrived at will follow. Please feel free to play yourself for comparative and experimental purposes:

1+-line: 9/43/.316**

All in all, she had a clean slate as far as Jake Bennett was concerned, and he thought no more about it. Although

Explanation: Using the straightforward method, the results would have been 17 HR (frequency of "a," also capitalized and first word of the paragraph)/35 RBI (number of all the leftover qualifying letters)/.281 (17 x3= 51, 51-35=17), 17-.300 = .283) but it was immediately apparent that the practically 1:2 HR:RBI ratio was unacceptable for any player unless it was for an extremely slow-footed player, be it 1B or C, and that player would not have that high a BA, and even when adjusting the ratio to 1:4, resulting in a 17/35/.267 line (17 x 4=68 - 35 =33=), 33 -.300 = .267) it was again felt the BA was too high, so, going the extra measure to be as objective as possible the ratio was raised to 5:1 which resulted in (17 x 5 =85 -35 = 50-.300= .250), which, while acceptable in a pinch or in a very short career, would be difficult to maintain throughout a lengthy career (it already having been determined by perusing a representative selection of ensuing paragraphs of >1 line that this would be the rookie season), not to mention extremely frustrating in what would no doubt prove to be a below than mediocre career. If there is any doubt, the *Encyclopedia of Baseball* might be consulted to find any precedent for similarly skewed statistics in a rookie season, and if there is, it is the participant's option whether or not to continue in this vein (and a "newbie" just might), but any experienced participant (unless a person with masochistic tendencies) most likely wouldn't for the aforementioned reason. In this case, discretion being the better part of valor, the participant (let's call him Jake) chose the next most frequent letter, which in this case was the letter 'e,' and when then putting it all together, the above stat line was reached using the following figures: (9 x 3 = 27 ((43-27 = 16) = .300 + 16 = .316, indicating the player had the potential of being at the very least the best hitter on the team. Indeed, the double asterisk indicates the player was Rookie of the Year, which makes that projection for this player valid.

2+-line: 17/71/.303

herself as much as possible, though not entirely a recluse, as evinced by her work as well as her weekly grocery shopping. What she did for fun was anybody's guess, most people figuring she didn't have any

Explanation: Again, using the straightforward method, the results would have been 23/65/.273, which, although the HR:RBI ratio was a tad high, would normally have been all right, but to keep the line more similar to the player's rookie season, the second most prevalent letter (the infrequent group in this case) was used, the infrequent letters, making a more representative line of 17/71/.303 (because the figure for this group was remembered after the initial count it wasn't necessary to do a recount, 17 was the new HR figure, then subtract 17 from the original HR figure and add that figure 6 to the RBI total, making the equation 23-17=6+65=71, 17x4=68, 68-65=3 + .300 = .303, resulting in a final line of 17/71/.303, all in all a successful follow up to the player's RoY campaign, and, more importantly, avoiding the dreaded sophomore slump. However, if subsequent paragraph scanning continues the pattern of lower HR:RBI ratio as it did initially in this case, then the decision must be made to go with that, with the notation that the player suffered an injury or got a lot bigger physically (without steroids) to explain this difference. Again, the *Encyclopedia of Baseball* could be consulted if it was felt that establishing a precedent was necessary, or not. All decisions are completely up to the discretion of each participant, although the ultimate goal is to mirror real players as much as possible.

3+-line: 29/119*/.332*

Normally the school didn't allow the terms of a child's status to be dictated, but this time they did. I can't be sure if Bobby had anything to do with it, but, one way or another, at his insistence, an agreement was reached that Gracie be transferred to her class. Though not one to gloat, Bobby was ecstatic and not a little emotional, feeling

Explanation: Although surprising for a breakout season to happen in a third (and only a 3+-line at that) season, the numbers could ring true for a player who looks like he might just be a Hall of Famer if not one of the all-time greats. If this was "only" a slugger, the 1:4 HR:RBI ratio would be used, which means the BA would be lowered to.303 (29 x 4= 116,) (119 ((RBI, total of all other letters) – 116) is +3 + .300 = .303, but since this player has a chance to be great, and this qualifies as a breakout season, the 1:3 ratio is used to raise the BA significantly, in line with this player's ability to hit for a high average, so the equation looks like this: 29 (HR) x 3 = 87, 119 (RBI) – 87 = 32, thus the .332 BA, with the asterisk indicating a league-leading category.

4-line: 31/131*/.338*

weren't going to be there much longer when we saw/heard the parents talking in low voices one particular day and constantly looking our way. Sure enough, that very evening, we were told to take a bath and put on our Sunday best the next morning. I knew it had to be true then though I knew no details and didn't want to.

Explanation: In this example, the equation is changed yet again to reconcile with the player's profile thus far; the ratio 1:3 was used, thus 31 x 3=93, 131 (RBI) – 93 = 38, .300 + 38 = .338, with the player leading the league in both RBI and BA, further augmenting his budding superstar status.

Statistics are then compiled at the end of a predetermined number of years (usually fifteen or more, the benchmark for longevity as a criterion for the Hall of Fame, asterisks are added up, one for each league-leading statistic, two asterisks for Rookie of the Year, and three for MVP. The asterisks are then added up for each player, with >20 being almost a shoo-in for the Hall of Fame.

There are innumerable caveats or occurrences for all the rules heretofore presented, such as injuries, slumps, even death, but as long as the game is played in good faith and the basic rules are followed, the statistics should be very representative of real players, and the game should prove very rewarding. In fact, oftentimes, the participant, depending on their knowledge of the game and its statistics (again, the *Encyclopedia of Baseball* being the fount of all things pertaining to this if one needs guidance), a similar player from history may immediately come to mind, and the formulae altered in order to emulate that player, again, as long as the basic rules are followed. In fact, this allows the "participant" (the person playing the game) to very easily tailor it to each individual, a somewhat desirable attribute for many game players. It cannot be stressed enough, the basic benchmarks must be adhered to, otherwise, it might as well not be played at all. It is felt that the intricacies of both the real game and this game will scare off all but the most fanatical about both to have enough interest and willpower to play out the string. To his chagrin, Jake had not found one person to even try it (and several who said he was nuts), most people not being great readers even if they loved baseball. And vice versa. Unfortunately, the only aspect of the game that can be feasibly represented is hitting. Pitching, like football, has not been proven to be successful using this method. As such, it is futile even to try. It's easier than it sounds, and everyone is free to develop their own version.

After a number of years of tweaking it, Jake had his routine down pat and rarely, if ever, varied it. As soon as he got home from work at 5:30, he jumped in the shower, then threw a slab of some kind of meat (pork and lamb usually though every now and then he'd treat himself to a steak) into the perfectly seasoned iron skillet he'd inherited from his mother. While that was cooking, he would prepare some sort of potato or rice dish, and a green vegetable, being a firm believer (again, thanks to his mother, who'd passed on not too long ago) that you should always have a green vegetable, a starch, and meat (and fish on Fridays, again courtesy of his mother, a devout Catholic, which he didn't often observe except during Lent), always some kind of combination of those three.

Dinner and the dishes would usually be over by 6:30, and then his nightly reading session (unless, of course, he decides to play his baseball game instead, which, realizing it was such a waste of time, he was trying to wean himself from, then all bets were off), safely ensconced in his imitation tawny leather Barcalounger, with his bookshelves within arm's length, when he would read straight through to midnight, at which time he would set his book (or books, sometimes he had two or three going at a time) down on his little end table, set the coffee maker for 7 next morning, and head off to bed.

In the morning, he'd fix a simple breakfast of cold cereal or oatmeal, pack himself a sandwich and chips, with an apple or banana, out the door by 7:45 and off to work. Every now and then, on a Friday payday, he'd go in with some of the guys to have breakfast at a greasy spoon, this being about the only indulgence he allowed himself.

Weekends had their own routine. Saturday mornings (even being hungover and with little sleep, he was up and at it every Saturday without fail) were devoted to housecleaning while he listened to the local college FM station, his musical tastes very esoteric, running to folk, contemporary, and psychedelic rock, and what is called "roots" music these days. He'd call into the station every now and then to put in a request, which, depending on which disc jockey was on, was usually granted. Nights he switched to a local program on an AM station that played jazz.

Sunday mornings (he rarely went to church), it was outdoor yard-work or minor house repairs, those he was capable of doing, and Sunday nights back to the FM station for the bluegrass show.

All this sandwiched around reading, of course. He thought nothing of reading for three or four hours at a stretch, which enabled him to read, in a good week, several of the books he was already very familiar with (*Moby Dick, Walden, A Week on the Concord and Merrimac Rivers, Catcher in the Rye, Crime and Punishment*) unless, again, he was playing his baseball game.

A fairly mundane, unexciting routine, but Jake preferred it that way. Not one to stick out in a crowd or, in turn, stick his neck out in any direction, Jake lived a very inward life, a necessity because he couldn't reconcile it with his outward one. Strangely, his life was like a dream. He felt like he'd been here before, but not in any sense the same way, especially outwardly, nor was he a participant. He merely watched it go by. That was one reason he read all those books: if he couldn't recall his real life by himself, he would ransack as many books as possible to try to find it, or perhaps even read his way into one.

For most of the time while at work, riding around in the DPW truck, Jake was in a reverie that usually consisted of books he'd read recently (*Rabbit Run, Wapshot Chronicle, Under the Volcano, Parade's End*) - or ones that stuck in his mind long after he'd finished them (*Moby Dick, Walden*, or that he thought might approximate past events in his life, or must have happened to him they were so similar, mostly concerning his home life and high school days (*Look Homeward Angel, Catcher in the Rye*) - of music he liked (Moby Grape, Savoy Brown, among many others), and moments he'd enjoyed real happiness, or, rather, joy, (something he had done in Little League, or the spelling bee he won in sixth grade, and the fantastic senior year he had running, undefeated record-breaker in cross-country and the 2-mile) always fleeting. But as of yet, there was still nothing he could put his finger on that proved he'd actually experienced any of this. Nothing that is, except that sign in Studs' place.

His work was of such an automatic nature no one around him seemed to notice these reveries. He could even converse while in the midst of one, made easier by the fact of his normal reticence or the unobservant natures of his co-workers, who, to their credit, did sense his oddness but chose not to persecute him, as they normally would another, because he was a "nice guy."

But lately, these reveries were of a mindless nature, almost trance-like, he couldn't conjure up any memories from his distant past, and it worried him, as you might expect. As a result of these reveries, he lost his purpose for reading and played his baseball game more and more often.

The one thing he never dreamed of or even thought about was the future. But that was beginning to change, little by little. Lately he'd begun to feel some stirrings of an unfamiliar nature whenever he was in the slightest proximity of the local librarian. Not all that surprising, he thought (when he thought about it). After all, she knew about his secret passion for books, had been complicit in procuring them for him, although she never showed any emotion when doing so. He still checked five books out each week, if only to play his baseball game with. It was strictly professional on her end, he figured, so nothing to worry about, which meant it wasn't going to alter his routine greatly. Still, it was so important to him he couldn't help but wonder if it meant anything to her at all. If so, there might be a problem, and he might have to look elsewhere for his books.

They'd never even talked (except for the time she reprimanded him), he only knew her as Miss Graham, couldn't even describe what she looked like (except for the hard-to-miss oat-blonde hair kept in a pony tail and round brown tortoise-shell reading glasses, kept on a chain around her neck), didn't know her age or where she lived, although it must be in the village, a prerequisite for employment there.

That was okay for now, perhaps forever, as far as he was concerned.

He did begin to ask around about her, though, and while no one in his circle seemed to know much, he did glean a little info from Studs, the local watering hole naturally being the source for all things nefarious concerning the town. Studs was no gossip, though. He only divulged things judiciously, on a need-to-know basis, and, even then, only to a certain few people. He liked Jake, why Jake didn't know. Most probably because he was a solid citizen and because they managed to while away the time of many a slow Friday evening (usually weather-related) talking about anything and everything under the sun.

Seems she came from Wilsonville, a village just a few miles east of them. There were rumors when she first came that she'd been in some kind of trouble there and had run away to escape it. She'd worked as a waitress for a while up at the Copper Skillet, a greasy spoon the DPW often frequented.

"Hmmm," Jake thought aloud, "Funny I never saw her there, as often as we eat there, and I can't imagine her working in a place like that. And now she's a librarian? How can that be? Doesn't add up."

"It's true, all right," Studs said. "You just might have missed crossing paths. I do remember she left town for quite a while and when she came back was a librarian. Surprised us all. Seemed like she'd done a 180 from when we last saw her."

'How's that?" Jake asked.

Studs paused before replying. "Isn't that obvious?" he finally said, sensing there might be something developing between them, at least on Jake's part, and not wanting to dash his hopes or sully her reputation any more than it already had been, fudging his response with what even Jake must know was a dubious answer, "Going from a waitress to a librarian seems like a big change to me."

While it still didn't add up, Jake didn't pursue it any further, at least for now. If he wanted to find out more, he'd ask her himself when and if he got to know her better.

What Studs hadn't told him was what a messed up young woman she'd been- out all hours, drinking and doing all kinds of drugs, sleeping around, that the real reason she'd originally left was she'd been made to as a condition of her sentence for drug possession, public intoxication, as well as assaulting a police officer. That last one had been a laugh, all the patrons of the Crow's Nest agreed as if she'd hurt anyone except maybe herself. No one knew who the complainant on the force had been, but they had a pretty good idea. Old Deputy Dempsey, Barney Fife (with a drinking problem and without the lovability) in the flesh. Tough guy pretender, he'd probably felt threatened by her righteous anger (and her stature- she was a big girl, at least bigger than him, although that didn't take that much) and overreacted, but then again, he would be frightened by a mouse.

Her sentence had been suspended on the condition that she go away and get help, and to her credit, she had and came back a changed, if not a happier woman. And as noted before but bears repeating, as a complete opposite of her former self, which wasn't always a good sign, exchanging one extreme for another. Of course, no one knew her that well. It could be more of a stereotype of a librarian than anything else. Everyone knew her to be pleasant and helpful, if preternaturally shy.

She'd "found" herself now, dedicated her life to helping others find their joy (or at the very least an escape from the mundane existence endemic to a small-town life) through books. Although she never let on, she would have much preferred working at an academic library, but the University required a second, advanced degree, which, because she didn't have the time, money, or inclination, she wasn't about to do. Besides, this suited her perfectly. She came to realize (although she often wondered if she'd just given up), she was only called upon out in Reference when a substitute was needed, or there was a specific request for a book outside the library system, the rest of her time being spent cataloging books to her heart's content, away from the public eye. And although she didn't spend much time at the Reference Desk, she was adept at "negotiating the question," i.e., finding out what the patron's often singular needs were by asking questions and generally making them feel at ease, which made it much easier to parse the myriad options for their specific informational needs. She had her own clientele, as it were, and, although sporadic, the other librarians resented the fact that they (her clients) immediately asked for her when they came into the library. And Jake Barnabo was by far her best customer.

She lived a simple existence, as Spartan-like as possible, in a rooming house on Spring Street by the dry cleaners with kitchen privileges, using the bus and "shank's mare" for transportation, keeping to herself as much as possible, though not entirely a recluse, as evinced by her work as well as her weekly grocery shopping. What she did for fun was anybody's guess, most people figuring she didn't have any.

All in all, she had a clean slate as far as Jake Barnabo was concerned, and he thought no more about it. Although she never let on, she sensed a difference in him lately, yet there was no way anything could happen between them, that was for certain. She'd leave town and start over if she had to. She'd done it before and could do it again, although she knew this time it would be increasingly more difficult. Better to let sleeping dogs lie, she thought bitterly to herself. She'd nip any further romantic aspirations (if there even were any, she might be overreacting, she realized, as she did with anything concerning her private life, with good reason) in the bud immediately next time she saw him, whenever that might be.

∞

One particular time, however, after trying to fulfill a very problematic and particular book request of Jake's, one that took many labyrinthine twists and turns and false starts and do-overs, she was ultimately unsuccessful (for the first time) only because the work in question seemed to have disappeared into thin air.

She wondered how he had even found out about it in the first place, and he didn't even remember, probably in one of the many literary reviews he looked at now and then at the Central Library in search of more interesting and difficult things to read.

Though somewhat disappointed, Jake didn't blame her at all. In fact, he was very appreciative of her painstaking and patient effort in attempting to retrieve said book, William Gaddis's The Recognitions, a 956-page 2 lb. 7oz. tome, thick as a brick, published in the mid-50s and relatively ignored. The irony of such a weighty volume disappearing into thin air wasn't lost on her nor on Jake when she reiterated it. The only local place that had a copy was the University Library, with which her library had no reciprocal borrowing agreement, so it looked like, for now, Jake was out of luck. Several of the antiquarian book dealers she dealt with had priced it, but the cost was way too prohibitive.

Somehow, though, she determined that one way or another Jake would have it. She'd witnessed firsthand the difficulty he (and she) had procuring the books he required. Funny thing about that, you were deluged with the best-sellers, so many copies in the drugstores, bookstores, radio ads, newspapers (even libraries were jumping on the bandwagon, have to inflate those circulation figures, don't you know) it seemed you couldn't avoid them no matter how hard you tried, whereas the really good books were as rare as hen's teeth, except in libraries.

Unbeknownst to him, one day she secreted the book in her satchel and walked out of the University library with it as innocent as you please. No one would miss it, and although it was strictly against the librarian's code, this was a special circumstance and she would not be denied.

The next time he came to the library, she immediately got his attention, telling him she had something to show him, but it couldn't be done there, and could they meet in private somewhere? He readily assented, wondering what it could possibly be, not getting his hopes up at that point that this wasn't more than it was- strictly business. They chose the park at the other end of town to meet that very evening.

When Jake arrived, she was already there. He spotted what looked to be a large book in her hand, and as he approached, she proffered the book to him as if she were a supplicant and he a sinner. It was a hardcover minus dust wrapper, light blue, and what he later would find out was a uroboros stamped on the spine, cover, and title page. It was in very good condition, and it was heavy! In short, it was *The Recognitions*, the book he had been looking for.

To say he was surprised didn't do the moment justice. His first instinct was to hug her, but thankfully he reined that in. His next thought, as he hefted the book with some difficulty, was to set the book down and leaf through it. He spotted a picnic table under a street light that looked like he would be able to do this, and Gracie, noticing this also, said, "Why don't we sit down and look at it?" which they did.

It was a fine, unusually warm spring evening, the kind that makes you think that all and anything is possible. The book was just what he hoped it would be: compact print dense with allusions, long sentences, and big words. In addition, he'd noticed some very promising paragraphs of all different sizes for his baseball game. He couldn't wait to get started.

It was then that Gracie told him how she had obtained the book and that he would have to read it as quickly as possible, taking all the notes he needed to, which Jake readily agreed to do. Not that they'd miss it, but you couldn't be too careful.

When all was said and done, it was clear something was developing between them, though neither would dare think, much less say it. But there it was. On the day Miss Graham agreed to let him keep the book as long as he needed, they dropped their guards, inadvertently looking into each other's eyes, and, totally unbidden, Jake popped the question.

"Would you like to have coffee sometime?" he asked.

Emboldened by her immediate assent, he asked, "How about tonight?"

If she had shown one second of hesitation, he would have hastily withdrawn the offer, but she didn't.

"It'll have to be tomorrow, I work until 9 tonight, and it's too late after that to go anywhere. When I get off work?"

Jake almost blurted out it was a date but caught himself just in time. "Yes," he said, "tomorrow night it is. I'll meet you on the steps outside at five."

Not wanting her to think he was one iota ungrateful, as he was walking away, he was about to turn and thank her again (he'd already thanked her many, many times), but, realizing they had an understanding, finally, let it go. No sense in being obsequious, he figured, though with her, he wouldn't mind in the least.

It was a good thing their first meeting was only for coffee, as the silence was deafening at first, both because of Jake's natural reticence and Miss Graham's vigilant guarding of her past. What did they talk about? The usual: the weather, their respective jobs, but also, incongruously, their plans for the future, Jake's (one he'd been fantasizing about doing for the longest time) to write a book, and Miss Graham's to become an expatriate living in the north of France, Rouen, specifically, Madame Bovary country.

And this opened up things a bit. Miss Graham asked Jake about the book he wanted to write and, although vague as to the subject matter or genre, did state "that it had to be something never written, making it necessary that he write it himself."

They then got to discussing *The Recognitions*, Jake reiterating that he loved it but would have to read it several times to fully grasp it.

"Besides," he said, "I have to keep myself from stopping three or four times on every page because he makes a reference to something I've never heard of. Looking through it, I began making annotations (I found a lot of them in my trusty *Webster's New Collegiate Dictionary*) on the first couple of pages to save time when I finally began to read it but finally decided to read it all the way through, looking up only those things I was really curious about, or that I thought were crucial to understanding the narrative, which in itself was a painstaking process. Then I think I'll go back and begin compiling annotations, which will be quite a project in itself. The book is so encyclopedic."

Although she was nervous when Jake said he needed to read it several times, she figured they'd cross that bridge when they got to it.

"I think that's a great idea," she responded. "While I'm no great reader, some of it caught my interest as I was perusing it out of curiosity and, naturally, had the same difficulties- though I'm not nearly as well-read as you- with so many arcane references I found just in the little bit I read."

"Yes," Jake agreed, "and I think it's a very worthwhile project to undertake, even though I have no idea how long it will take. Hey," he continued, "maybe that's my book right there! I'll call it "A Reader's Companion to William Gaddis's 'The Recognitions'"! Wouldn't that be something! What do you think?"

"Jake," Miss Graham cried enthusiastically, "that's an even better idea! And I can help you track down the resources you need to do it! I'm sure most of them can be found in any decent library's reference section- even ours- and, if we can't track something down, we can go to the Central Library or the University Library and look. Oh, this is so exciting!"

Needless to say, even though Jake hadn't known Miss Graham all that long, and even then in a strictly professional capacity, where he'd never seen her display any sort of emotion, he hadn't seen anyone so enthusiastic about something (especially concerning him) in a long time- if ever- and was not ashamed to say he found it very attractive.

As if realizing how untoward her outburst was, Miss Graham blushed deeply, lowered her head, and was silent.

Jake, noting the gaping lull in the conversation, hurried to demonstrate his own embarrassment at presuming he even had the capability of realizing such a grandiose project by doing what he often did, downplaying his abilities and ideas.

"Maybe it's already been done," Jake said. "I'll have to make sure it hasn't. I was going to say I was wondering if there would be any interest in it if I wanted to try to publish it, but then realized that wasn't important right now; what was important was doing it for myself."

Miss Graham, who seemed to have recovered somewhat, agreed, telling him she could help him with that and reiterated she'd help him elsewise in any way she could.

All in all, a great beginning, in fact, beyond each of their wildest expectations.

Circumspect in all things, they took it slow. Painfully slow, both in their relationship and his project, the first purposely, the second necessarily, so. In other words, for now, it was strictly business.

First things first. Now that Gracie had gone to great lengths to obtain the book for him, and now that he had bragged about his ambitious project, he'd better come through. The problem was that he doubted his ability to do either. Nevertheless, he began.

It was infinitely more difficult than he thought. He found himself having to reread each sentence several times and slowly. He did like it, though, and admired the obvious intelligence of the author. There were already several allusions on the very first page, but he decided to stick to his plan- read as much as he could at a time, then come back and mark each unfamiliar allusion as he came upon them and compile lists of these to look up after he'd gone through the entire book. He figured it would take a month at least to get through it but he didn't mind. It would keep him honest and his mind off Miss Graham.

In what almost became a ritual would eventually be played out for several months, with much paperwork, numerous phone calls, and finally, some negotiations.

What negotiations might you ask? Early on, Jake had realized he would need a lot more time to read, comprehend and actually finish the book, not to mention the copious note-taking, which was the reason he needed more time. Gracie, after many misgivings, finally agreed and told him to take as much time as he needed.

More than that, he already knew it was going to be his favorite novel ever. It was the kind of book he'd been waiting for his whole life-dense, rigorous prose that immediately took you into a world you'd never experienced but had somehow imagined, meager as he thought his imagination was – something that totally absorbed him. He did wish he caught at least some of the references, but he didn't have a clue. There were persons, places, things, as well as foreign phrases, concepts, literary allusions (really, allusions of every kind), even words (and he prided himself on having at least a better than average vocabulary) he'd never encountered before. Oh, every now and then, he came across one he had at least a casual acquaintance with, but not enough to know why the author had used it. He desperately wished he'd paid more attention in high school, but he was going to catch up. Look how far he'd come already!

He even suspected maybe Gaddis was doing some kind of stream-of-consciousness, free association, playing tennis with the net down sort of thing. He'd never been able to get through *Ulysses* or *Absalom, Absalom!* for that same reason, but at least with those, he didn't feel any urgency to understand them or figure that perhaps he'd come back to them later, which was not the case with this book. He was locked in, hooked, thrilled, whatever adjective you want to use. Even though he realized he'd have to read it over and over again to even attempt to fathom it (something he might not even then ever accomplish), he knew it was worth it. He trusted the author and believed each of the almost 400,000 words had a purpose. And it was so interesting, which was the main thing. It read like scripture to him. He'd found his novel, replacing *Moby Dick* in that category. He now had a paradigm in four categories: *Walden* in nonfiction, *Pilgrim's Progress* in children's literature, *The Recognitions* in fiction, and *Leaves of Grass* in poetry, all four eclipsing *The Bible* in influence for him, with *Walden* being his overall favorite. He had yet to discover a philosopher congenial to his needs (technically, he didn't deem Thoreau as one), but felt he eventually would. Perhaps this was just a matter of the right book at the right time, and it, too, would eventually be surpassed, but he didn't think so.

All this made it an even deeper experience- it was a weighty tome he'd have to study and would result in his first book if everything went right. He wished he could tell someone about it, but Grace was the only one who knew or who would even care. But, as before, he had to get through it first.

Slightly more than a month later, Jake completed his first go-round with the book. It had exhausted him. The moment he finished the last sentence, his first impulse was to call Grace but then he thought better of it. Not to rush things was his motto, and he was certain Grace concurred. Besides, he needed a few days at least to mull the book over. He knew she'd ask him questions about it, he only hoped she didn't ask what it was about. Even that was complicated.

Finally, the next Saturday, he called her. She seemed thrilled both that he finished and that he called, and they agreed to get together for an impromptu dinner that very evening.

Grace asked him first thing about the book, just generally, thank goodness, and he told her: it was about a lot of things, he began, Gnosticism, art forgery, counterfeiting, music, and the history of Christianity. It was mostly set in Greenwich Village in the forties and in Spain at the beginning and end, but, he freely admitted, he had absolutely no idea what it meant, at least not yet, and he wasn't even sure of what happened in the end, which was extremely frustrating. Of course, this wasn't the first time this had happened, the most embarrassing one being when he'd hadn't known Robert Cohn had literally lost his balls in *The Sun Also Rises* until a critic mentioned it in an article he was reading about the book. Then he had to go back and scan the book until he found the part that says he did, and if he couldn't understand Hemingway's pellucid prose, how in the hell could he parse Gaddis's Boschian style?

"But I will," he promised, knowingly, "and I'll help others understand, too," partly referring to his project. "It's worth reading over and over. He's so intelligent, knowledgeable – brilliant, really - I've never read a book like it. There's just so much in there."

He also informed her he had just completed a rudimentary synopsis and, anticipating she'd have many questions, had almost been tempted to just give it to her and would when he saw her next but had thought better of it. They had so little time together. He didn't want to "waste" it talking about his piddling contribution to the Gaddis canon that would never see the light of day. He'd give it to her in the library the next time he went.

"Well, I'm glad you came to that conclusion," Grace said archly, "because whatever else would we have to talk about if not that? I'm kidding," she added quickly when silence ensued.

Grace seemed satisfied with his brief, if halting answers, didn't even ask any questions or volunteer that she'd like to read the book, but this seemed to open things up even more between them. They continued to discuss their future plans- Jake's still nebulous at best, but Gracie's much more definite, even if she'd have to scrimp and save for the foreseeable future to realize them.

Grace (Jake finally felt comfortable enough to call her by her Christian name- after asking first- although it would be sometime before he employed the less formal, more familiar Gracie) was as forthcoming as he'd ever seen her (which augured well for their relationship he noted), stating bluntly that she wanted to get as far as way from this town, city, and state- nay, country, so she could start fresh in the north of France, which, although expensive, was her place of choice, mainly because it was Madame Bovary country. She'd fallen in love with both the book and Emma, though she told no one. The pastoral beauty, food, and, of course, wine were also positives for her. She'd learn just enough of the language to get by. She planned on living a simple, quiet life alone, tending to her gardens, vegetable and flower, perhaps even keeping some farm animals- a cow for butter and milk and chickens for eggs.

Jake, while he didn't let on, was pretty taken aback (his heart sank if you want to know the truth) when she said (very definitively) "alone", but who knew what was in the stars? He certainly didn't, or what he even wanted. Things could change, and he was pretty sure he wanted them to.

As they walked back to their respective places under a harvest moon, they were silent until they reached Grace's place, where they parted amicably, if not formally, with no immediate plans to see each other in the foreseeable future, though each had a definite feeling they would.

Still, as they will in a small town, people in the town began to notice them together, and, noticing, began to talk. Studs was the first to point this out very matter-of-factly to Jake. Jake nodded his head slowly as if to say, OK, what of it? at which point Studs raised his hands in the air, shrugged his shoulders, and said, "Don't shoot the messenger."

Luckily, Jake still had no inkling about her past. But unfortunately, Studs knew that inevitably that was going to change, and probably sooner than later. 'Poor bastard,' Studs thought to himself. 'It would be a real test for Jake. Himself, the few times he'd run into Gracie, she'd been very pleasant and, not one to countenance gossip, he had no problem with her at all. In fact, she seemed pretty nice to him. Big girl, big hands. She could take care of herself,' he had no doubts about that. It made him feel even better about her.

When he got home that evening, Jake, who had a phone in the house he seldom used (it was only for when he was "on-call" at the plant), toyed with the idea of calling Grace to let her know what he'd just heard but realized he didn't even know if she had a phone (she wasn't listed in the phone book when he tried to look it up), and said to himself, 'No, I don't want to get in the habit of doing that. I don't think she'd want that either. Besides, I don't want to scare her off.'

In addition, he had plenty to do now that he was set to embark on his research project, for which he'd purchased several notebooks and sharpened his pencils, something he was eager to get started with. It was a project that (for now) didn't require much creativity (luckily, because it was something Jake didn't feel he had in great supply) and, being something which would take a bit of mental slogging, would keep him plenty busy for the foreseeable future. And to his credit, he made plans to set to it assiduously as any eremite.

But the rumors just wouldn't go away, and not only would they not go away, he couldn't get away, as all the rumors emanated from work. In fact, it seemed every day he heard a new detail or aspect about Grace's past.

It was the bit-by-bit nature of the whole thing that was really getting to him. He'd much rather have the whole thing at once, some kind of narrative, not this piddling drib drab of innuendo. Get it out, mates, let's hear the whole thing, was his thinking. He could take it.

Instead, he was taking all these fragments he heard and trying to piece them together by himself, and it wasn't working. It made no sense at all.

No one was doing it intentionally (at least it didn't seem so). It was just the usual run-of-the-mill gossip bandied about to while away the time when things were slow at the DPW, normally while riding around on a rainy or snowy day or on a Friday payday, goofing off the rest of the day until they got back to the plant and received their paychecks. And while it was interminably boring and a monumental waste of time, it was a long-held, time-honored tradition, one he knew he couldn't easily shirk.

One day Jake overheard one of the guys talking about a "loose woman" he'd known who all of a sudden several years ago had shown up in town acting like she was all that when he knew the real story about her.

The other two guys in the truck huddled around him at his bidding, whispering so Jake couldn't hear what they were saying. He knew they were talking about something that concerned him. It was hardly even subtle. One guy, in fact, looked over at him and had to stifle a laugh. This was followed by an ostensible *shuuuussshhh* from the principal interlocutor.

Jake didn't pay it any mind, figuring it was the normal bragging about imaginary sexual conquests. But one guy, Russ, from another truck, wasn't about to let it alone. How he even knew they had even been discussing it is anybody's guess, but there it was.

So, the first concrete thing he heard was when Russ pulled him aside and gave him an unwanted and unasked for heads up. He didn't know Russ all that well. He was thought of as a bit of hard-ass and a little weird about religion, wasn't all that well-liked by the guys, and Jake had rarely ever spoken to him.

"Just wanted to let you know," he said, "the guys around the plant have been talking about your friend, the librarian. Now I don't like gossip any more than the next man, but they were saying some pretty crude things about her, and I thought you should know."

Jake, totally flummoxed, didn't know what to think, but if he thought anything, he didn't let on what it was. In fact, he said nothing, just acknowledged Russ with a nod and walked away. He had a feeling it wouldn't be the last time, either, and he would be right. He really didn't care what they said about her. He wouldn't believe it anyway. He just didn't want it to get back to her, which it probably wouldn't, as none of them had or were likely ever to darken the library's door.

But to be certain, he wanted to nip it in the bud, and he knew just how to do it by going to the center of their universe, Stud's Place, and get it straight from the horse's mouth. Studs saw him coming and did a double-take. It wasn't a Friday Jake realized Studs was "saying," with that gesture, but he was in no mood for pleasantries. He got straight to the point, and again Studs held his hands up as if in abeyance.

"Hey," he said, "I tried to tell you, but you didn't want to know."

"I still don't want to know," Jake said, "I just don't want any more surprises. Give it to me straight and slow. And don't leave anything out. I want to know everything."

"If you insist," Studs said, "but you'd better sit down, it's pretty rough, and I don't know many details, just what I've heard and observed. Might as well start with that about-face I mentioned a while ago. It's as good a place as any. As you know, she's not from around here but rather over to Wilsonville. You ever been there?" he asked parenthetically.

"Well, I digress," Studs continued after Jake nodded, admitting that he didn't know anything of her time in Wilsonville, just that she'd shown up out of the blue, alone and, from the looks of it, pretty downtrodden. The rest is, in a nutshell, pretty sad, but not without a somewhat positive ending, as you probably know all too well. Do I need to continue?" he said, grimacing when he noticed the exasperated look on Jake's face.

"OK then," Studs continued, "not gonna sugarcoat it. She was pretty messed up right from the start- out all hours, drinking and doing all kinds of drugs, sleeping around- even with women (it was Jake's turn to grimace at that), until finally she got popped for drug possession, public intoxication, as well as assaulting a police officer. All in one night, mind you. The judge suspended her sentence on the condition she goes away and gets help, and, to her credit, she did, and is as you see her today."

Assaulting a police officer? Jake said incredulously.

"Ah," Jake said, dismissing it with a wave of his hand, "it was Deputy Dempsey- you know him don't you? - it was his word against hers, and no one ever believed- she's a lot bigger than him, mind you- it happened."

Jake didn't know that particular deputy, had no occasion to, having never been in trouble with the law. Grace was a big girl, he had to admit, and he'd never seen that side of her, but he suddenly realized that her intense shyness might be a result of her somehow being afraid of her own strength. He could definitely see that.

"And was she able to support herself just waitressing?" Jake asked.

Studs looked away quickly as soon as he asked the question, but Jake, sensing there was more to the story, persisted.

"Come on, Studs," he said, "tell me all of it."

"You sure?" Studs said, "it's gonna hurt, be forewarned."

"Tell me," Jake said, shaking his head resolutely.

"Hmmmmm," Studs said, "how shall I put this? Well, it seems- that's what the rumors say at least- that she had several "sugar daddies" among the wealthier men in town. I didn't see any of that because they mostly hung out at the hoity-toity joints uptown- the Eagle Beagle and the Country Club."

While he felt mostly sad, it wasn't that he hadn't already imagined something worse than that- except for the "sugar daddy" part- he had. He'd like to know more about that. At least then, he'd be able suffer exquisitely.

"How old were these men," he asked, "and I suppose you don't have any notion about who they were?"

"Like I said," Studs replied, "these were rumors I heard. Nothing to substantiate them. Sorry kid."

"Ah, that's all right," Jake said. "Water under the bridge, I guess. Speaking of water, give me a glass of one with some bourbon in it."

Studs was surprised, as it was so unlike Jake to break his routine, the stuff of legends. You could almost set your watch by his comings and goings.

"Whatever you say, Jake," Studs replied. "You're the boss. One bourbon and water coming up."

It must have hit Jake harder than he thought. As a matter of fact, he was kinda blue all of a sudden and knew before the night was through that he was going to get thoroughly stewed. It was payday next day anyway, so he didn't care, he'd be able to sleep or hide all day if he wanted to on the bench seat just behind the front seat in the DPW truck. Or he could just call in, he had enough sick days coming, and boy, was he going to be sick. He was going to get so stinking drunk, plowed, shnockered, lit, shit-faced, looped, falling down drunk, what have you, he was gonna be one or all of those.

Although Studs frowned on public intoxication (Jake often kidded him about that being a conflict of interest, him being the cause of it after all - "ill-gotten gain"- he called it, which pissed Studs off royally), Jake knew he'd make sure he got home alright and cut him off when he thought he'd had enough.

True to form, Studs kept a wary eye on him, wondering if this anomalous occurrence (Studs was a reader with an above-average vocabulary) was going to preclude (he sometimes got a bit bombastic) his Friday night "visit", breaking his string of (he stopped and looked at his watch for some reason) 312 straight Fridays of perfect attendance.

Jake responded that he hadn't thought that far ahead, but as he never got drunk more than that one Friday a week and suffered from excruciating hangovers, probably not.

"Won't be the same without you, buddy," Studs said, "that's all I've got to say on the matter- except that I think if you left now, which you probably should, you'd be fine for another (excuse the pun) round tomorrow, keep that impressive Friday streak alive. Just sayin'."

When Jake woke up the next morning, he was in a strange bed with an excruciatingly painful hangover. When he gradually got his bearings, he realized he was in the room in the back of Studs' place. He had passed out on a cot, skanky as it was. There didn't seem to be anyone around, as he heard no sounds at all to indicate there was.

Ohhhhhhhhh, he said to himself, putting his hand to his brow, feeling his skin blanch and sweat as a wave of nausea swept over him. He had to get up, get a drink of water, get moving, keep moving, he couldn't lay there any longer. When he finally resolved to do so, he moved gingerly so as not to be rocking on the wave of the floor beneath him. He dreaded having to go in the bar to get some water- the smell of the booze, beer, and cigarettes would set off another wave of discomfort he wasn't sure he could face, but knew he must as there was nowhere else in the place that he could see to slake his thirst.

He was just able to make it behind the bar, grab the soda gun, shakily get a glass from under the sink, and squeeze the trigger, squirting a great deal of liquid all over the place until he finally filled the glass with water, which he lifted with a shaky hand to his lips.

'Copper mouth,' he groaned, then took another mouthful of water and spat it into the sink much as you would at a dentist's office. He shuddered all over and groaned again, and when memories of the night before came throbbing back, put his hand to his head and groaned even louder. 'Ohhhhhh noooo, it can't be true, it's just a bad dream,' he rationalized to himself, all the while knowing it wasn't, and, finally acknowledging it, rested his head on the bar as his heart sank.

Everything he'd heard about Gracie came rushing back and at first, seemed overwhelming, but then not so much. She didn't need his disapproval, and he'd make sure she didn't get it. Who was he to judge? As far as he was concerned, nothing had changed between them one bit. He hadn't told her much about himself, either (not that there was much to tell), so as far as he was concerned, they were even-Steven. Now, if only he could get rid of this deadly hangover.

To that end, Studs walked through the door that very moment.

"You're up, I see," he said. "Hair off the dog?"

"Noooooooooooo," Jake groaned.

"That bad? I'm not surprised now that I think of it. I had to pour you onto the cot in the back. You kept saying, 'I don't care, I love her- her and the book she got me. I assume "her," he said with air quotes, meant our mutual friend, who shall remain nameless, but I have no idea about the book."

Jake implored him with his eyes to stop talking.

"I suppose you'll tell me when you're ready. In the interim, I'll fix you a Bloody Mary sans Mary," Studs said, "that should do the trick. Then we'll see about getting something in your stomach."

When Jake turned slightly green, Studs hastened to make him the drink, lacing it with plenty of pepper, tobacco, lemon, Worcestershire, and lots of ice.

Jake chugged it down and found it bracing enough to allow him to take the next step, whatever that might be.

"Looking better," Studs said. "Now a little food is in order, The Skillet, I'm thinking, get plenty of grease in you to absorb all that alky-hall."

Jake could only shrug his shoulders and mutter whatever under his breath.

The Copper Skillet, the greasy spoon all the working stiffs frequented, was deserted on this early Friday morning, which surprised Jake. He was relieved and hoped they could finish before the crowd started filtering in.

Studs watched him looking around warily and said, "You think this is Friday, don't you?"

"Um, yeah," Jake said, " 'cause it is."

"Think again, bucco," Studs said. "It's Saturday. You missed a day, my friend."

Needless to say, Jake was appalled. Nothing like this had ever happened to him before. Quickly toting up the damage, he found it to be minimal. He missed a day of work, hadn't called in, hadn't gotten his paycheck.

"Don't worry," Studs said, again reading his mind. "I called in for you. Told them you were too sick to come to the phone. Jerry (Jerry Coffmann, the dispatcher) is a friend of mine. So no worries there. You ready to order?"

Jake hadn't looked at the menu. He knew it by heart but wasn't sure he even wanted to eat. But when the waitress (a new one most likely, as he'd never seen her before) approached, he didn't want to make her feel bad and said, "Two poached eggs, buttered rye toast, corned- beef hash, and some coffee, please."

"Put plentya butter on that toast, and I'll have the same, miss...uh, Jenny," Studs said, looking at her name tag.

"Not a bad looker, either," Studs leered gently as she walked away.

Jake didn't acknowledge this. His mind was elsewhere, thinking of the new project he was about to embark on. But first, he had to read the book over again, and get familiar with it, so he knew what to look for. He had a quick flash of despondency. Who did he think he was, trying to understand such a learned book and then write his own book about it? And why did he even want to write it? But he did and would obey Faulkner's dictum: don't write until you can't not write. Double negative there, Billy boy, but you're allowed. You could do anything you wanted. Besides, you're not really writing a book. You're compiling a list of references and defining as many as you can. You're providing a service. One word at a time, focus on that, and gradually you'll be finished. He hoped so. He didn't know if he could take another disappointment this soon.

He said nothing when the food came, merely bolting it down and gulping the hot milk-sweetened coffee. "I gotta go," was all he said to Studs, placing a five-dollar bill on the counter. "See you around. And thanks."

By the time he got back to his place, Jake was nauseous and as he looked at his pale face in the bathroom, he broke out into a cold sweat. 'Ohhhhhhhh,' he groaned again, 'I'm gonna get to bed, sleep it off, forget about everything.' Before he did, though, he checked the end table by the couch to make certain the book was still there. Why it wouldn't be, he had no idea, except that a bad hangover left him paranoid. As he hefted it, he felt the familiar thrill of anticipation he got when embarking on a new project course through his body, but this time knew it was going to be a big undertaking, by far the biggest he'd ever attempted. He resisted the urge to open the book and make a tentative start, not in the shape he was in. No, he needed to rest up so he could be at full capacity when he began in the morning- after a good breakfast, of course. He also fought back the thoughts concerning Gracie that were threatening to overwhelm him, crawling into bed beneath the cool, clean sheets and curling up in the fetal position. Thankfully, he was asleep before he knew it.

He awoke on Sunday fresh and rested. He boiled some water for his Taster's Choice freeze-dried instant coffee, toasted and buttered some rye bread, and whipped up some scrambled eggs, which he drenched with tabasco sauce. He perused the morning paper for the ball scores, the sports section being the only part of the paper he read unless something else caught his eye. He put the paper down:

He realized he couldn't put it off any longer. It was time to begin.

Jake set out first to compile an exhaustive list of names, foreign phrases, words, people, places, excerpts from obscure texts, mostly in Latin, he needed to look up, poring over the reference books in their library at night during the week and on weekends for an explanation, and gradually beginning his annotations as he went along: brief, succinct, discrete (for now, he imagined he'd have to tie things together at some point, begin to put them in categories. It was a huge undertaking, with hundreds and hundreds of entries.

When he first showed them to Grace, she seemed undaunted. A month later, deciding (jointly) he had a promising start, they decided once more to go out, this time to dinner. Jake brought the accounting ledger he'd used to note down the references, along with their explanations, in neat if minuscule printing in pencil, and presented it to her when he met her at the restaurant. Still mired in reticent shyness, they nevertheless managed to have a good time, recapping his herculean labor of the past month, reading out entries aloud, realizing it was only a start. He'd barely touched the surface. The majority of what was there he couldn't find any description of, so the hard work was just beginning, and he and Gracie would be ransacking some libraries in the near future.

And he still owed her a synopsis. She hadn't mentioned it, but it felt like the elephant in the room. He tried to rationalize it by thinking maybe it wasn't even necessary. He'd never seen a similar book if one even existed. But the more he thought about it, the more he realized it probably was pretty important. In any case, he had promised Gracie a synopsis and a synopsis she would get. But before he could even begin it, he saw a little item in the back of the *New York Times Book Review* announcing the publication of a book entitled *A Reader's Guide to William Gaddis's The Recognitions!* His heart leapt in his mouth as he figured it was all over, and he started feeling sorry for himself, woe is me, etc. Once he got that out of his system, he decided he would tell no one and get a copy for himself. He went up to the local Ulbrich's on Main Street, but they didn't have a copy, so he ordered one, which would take two weeks, he was told. He decided to try doing his own synopsis but still hadn't read the book enough to get an overview, or even an idea of what was really happening, so he ended up with a rudimentary outline, describing the most basic things, such as Camilla died, Wyatt was raised by his Aunt May, who was a staunch fundamentalist, a crazy party in Greenwich Village where many of the characters in the novel were introduced, among them Anselm, a very cynical poet, and Stanley a composer and organist of Church music, Agnes Deigh, a book critic, Ed Feasley, a cutup living off his dad's money, and the Big Unshaven Man, who cadges drinks off people who think he is Hemingway; Wyatt begins to engage in art forgery and sells it to Recktall Brown, who is involved with an art critic named Basil Davenport, Otto Pivner, a big poseur is introduced, Wyatt is married to Esther but cheats on Wyatt with Otto, Otto is writing a play using verbatim conversations with Wyatt as his material. The parties are crazy, Wyatt, as well as his father, are getting more demented as the book goes on, Esme, a paranoid schizophrenic as well as a heroin addict who models for Wyatt, falls in love with him, to which he is oblivious, she sleeps with Otto and Chaby Sinisterra, and tries unsuccessfully to off herself, and ends up in a Bellevue psych ward; in the end Wyatt (now called Stephen) goes to Spain and ends up in the same monastery as his father had been in when he was seeking consolation after Camilla's death. The cathedral where Stanley finally gets to play his church music on a grand organ, which literally brings the church down on him.

Jake continues to lay low, taking vacation time, until the book arrives. He reads it and is shocked at how many things he missed, which totally discourages him into finally abandoning the project altogether. As one final act, he plagiarizes the Synopsis, which is far better than anything he could ever have done. He shows it to Gracie, hoping to impress her:

SYNOPSIS

Part I

Reverend Gwyon and his wife Camilla sail from Boston to Spain; Camilla is stricken with acute appendicitis. Frank Sinisterra, on the lam from counterfeiting charges in America, poses as the ship's surgeon, operates on Camilla and she dies. Reverend Gwyon has his wife buried in a cemetery at San Zwingli. After months in a monastery seeking solace, he arrives back in New England with a Barbary ape. His son Wyatt is four and, with the loss of his mother, is tutored by his Aunt May, Reverend Gwyon's sister.

As Wyatt gets older, he develops a talent for drawing, his education becoming an intermixture of Aunt May's Protestant devotional books, arcane studies from his father in comparative religion and alchemy, and adventure tales from his maternal grandfather, the Town Carpenter. Aunt May condemns his artistic endeavors and instead prepares him for the ministry, for which he is reluctant. She dies when he is twelve, and though he abhors Christianity, he leaves for divinity school when he comes of age, though not before suffering a grave illness, his recovery from which involves the sacrifice of the Barbary ape. He spends the months of convalescence painting, developing two projects which, though unfinished, are mentioned throughout the novel: a copy of Bosch's tabletop painting *The Seven Deadly Sins*, and a portrait of his mother Camilla.

When he returns from divinity school, he decides to go to Europe and study art instead. To pay for this, he finishes the Bosch copy and exchanges it with his father's original, selling it to his future employer Recktall Brown.

Several years later, Wyatt is in Paris, having left Munich, where he was studying art, to avoid the homosexual advances of a fellow art student. In the meantime, his art teacher, while being a very good teacher, also (unknown to Wyatt) sells one of Wyatt's paintings as a rediscovered Memling. Wyatt paints alone at night. Shortly before a showing of his paintings, an art critic offers favorable reviews of his work for 10 percent of Wyatt's royalties. Wyatt refuses and none of his paintings sell. Then he finds out that his imitation Memling has been "rediscovered" as an original, and he decides to quit the art world and leave Paris.

Several years after that, Wyatt is living in New York with a woman named Esther, an aspiring writer. He works as a draftsman but sometimes designs bridges for which his supervisor, Benny, takes credit for. His marriage is a failure, compounded by the appearance of Otto Pivner, a wannabe playwright who recently graduated from Harvard. Sick of his job and his wife (who he probably knows is sleeping with Otto), he leaves to forge paintings for Recktall Brown. Otto moves in with Esther, then leaves her after a year or so, and his place is taken by an adman named Ellery.

Otto works on a banana plantation in Central America, during which time he is writing his play *The Vanity of Time*. He looks forward to returning to America triumphant, tanned, having finished his play, and wearing a black sling which he purports having gotten from having been in the middle of a revolution.

Upon returning Otto is invited to a Greenwich Village Party, where he meets many of the novel's characters: Arny and Maude Munk, a childless couple ineptly attempting to adopt a child and never succeeding; Herschel, a witty ghostwriter; Agnes Deigh, a literary agent; Hannah, an overweight Village artist who likes Stanley, a staunch Catholic and composer of organ music; Anselm, an acne-ridden poet, as well as other assorted minor characters from the Village who appear at parties throughout the book: a critic in a green wool shirt; Buster Brown; Sonny Byron; Adeline Thing; Ed Feasley, a practical joker who went to college with Otto and now lives off his father's money; Big Anna, a flaming homosexual; Mr. Feddle, a muddled old man who writes poetry he pays to have published; Esme, with "manic depressive with schizoid tendencies," as well as a heroin addict who models for Wyatt.

Otto awakes the next morning in Esme's apartment and goes out for a few hours and when he comes back, Esme has just awoken, so Otto goes to a nearby drugstore for coffee; Esme does not remember taking him home, and he learns he has a rival in Chaby Sinisterra, Frank Sinisterra's son. After making love, Otto and Esme both dream of Wyatt, and Esme goes to see him when she wakes up.

That afternoon, Fuller, Recktall Brown's Negro servant, is walking Brown's dog, and once more buys a train ticket to escape from Brown's domination. Upon returning, Brown asks him for the ticket. Basil Valentine, an art critic who works in conjunction with him, is thereby first doubting then authenticating Brown's commissioned forgeries. Valentine has come to meet Wyatt, who finds in Valentine someone more sensitive to the implications of forgery than Brown. Valentine is intrigued with Wyatt, and a tenuous rapport develops between them. Valentine's plan is for Wyatt to forge a work by Hubert Van Eyck, a painting Wyatt does never actually paint.

Back at his Horatio Street studio, Esme has come to model for Wyatt, only to find she is not needed. She puts her arms around him, but he rejects her. She goes home and injects herself with heroin, and tries to write some poetry. Failing to write anything, she begins writing the opening lines of Rilke's First Duino Elegy, only to be interrupted by a knock on the door.

Part II.

Mr. Pivner (Otto's father) leaves the office for his lonely apartment. After taking his insulin injection, he listens to the radio and, as is his habit, reads the news. Mr. Pivner is excited because Otto has written to say he will call to arrange a meeting (Otto, for some reason has never met him), and awaits his son's call with great anticipation.

In her office, Agnes Deigh rejects Otto's play, saying diplomatically she liked it a great deal, without in reality never having read it.

A despondent Otto leaves her office and goes to Esme's, where he finds Chaby, who is just getting dressed. Otto takes Esme out to dinner, where they meet Max, Anselm, Ed Feasley, and a few others from the earlier party (including the Ernest Hemingway doppelganger). Otto calls his father for a rendezvous. Wyatt brings the damaged painting to Brown's. Brown returns home to find Wyatt drunk and attempts to dissuade him from abandoning his forgeries. Leaving, Wyatt suppresses a sudden desire to kill him.

Wyatt then goes to Esther's to retrieve the forgery fragments left there the night before.

Wyatt arrives with the fragments at Valentine's. Drunk, distracted, and disturbed, he rambles on disjointedly and finally steals Valentine's golden bull from behind his back and heads for the train station, planning to return to his father in New England and resume his studies in the ministry.

Wyatt arrives back home at dawn and makes his way to the parsonage and comes upon his father in front of the parsonage addressing the sun. As lightning strikes the barn, Wyatt demands of his father: *Am I the man for whom Christ died?* Receiving no answer and realizing his return has been a mistake, Wyatt boards the train back to New York, but not before buying a "griffin's egg" at The Depot Tavern. Returning, Wyatt goes first to Browns, who is away on a business trip, and Wyatt discovers Fuller using sympathetic magic in an effort to destroy his employer.

Otto finds Esme having breakfast with a pornographer, and Stanly and Max arrive. Otto pays for all five breakfasts. Otto takes Esme for a walk and, failing to get a commitment from her, proposes marriage. Esme doesn't take his proposal seriously and leaves him. Esme goes to Wyatt's Horatio Street studio where he may or may not be, wanders around talking to herself, kicking the griffin's egg, dons Camilla's earrings, makes herself up garishly with Wyatt's paint, and writes him a letter. Assuming she doesn't exist for him except as a painting, she goes home and attempts suicide. Otto learns of Esme's attempted suicide and, vainly assuming he drove her to it, rushes to her place to forgive and console her, finding Chaby there as well. Esme has lapsed back into schizophrenia and thereafter refers to herself in the third person. Otto learns she has been modelling for Wyatt, and after reaffirming his need for her and loathing of Chaby, he goes off to meet his father.

Frank Sinisterra is preparing to meet a contact to pass on five thousand dollars of counterfeit twenties, of which he is particularly proud. Before leaving, he dons a green scarf (left by Otto at Esme's and taken home by Chaby). Mr. Pivner also prepares to leave- also with a green scarf, by which he and his son will recognize each other. He accidentally breaks his last container of insulin but plans to pick up another one on the way and take his injection in the men's room where he is to meet Otto. Unfortunately, he begins to lose consciousness once he has entered the lobby; he is mistaken for a drunk and ushered out a side door by a hotel employee. Otto meets Sinisterra, believing he is his father, and SInisterra believing he is his contact, Otto believing the five thousand dollars is an unusually generous Christmas present. Sinisterra meets his real contact, and they wait for Otto to leave the bar, and follow him when he does. Otto is arrested for soliciting an undercover policewoman. Having cleared up this misunderstanding with the police, Mr. Pivner returns to the hotel. He waits until it is obvious Otto is not coming, then reluctantly goes home, planning to return the next night.

On Christmas Eve Wyatt and Valentine meet at the zoo. We learn that Wyatt burned everything in his fireplace and planned to expose his forgeries at Brown's Christmas Eve party.

Esther's Christmas Eve party is an occasion to meet one of her favorite authors. The guests are pretty much the same as at the earlier party. Wyatt shows up unexpectantly to collect some of his old clothes. Esther is at first hoping he will stay until she realizes he hasn't changed. As the party unfolds, a little girl downstairs keeps returning for more sleeping pills from her mother; a baby and a kitten wander under the guest's feet; Stanley redoubles his efforts to bring Agnes back to the Catholic fold. By now, the guest of honor has arrived, followed by a bedraggled Otto. The party comes to a chaotic end. The kitten is killed when Agnes sits on it, Maude Munk steals the anonymous baby while her husband has a homosexual encounter with another guest; Esther realizes that Ellery has made love to another woman named Adelaide during the party; Esther retreats to her room with a black critic who asks her to watch as he masturbates. Anselm goes into a restroom in a subway station and castrates himself; Stanley is arrested when he tries unknowingly to pay for a drink with Otto's counterfeit money.

Wyatt arrives pounding on Valentine's front door, wanting to retrieve the forgery fragments so he can expose them at Brown's party. Wyatt had already been at Brown's party but failed to convince anyone of the forgeries. Brown has gathered a number of art critics to view Wyatt's latest forgery. Brown, drunk and restless, climbs into his treasured suit of armor and crashes down the stairs to his death just as Wyatt returns. Wyatt has discovered Valentine has burned the fragments, making it impossible to clear himself. Wyatt stabs Valentine (though not fatally), then decides to leave the country. He goes off in search of Esme. Otto is looking for Esme at the same time but unable to get into Bellevue at that time of night, goes to Horatio Street in search of Wyatt. In front of Esme's apartment, Otto finally sees Wyatt. Otto does not tell him where she is, so Wyatt leaves him.

On Christmas morning, a deranged Reverend Gwyon treats his congregation to a Mithraic ceremony. He is sent off to an asylum, where he is apparently killed. Dick, his young replacement, sends his ashes to the monastery in Spain he went to after Camilla's death.

Part III.

Otto, on the run, has returned to Central America with his counterfeit money. This time he does witness a revolution, and after being knocked unconscious by a falling horse, he suffers from Ménière's syndrome. Disoriented and wearing a sling for a real broken arm, Otto now calls himself Gordon after the Byronic hero of his play.

Mr. Piver is arrested for counterfeiting, Agnes Deigh makes a failed suicide attempt and Benny commits suicide on a television show. Elsewhere, others are preparing to go to Europe, Stanley to Italy to play his organ concerto at a chapel there; Max and Hannah to Paris; Anselm to a monastery to write his confessions, and Frank SInisterra back to Spain again. Stanley takes Esme with him as a stowaway when he finally boards the ship for Europe. Also on board is Basil Valentine. Those who remain in New York, like Ed Feasley, Maude Munk, and Ellery, are seen wallowing in ennui.

Sinisterra is in Madrid posing as a Mr. Yak, whose passport he probably bought, looking to obtain a corpse for a scheme he has hatched. Wyatt happens to be there searching for his mother's tomb. When Sinisterra discovers Wyatt is the son of the woman he inadvertently killed thirty years before, he takes him under his wing. He gives Wyatt a passport with the name Stephan Asche. Wyatt/Stephan is talked into assisting Sinisterra in his machinations but has little interest at the point beyond white wine and prostitutes: first a flashy blonde names Marga, then a simple girl named Pastora, who wants to have a child by him. Sinisterra and Stephan carry out their abduction of a corpse. But, upon returning and hearing the authorities are looking for a counterfeiter, Stephan flees, leaving Sinisterra to complete the counterfeit.

Stanley's maddening adventures at sea are featured in this chapter. Esme has made contact with Valentine and increasingly proving a trial for Stanley. At one point the ship stops to retrieve survivors of the shipwrecked vessel; one who is dying resembles Wyatt, and Esme, believing it is he, faints. Stanley takes her back to their stateroom, but she insists on seeing the sailor, and Stanley has to restrain her physically (experiencing an orgasm in the process). Esme later hears a priest administer last rites to the dying sailor. He dies during the night and is buried at sea. Esme convinces it is Wyatt being buried, runs to the railing, and Stanley pursues her, afraid she is going to jump. Instead, as we learn later, Stanley himself attempts to jump overboard. Stanley awakes in the ship's hospital (having been prevented from jumping overboard by an Italian waiter), apparently in the same bed where the sailor died.

Back in Spain, a somewhat deranged Wyatt is staying at the monastery restoring paintings, apparently, scraping off the paint to "restore" them to their original form. Stephen went briefly to North Africa, where he ran into his former companion Han. Han thinks Stephen has come to join him in the French Foreign legion, becomes resentful when he finds out otherwise and attacks Stephen, who shoots him. He then flees back to the monastery to live through his guilt, "to live deliberately" and to "simplify" (Thoreau). He is last seen leaving the monastery, apparently to find his and Pastora's daughter, finally achieving a positive direction in life.

Epilogue

Wyatt's story is finished; there is nothing left but to follow the fate of the rest of the characters, which is not too pretty. Esme dies of a "staphylococcic infection." In a hospital in Budapest, Valentine is dying for no apparent reason. Back in Barbados, where Fuller now resides, Otto/Gordon learns his counterfeit money has been stolen, and is told he must start all over again. On Easter Sunday, Stanley goes to the church at Fenestrula. Not understanding the priest's warning against using bass notes and dissonances, Stanley pulls out all the stops and begins his music; the church collapses, killing him instantly. The music, however, survives, "and it is still spoken of, when it is noted, with high regard, though seldom played."

He tells her at the end about the book that has been published, never letting on he plagiarized the synopsis. She is very impressed with it and thinks he will finish the book.

But aside from all this, toward the end, they were both worn out. Jake wasn't sure why but he could see her gradually pulling away, and he had to admit he was ambivalent after finding out the things he'd found out about her, which hardly redounded to his credit. And once that began to happen, they both abandoned the project, Gracie because she didn't like the closeness of their relationship and felt dependent on it for fulfillment in her life, and Jake because he felt the hopelessness of it all, both the book and their relationship. He'd never get the true import of all the allusions the novel was studded with. You couldn't simply look a person up in the dictionary or encyclopedia and expect to see the ramifications of why that particular person was chosen for that point in the novel; there were quite a few references they couldn't even track down no matter where they looked, and in spite of all the references he'd listed, he knew there were many more he missed, especially the literary allusions, and the exposition of all the different topics (art, religion, alchemy, music), in the broadest terms; even some of the words he knew the meaning of, some seemingly simple words such as 'recourses, carnation, etc.' were in a different usage than he'd ever seen, and he couldn't track down that definition of the word, and lastly all the foreign phrases which they had no hope of translating.

So, Gracie went back to Wilsonville and Jake to the DPW. While it had been a worthwhile undertaking, he'd been foolish to think he could make a book out of it and even more naïve in thinking he and Gracie could make a life together. As far as Gracie was concerned, it was a lesson learned. She was going to focus on working and getting out of the country. No more entangling alliances for her, thank you very much. She moved into Mrs. Miller's boarding house on Main Street, bringing only her clothes and twelve books (the 11 volumes of *The Golden Bough* and *Madame Bovary*). Luckily, she had a room with cooking privileges and could confine her comings and goings to work and the grocery store. Now it was simply a matter of keeping a low profile and saving enough money to leave the country. She didn't care how long it took. She would do it.

Jake, spending the rest of his days at the DPW, was able to purchase a copy of *The Recognitions*, it having been rediscovered in the early 80s. He never thought of trying to write another book again.

EPILOGUE

Not so bad, really. Just like many small towns in America, some better, some worse. Still, this was a worthwhile enterprise, if only to get the story out, a story that needed to be told. Of course, it's possible no one will ever read it, which would be unfortunate. It would be interesting to hear from some of the people who recognize themselves in the story (which is entirely fictional), and see what their version is. It is highly doubtful anyone could challenge this account, not unless they were away at the time, or had a faulty memory, or accused the author of merely making it up, the latter merely proving his point. That would be the highest compliment. Let the story stand as it is written. It is what it is.

Johnny and She never made it to the city. In the end, Johnny was too intimidated to go somewhere sight unseen, and Sheila wouldn't go without him. She ended up singing in some local watering holes, but that was about it, even though everyone said she was great. They ended up married to other people, with no children, living out their desultory lives, Johnny at the supermarket, where he eventually became produce buyer, She at the hair salon in Wilsonville, later to become its owner. It was a damn shame because they thought they'd be together forever, and many people thought She had the talent to go places. Small town often catches up with you. If you don't go when the chance comes, you never will. Hard, if not impossible, to shake the dust off your feet. She even kept the agent's card and took it out every once in a while to look at and wonder what could have been, though secretly knowing she must not have had what it takes, or she would have tried every which way to fulfill her dream.

Jim Weatherly thought he'd seen everything, but nothing like this in a small town. If you had told him that Joe Wilson and Bill Burnham were lovers, he wouldn't have believed it in a million years. But there it was. Old Dudley, the night watchman in several places in the village, had spotted them while doing his rounds one evening around midnight, splashing and cavorting nude in the pool at the Village Rec Center. He saw them kiss and embrace when they got out of the pool and head for the sauna arm in arm. He saw it several times before he said anything until he spilled his guts at SpaƆey's for the price of a draft beer. "So what's it to ya?" Swede Patrick asked, acting like he didn't care one way or the other when secretly he couldn't wait to tell his family (he came from a large family) about it. Once they heard about it, it spread like wildfire.

It ruined both men's reputations, although Mr. Wilson didn't seem to care, holding his head up defiantly as he went through town, still haunting the drugstores in the village, looking at price labels. He was no longer on any of the many Boards he had served on, but he seemed totally devoid of any emotion. He died not long after.

Mr. Burnham, on the other hand, blew his brains out one evening in his study.

Toby Klein never went to college in the normal way, doing odd jobs around town, seemingly a forlorn as well as bitter soul. His parents both dead, he lived alone in the house he grew up in. Eventually, he sold it and moved to an apartment in the city, set up pretty well financially for the foreseeable future. He enrolled in night school at the University, where he fell in with some student radicals, members of the SDS in fact. It was his habit to go to the student rathskeller after work (he worked for a janitorial service) and have a Carling Red Cap or two before class. It was there he met several of the members, who were constantly recruiting. Toby was no dummy, he knew what was going on in the country, the nationwide civil unrest, and the Viet Nam War, and he was more than happy to put his shoulder to the wheel and join the cause. He got mixed up in a plot to steal and dispose of all the area draft records, got caught, and spent several days in jail, after which he posted bail and was ultimately let off on a suspended sentence. He never married.

Sheriff Grimes finished out his term after the Gracie debacle, and to everyone's surprise, he and Mrs. Grimes retired to Florida in the winter, coming back for the pleasant summers. He'd had enough of the politicking, the cold weather, he wasn't getting any younger, and he'd never really gotten over what happened to Gracie and the aftermath-inconclusive forensic evidence, no one charged, and no witnesses. They rarely ever saw Johnny, though they were glad he was settled down with a family. He knew where they lived and that he could always come to them for anything he needed, but visits were not forthcoming.

It was a shame because Mrs. Grimes had been looking forward to grandchildren, and now she hardly knew them.

The Fearsome Foursome were whittled down to three, with Pierre even more reclusive and Swede Patrick disgraced into persona non grata status. Paul Brennan had gone on to become a fire-breathing nondenominational pastor, joining Abby and Gail at the hippie commune in Zoar Valley.

Even though Gracie returned to her hometown of Wilsonville after fifteen years or so in exile, nobody knew it was her. Why would she come back to a place with so many bad memories, a place where she was so reviled, and the feeling was mutual? She supposed it was another case of better the devil, you know. And she had worn out her welcome in Edgerton if you want to know the truth. Plus, she wanted to be back where her father (her only family) was if only to tend his grave. And if anyone should recognize her, f'em, it won't bother her at all.

Besides, things were changing so constantly there you could have as much anonymity as you wanted. People came and went so quickly that there were very few people left here from when Gracie was a kid, either dead or moved on to greener pastures. She dyed her hair black, wore it butch short, and no makeup. No one has recognized her as yet, and she doesn't think anyone will. She could be a guy for all they know. Maybe they won't even care even if they do recognize her. She lays low as much as possible, doing her grocery shopping at odd hours when she knows few people will be at the A&P. The fewer, the better. That's the only time she goes anywhere, other than camping, where she doesn't have to worry about seeing anyone.

Also, Gracie had a friend in Sheriff (now retired) and Mrs. Grimes. They'd protect her, keep her secret. Like her friend Toby, he thought he owed her something because of what happened at that castle, but he really didn't. There was nothing he could have done to prevent it. She just wished the Sheriff could keep his damn gung-ho deputy from rousting her any time he had the chance when she was camping on Wilson's land, but she guessed he no longer had any say in the matter. And Mrs. Grimes, who for some reason had taken a shine to her early on in life, had always been there for her. She's the daughter- child- she never had, it seems, which was a lot to live up to. She was sure she'd unintentionally disappointed her many times. What made it worse was she heard their adoption of a boy hadn't gone so well.

If it wasn't for them, she didn't know what she'd have done. She was able to keep a low profile, the Sheriff having given her a job at Police Headquarters, working for him. He maintained an office in the police building as president of the local PBA. She performed file-keeping, fact-checking, answered the phone now and then, as well as keeping sure he made and kept his appointments.

So overall, it wasn't not so bad and, given her past, could have been a lot worse. Everyone left her alone and she them.

Sure, nobody knew her. Nobody knew anyone for that matter. She's finished with the human race. All she lives for now is nature. Trees, rocks, birds and things. Doesn't want to study it. Just be out in it. If she learned a few things about it along the way, so be it. Except that she has to make a living, she'd be out there 24/7. Doesn't have to be wilderness, any treed area or park- any greenspace, really -will do, although God knows there's little enough of that around here.

She walked everywhere. If she can't walk somewhere, it's not worth going to, and she doesn't go.

She still went camping every weekend just as she'd always done since she was in the Girl Scouts (it was the only thing she liked about Girl Scouts)—nothing exotic, just the woods on the end of town for the most part. It's posted, and she'd been evicted many times from there, but she kept going back and would keep going back until she couldn't any longer. It's the last vestige of the uncivilized past remaining, and she's sure that once the land, held in escrow until Mr. Wilson's estate was out of probate, was up for grabs, it would be parceled out for "development." It's just a matter of time. Then she'd have to leave for good.

She grew up tough. A tough childhood, a tough life, had made her strong. She wasn't looking for any sympathy, mind you. And no humans mean specifically no men.

Although she could do without women, too, if you want to know the truth. Just not as much. They are, as a rule, smarter, gentler, and better listeners, and she had a lot to say, that's for certain. If they didn't have those qualities, she wanted nothing to do with them, and she could usually tell right away.

And she didn't dwell on all that any longer. She couldn't afford to. Her goal right now was the same as it's been for some time - to have enough money to not only get out of Wilsonville but the country period, settle somewhere in the north of France, specifically near Rouen, where Madame Bovary lived. She's wanted to go there ever since she read the book, instantly identifying with Emma as another woman of ill repute as if that made her a bad person. She'd just had bad luck with men. Who hasn't? It was simply the wrong place at the wrong time for her, and she couldn't take it any longer, so she did the only thing she felt was left for her to do.

It was her favorite book ever, recommended by her friend Jake. She'd read it over and over, thoroughly imbued herself with it. You might think it curious that she wanted to go there for a new beginning, as we all know what happened to Emma Bovary, but she looked on it as a sort of vindication of her if she could live out her days there in peace and quiet. You might think of that as morbid, too, but it wasn't, on the contrary, because that's all she desired out of life at that point. Her anger had largely been subsumed, to be replaced by an ineffable sadness mirrored in her face and being. It wouldn't be too much longer, another year, when she'd have worked long enough to collect her pension. And a generous pension it was courtesy of the state. But she felt she'd earned it and then some. Once she'd saved enough money and got it, she'd follow Sheriff and Mrs. Grimes out of town, destination Madame Bovary country.

Made in the USA
Middletown, DE
30 July 2022